Praise for The Girl in the Mirror

"*The Girl in the Mirror* is the first installment in the Sarah Greene Mysteries series, and while the book plays with the usual mystery genre conventions, it has the added intrigue of supernatural elements. It's an excellent first entry to this exciting new series, set in the California town of Dos Santos where a shady history lends itself to all kinds of paranormal drama for protagonist Sarah Greene. Author Steven Ramirez weaves a gripping mystery at the center of the novel, and the unpredictable twists keep the pages turning well into the last act."

IndieReader

"*The Girl in the Mirror* is a well-paced paranormal mystery that delivers chills, laughs, and romance all in one go, and gives the reader a heroine to root for. The character of Sarah begins as a woman unsure if her choices in life are the right ones, but through her trials she becomes stronger and more confident in herself and her abilities. Ramirez delivers highly readable prose that is both funny and unnerving when it intends to be."

The BookLife Prize

"*The Girl In The Mirror* is a spooky, supernatural thriller. The first page drew me into the story and kept me there until the end, with the suspense building on each page. This is a well-paced story, with plenty of action and a great plot filled with twists and turns that keep you hooked."

THE GIRL IN THE MIRROR

Also by Steven Ramirez

Tell Me When I'm Dead—When a plague decimates the town of Tres Marias, recovering alcoholic Dave Pulaski, his wife, Holly, and a band of soldiers must kill the living and the dead to survive. "*Tell Me When I'm Dead* is a gritty, pulse-pounding read that never loses its sense of humor, for an original and well-rounded work of zombie fiction."

Dead Is All You Get—Fighting to protect his wife, Holly, from the hordes of undead, Dave Pulaski discovers the truth behind the contagion—a revelation that will drive him past the limits of faith and reason. "Steven Ramirez has driven a stake into the brain of this genre and created something new that is definitely worth the effort, and demands a read from fans of zombie fiction."

Even The Dead Will Bleed—In Los Angeles, Dave Pulaski is on a mission to rescue an innocent girl from a secret facility experimenting on humans, then kill the man responsible. But he encounters dark forces that will deliver him to the brink of hell. "The brutally terse and matter-of-fact style of narration creates a constant mood within the story that is hard not to admire, and matches up with other masters of the thriller genre."

Chainsaw Honeymoon—At fourteen, Ruby Navarro is on an insane mission to get her parents back together, and she needs her two best friends, her dog, an arrogant filmmaker, a bizarre collection of actors, and a chainsaw-wielding movie killer to do it. "In the form of Ruby, Ramirez imparts to readers all the confusion brought about by puberty; the emotional neediness camouflaged by sarcasm; the obsession and continuing frustration with boys; and the bonds female teenagers forge with one another."

Come As You Are: A Short Novel and Nine Stories—Seventh-grader Ivan Stein finds a notebook controlled by demonic forces that will inflict suffering on the good as well as the bad and take his soul as payment. "Impossible to put down until the last page is read."

About the Author

Steven Ramirez is the winner of a 2019 Best Indie Book Award (BIBA) for *The Girl in the Mirror*, the first novel in a new supernatural suspense series, SARAH GREENE MYSTERIES. And he wrote the acclaimed horror thriller series TELL ME WHEN I'M DEAD. A former screenwriter responsible for the funny, bloody, and action-packed movie *Killers*, he has also published *Chainsaw Honeymoon*, a romantic comedy, and *Come As You Are*, a horror collection. Steven lives in Los Angeles.

Want to learn about new releases? Sign up for the newsletter at stevenramirez.com/newsletter.

Author Website
stevenramirez.com

facebook.com/StevenRamirezAuthor

twitter.com/byStevenRamirez

goodreads.com/byStevenRamirez

THE GIRL IN THE MIRROR

A Sarah Greene Supernatural Mystery

STEVEN RAMIREZ

Glass Highway
LOS ANGELES, CALIFORNIA

Glass Highway
Los Angeles, CA
stevenramirez.com

Publisher's Note: This is a work of fiction. Names, characters, places, and incidents are a product of the author's imagination. Locales and public names are sometimes used for atmospheric purposes. Any resemblance to actual people, living or dead, or to businesses, companies, events, institutions, or locales is completely coincidental.

The Girl in the Mirror / Sarah Greene Mysteries Book One / Steven Ramirez.—1st ed.
ISBN: 978-1-949108-03-3
Library of Congress Control Number: 2019903351

Edited by Shannon A. Thompson
Cover design by Damonza

For Daphne, who taught me dread.

They kept coming at him from the air, silent save for the beating wings. The terrible, fluttering wings. He could feel the blood on his hands, his wrists, his neck. Each stab of a swooping beak tore his flesh. If only he could keep them from his eyes. Nothing else mattered. He must keep them from his eyes.

Daphne du Maurier, "The Birds"

THE GIRL IN THE MIRROR

One

IT WAS the screaming that woke Sarah Greene. *Her* screaming. Sitting up, she tried calming her jackhammering heart by using a breathing technique she'd learned from a psychologist years ago. A slow, steady breath through the nose… Hold for three seconds… Purse the lips and exhale slowly… Relax and repeat. That always helped, even though she'd felt Dr. Bates had been a condescending bitch. *There's no such things as ghosts*, she had said through impossibly huge black designer frames and thin, pale lips that reminded Sarah of a Muppet. Did Muppets have lips?

Her bedroom was dark except for the glow from the colorful guardian angel night-light she'd had since she was a kid. The only reason she still used it was in case she had to get up in the middle of the night to pee. Or that's what she told herself. Maybe the real reason was that her mother had bought it for her when Sarah was suffering from night terrors. What time was it? She switched on a light and grabbed her phone from the nightstand. Just after midnight. She'd only been asleep, what, forty-five minutes?

"Gary?" she said.

She heard a thump from somewhere far off. Then, the familiar rapid padding noise as her sleek, gray tabby with the broken black stripes and cool green eyes bounded into the room. The cat leaped onto the antique iron double bed and maowed. She brought him close. That always made his eyes squishy, while magically pull-starting the purr machine.

"That was a bad one, Gary."

Realizing it would be hours before she could get to sleep again, she set the cat aside and threw back the sheet and duvet. She sat there, observing the goosebumps on the tan, muscular legs she'd developed running five miles a day. She didn't recall why but she'd decided to sleep in the over-size Knicks jersey Joe had given her when they were first married. The man was a New Yorker through and through. Had she been thinking about her ex-husband again?

"Goosebumps aren't sexy," she said, lifting a bare leg and modeling it for the indifferent feline.

She talked to Gary a lot, she noticed. Pathetic when you stopped to think about it. But he seemed to listen. Sometimes. Eventually, though, he got bored and hopped off the bed, looking for something better—like a game of Duck, Duck, Goose.

"Typical guy."

Sarah remained on the bed, waiting for the inevitable after-images she knew would follow. That's the thing about nightmares. They're never over until the sun comes up.

And she'd been having this particular one—or variations of it—since she was fifteen. That was when her best friend Alyssa died in a car crash. Exactly one week later, she appeared in Sarah's room. Sarah remembered she hadn't been scared. Instead, she cried. A few nights later, she had The Nightmare for the first time.

Now years later, she felt the familiar tingling dread—a cloud-like gloom gathering behind her eyes. Then, a parade of stilted pictures appearing like something out of a demented slideshow organized by evil clowns with French accents. A flash grenade of white-hot light sent her hurtling into a roiling vortex of familiar images.

She was standing in a place she didn't recognize, surrounded by dark, smooth walls. Though she was alone, she could feel a presence —something malevolent. Now, a whisper of wailing voices.

A dark, reddish light glimmered behind the walls, and she could see something moving. People. They were naked, their eyes filled with terror. She turned in a complete circle and saw that they were all around her. She could hear a deafening scraping noise as the walls began moving in on her. Thousands of hands tried to grab her. She opened her mouth to scream.

Coming out of it, Sarah could feel herself getting anxious again and decided to take another calming breath. Eventually, she pulled on a pair of jeans and made her way to the kitchen where she found the cat playing with a plastic bottle cap that had somehow missed the trash.

Now what? Coffee? No, she'd never get back to sleep. A drink? Hmm. She had a bottle of Talisker 25 Year Scotch Joe had given her on her thirtieth birthday. Pretty pricey for a guy who was famous for replenishing his underwear drawer once every decade, and only if Penneys was having a sale. Okay, maybe a quick one. That stuff needed to last until she turned forty, which was seven years away. Shit, forty…

She found a juice glass in the cupboard—she wasn't big on formality—and was about to grab the bottle when the temperature in the room dropped suddenly and the lights flickered.

"Come *on*."

Seeing her breath, she looked down and noticed Gary

staring intently at something. Turning, she saw it, too. The wispy image floating not ten feet from Sarah seemed solid at times, then transparent. Each time it tried to materialize fully, the lights dimmed.

Wordlessly, she dropped the glass, and it shattered on the floor, startling the cat and sending him skedaddling out of the room.

"Alyssa?" she said.

The last time she'd seen the girl, she came to warn Sarah—no, to *prepare* her—for her mother's impending death from cancer. Then as now, Sarah felt a deep sense of longing she hoped she would get over after seeing her best friend in the world lowered into the cold ground on a wet January morning. Two years later she would return, only now the coffin would contain her mother.

Alyssa Cortez was wearing the dress her grieving parents had picked out for her—white with little pink rose-buds around the collar and the gold crucifix they had given her for Christmas. Her dark hair was long—exactly the way she'd been wearing it since second grade. She was barefoot and *still fifteen*. Sarah recalled how in high school they used to spend so many hours in her old room painting each other's toenails and scaring each other with made-up ghost stories. Outside, Sarah's younger sister, Rachel, would try to horn in on the fun, but to no avail. That seemed so long ago.

"Sarah, you're in danger," the apparition said, its voice muted, as if she were speaking through a closed door.

"What? But how—"

"Be careful when you help the girl." Her voice was clearer now. "I hope… I'd really like to see you again."

Her image became unstable. Like a sigh, it faded into nothingness. Sarah reached out to her friend, hot tears streaming from her eyes.

"Alyssa, wait!"

But she was gone, and Sarah was alone.

The Cracked Pot was dead. Like Denny's on Blue Monday. Only woozy denizens desperate for a caffeine fix could be found hanging out at that hour because it was the only place in Dos Santos that was open. And the coffee was good, though you had to wait forever for a refill because each cup was "crafted" by hand.

It was one-thirty in the morning. Sarah sat across from her ex-husband and current business partner, Joe Greene, with two cups of steaming Guatemalan Antigua separating them. The beans had been roasted out back in a little shed earlier in the day, which was why the coffee was so damn good. She took a sip. Screw it, she wasn't getting back to sleep anyway.

Sarah thanked God Joe never complained whenever she called him up in the middle of the night to meet her so she could dump her latest problems on him. Come to think of it, he had never complained about anything—even when she informed him that she wanted a divorce. Hell, he'd been downright conciliatory about the whole thing and offered to help her find an attorney. She'd stayed mad about that for a long time. What? He couldn't wait to be rid of her?

She added more half-and-half to her cup, watching Joe drink his black. She had decided to wear her white cashmere sweater with the skinny jeans. In the old days, Joe would always tell her how much he loved that sweater—the way it hugged her every curve. Damn him, he even looked handsome just having fallen out of bed: graying hair that he always wore short, beard stubble, lean muscles bulging through his black T-shirt from all the physical labor. A softer Henry Rollins, she decided. And hot—*stop it, Sarah.*

"So, what happened?" he said, clueless as to where her mind was at the moment. "The nightmare again?"

"Yeah."

Coming down from her lustful feelings, she sighed dramatically and picked at a red spot on her cup that was in reality baked into the enamel.

"Sarah, you've had these before. It'll pass."

"I just wish I knew *why*, though."

He noticed she was holding the St. Michael medal she always wore around her neck. "I feel like you're not telling me everything."

For a guy, Joe had loads of intuition. "What? No, I… Okay, fine."

She lowered her voice, though the scruffy, tatted-up twenty-something server with the gauged earlobes was way over on the other side of the restaurant taking an order from that odd elderly couple she recognized from the local hardware store. They always seemed to be purchasing light bulbs, she remembered.

"Later in the kitchen, I, uh, I saw Alyssa."

"Your dead friend from high school?"

"Uh-huh. She was there. Almost in the flesh. Gary saw her, too."

Sarah never felt uncomfortable telling Joe about these episodes. They'd known each other for fifteen years—had it been that long?—and he had learned to accept that she was "special." In fact, he'd once told her he was glad to know there was an afterlife. Said it gave him hope.

"Was it like the last time? Did she speak to you?"

"She told me I was in danger."

"Anything specific?"

"Kind of. Apparently, I'm supposed to be helping some

random girl. I immediately thought of Katy, but then I wondered why Alyssa wouldn't have come out and said my niece's name."

Joe drained his cup and spun it back and forth between his hands. Sarah knew he did that whenever he was mulling something over. One time, he'd tried it with a wine glass at a fancy restaurant. Disaster. It wasn't a total loss, though. While a busboy cleaned up the mess, Joe proposed to her.

"I dunno," he said. "Maybe one of Lou's cases?"

"I don't think the police chief will be asking for my assistance anytime soon, not after that last fiasco. Anyway, I got the feeling this is something else. That something's going to—"

"Drop into your lap?"

"Yeah, exactly."

"I guess we need to wait and see. You want another cup?"

"No, I'm good. We should go."

They stood, and Joe looked around for the server but didn't see anyone. He opened his wallet and threw down a ten-dollar bill.

"Isn't that too much?" she said.

"Whatever."

Outside, they stood in the October chill between two vehicles—her classic black 1963 Ford Galaxie 500 XL and his late-model gray Dodge Ram truck. It occurred to Sarah that she'd never seen Joe driving a regular car. And the only time he'd put on a suit was when they got married. She had worn a white dress her dad had bought her in Santa Barbara.

Though Joe was Jewish, he had agreed to get married at Our Lady of Sorrows, the Catholic church where Sarah had been baptized, received her First Communion, and made her Confirmation. She'd been so happy back then. Though she didn't like to admit it—and she would never tell Joe this—sometimes, she thought the divorce might have been a huge mistake, especially since they were in business together again. But there was still the question of children.

"You going to be okay?" he said, taking her hand. Though they were rough, she loved the feel of his calloused fingers.

"I don't know."

"Want me to stay over? I promise I'll confine myself to the sofa."

She wanted to but she didn't. Technically, it would be a sin if they had sex again. She should know. Since the divorce, they'd found each other in her bed—or his—more times than she cared to remember. And each time in Confession, she promised Father Brian it wouldn't happen again.

"I'll take that as a no," he said, and dug out his keys.

"Wait." She took both his hands in hers and rolled her eyes at what she was about to say. "I'd feel better if I wasn't alone tonight."

"Okay."

And that was that.

As she swung open the front door, Sarah found Gary in the foyer, sitting on the hardwood floor and maowing. Sometimes, it irked her that the cat seemed to love Joe more than her. And it didn't help that the guy immediately picked up the purring animal, scratching him behind his ears as Gary kneaded his paws in the air.

"Next time his litter box is full, *you* can change it," she said, walking off.

Joe set the cat down and stepped into the kitchen. He knew where Sarah kept the scotch and brought it out along with two whiskey glasses. They both needed something to counteract the caffeine, he reasoned. He could hear her opening a closet and guessed she was taking out the extra bedding. Winking at the cat, he poured out two drinks and brought them into the living room where he found his ex-wife arranging the pillow and comforter on the sofa.

"I'd put you in the guest bedroom, but I'm using it for storage."

"It's fine."

As she turned around, he offered her a glass.

"Hey, I was saving that," she said, snatching the glass from him.

"I can always buy you more."

"So, when did you become Mr. Moneybags?"

"It's a write-off."

"I don't think Rachel will see it that way."

"It's no problem. I'll bury it in some construction costs. Your sister will never know."

"Like hell."

She shoved the comforter aside. They sat and, clinking their glasses once, tried the whiskey. Its warmth relaxed Sarah. She grabbed her phone and fired up some straight-ahead jazz.

"John Coltrane?" he said.

"Sonny Rollins. When are you going to learn?"

"I told you, I like country and western."

"You do *not*," she said, laughing.

Like an old married couple, Joe put his arm around his ex-wife as she laid her head on his chest and, playing with his ear, listened to Sonny pouring his heart out on "You Do Something to Me."

"You need a girlfriend," she said.

"What for?"

"So you can move on. Even though you're never going to find anyone as sweet as me. And funny. I've been told I'm funny."

"Are you kidding? That's the only reason I let you hang around the office."

"Excuse me?" she said, straightening up and fake-punching his shoulder.

"So, how come *you* haven't moved on?" He arched his eyebrows, making her snort as she raised her glass.

"I'm…working on it."

"It's been two years, Sarah."

"It has *not*."

"The divorce was final in July. Then in September, we talked about doing that annulment thingie."

"'Annulment thingie?'"

"This is October. You're thirty-three, so, two years."

"Oh shit, you're right." She drained her glass and got to her feet. "I need another drink."

She brought back the bottle and set it on the retro 1950s Italian coffee table she'd found in an antique shop in Ojai. The smooth metallic top was decorated in a series of inlaid gold squiggles that reminded Sarah of lovers embracing, which was why she'd bought it on the spot.

They each had two more scotches. Before Sarah knew it, they were making out on the sofa like a couple of high school kids after the prom. Soon, she was leading him by the hand to her bedroom. Gary was already positioned on the duvet. She gave him the stink eye, and he took off.

It was cold in the house. They undressed and slipped in between the cool sheets. Joe's body felt so good to her—

familiar and strong. As they kissed, she felt his rough hands all over her and no longer thought of the nightmare or the apparition. All she wanted was Joe—her friend, her lover. Her protector.

Afterward, they slept in each other's arms, warm and dreamless. Tomorrow, Sarah would make the drive to Santa Barbara to see Fr. Brian. It was the loneliness, she would tell him. The awful, soul-crushing loneliness. And being the awesome priest he was, he would forgive her sins once again.

Two

After her morning run, Sarah made the short drive to Our Lady of Sorrows in under ten minutes. Joe had left her house early to shower and change so he could meet with Greene Realty's construction crew about a new property they were renovating. She recalled that he'd told her very little about the place, and when she pressed him for details, he got all mysterious and quickly changed the subject. Whatever. Let him have his little secret. She'd pry it out of him eventually.

Sarah smiled at the memory of waking up in Joe's arms. It occurred to her that whenever she was with him, she was never afraid. He was strong, sure, but that wasn't it. There was something about him—a kind of *spirituality*. Which was hilarious because Joe was the least spiritual person she knew. He'd barely made it through his bar mitzvah and, to hear his father tell it, always mumbled his way through the prayers during High Holy Days.

Taking the 154 south toward Santa Barbara, Sarah had to pass Resurrection Cemetery, a place she'd avoided since moving to Dos Santos a year ago. Religiously. They'd been burying people there since the Spanish first arrived in California, and she was aware that ghosts regularly haunted the twenty woodsy acres.

The cemetery was the whole reason Sarah had hesitated when Joe asked her to move to Dos Santos and rejoin the real estate firm. Well, that and the fact that she wasn't sure it was a good idea for them to be working together again, with him handling the construction side of things and her selling houses. She'd been gone a year, and before that had been a co-owner of Greene Realty the whole time they were married.

After five years of marriage, she'd gone off on her own, neglecting to reclaim her maiden name. Had she secretly missed working with Joe? In any case, she had no intention of seeing more spirits than absolutely necessary. Eventually, though, he won her over, and she moved to Dos Santos.

Dark clouds were gathering as she found parking just off Anacapa Street several blocks from the church. Watching them scud across the sky, she thought again about the previous night's activities. Nightmare. Apparition. Amazing sex. That about summed up her life. Why hadn't she given up on wanting a normal existence? Because she *was* normal, she insisted. Prone to paranormal activity, sure, but normal just the same. She wondered if she should mention Alyssa's appearance. Fr. Brian had always been sympathetic, though he was unclear on how these things worked or what they meant vis-à-vis God's grand plan.

The first few drops of rain fell as she got out of her car and made her way to Our Lady of Sorrows, walking past Notre Dame School, which she'd attended for eight years. She stopped and stared at the field. Girls in belair plaid skirts, white polos, and navy sweaters were playing soccer on the wet field. Boys in navy pants and ash polos were playing basketball on the slick, newly paved courts. Some things never changed.

Several teachers with umbrellas watched from the sidelines. When she looked closer, Sarah thought she saw her fourth-grade teacher, Mrs. Lech, standing a ways off from the others. She was wearing knit pants and a sweater and carried no umbrella. She had died of a heart attack when Sarah was in middle school.

When the old woman turned to look at her, Sarah could see that half her face had rotted away, leaving the teeth exposed in a nerve-shattering grin. Breathless, Sarah hurried down the street toward the church.

Walking briskly toward Fr. Donnelly's office, she stopped when she noticed a little girl with long, dark hair pressed up against a wall as another girl blocked her way. Sarah guessed they were both in second grade. The other girl, who was taller, was saying something to the shorter one. And whatever it was, it was making her victim cry.

Sarah approached them and faced the larger of the two. "Everything okay over here?"

"Fine," the tall girl said, and walked away.

Sarah faced the smaller one and, crouching down, wiped the tears from her cheeks.

"You okay?"

"Yeah, I guess."

"Was that other girl being mean to you?" No response. "Mm-hmm. Well, you have a guardian angel, right?"

"Yes."

"And so does she. Tell you what. I'm going to have a word with *her* guardian angel about this. No bullying. That's the rule."

The little girl brightened. "You can talk to angels?"

"Well. Sometimes. They don't always listen, though."

Sarah scrunched her nose. "Too busy with God stuff, I guess. But I'll try, okay? For you."

"Okay."

"What's your name?"

"Emily."

"Okay, Emily. Take care now."

Sarah rose and watched as the little girl skipped away. She stopped abruptly and turned around.

"Hey, what's your name, anyway?"

"Sarah Greene."

"Bye!"

As Sarah stepped into the office, the assistant, Mrs. Ivy, recognized her and waved her through. Sarah knocked and stood in the doorway of the small cramped office. She loved this place. The smells of old books, British Sterling cologne, and coffee hung in the air like so many comforting memories. Fr. Donnelly was on the phone, and when he saw her, he motioned for her to come in and take a seat.

"That's what you said the last time, Neal. No, I— Can you get over here and fix it? I don't have to tell you how many elderly parishioners we have. I don't want the Hosts sticking to their tongues during Communion, *capiche*? Tomorrow morning? Great. See you then."

He shook his head as he put down his phone and smiled at Sarah.

"Furnace again?" she said, closing the door and taking a seat.

"We can't afford to replace it."

"I keep telling you, Joe knows people. He could probably get you a sweet deal."

"We'll see. What can I do for you, Sarah? Oh dear, don't tell me."

Sarah had known Fr. Brian Donnelly all her life. He

had baptized her, given her First Communion, and married Joe and her. It was rare that a priest could remain at the same parish for more than five years, and she sometimes wondered what sort of pull he had with the archdiocese. Nearing seventy, he still had a full head of white hair. And his blue eyes, though intense and penetrating, were kind and full of humor.

"Joe and I…"

"So, do you want to make your Confession here or out in the confessional?"

"Here is fine."

She felt awful having to do this again so soon. She'd planned to put on a formal defense, attempting to convince the priest—and therefore God—that sex with Joe was the only thing standing between her and the loony bin. But what was the use? It was a sin, period. They were no longer married. She might as well have picked up some loser at a bar in Isla Vista.

"Did something happen to trigger…those feelings?" he said.

"What? Oh…" She sighed and began toying with his desk calendar. "Nothing. I saw my dead friend. And, um, Mrs. Lech a few minutes ago, outside."

"I haven't thought about her in years. How did she look?"

"Not so good."

"Oh. And when these things happen, you take solace in…relations with your ex-husband?"

"I guess."

"How does *he* feel about it?" Strange, he'd never asked that before. "I mean, a non-Catholic who isn't religious."

"You mean a Jew."

"Sure."

"He's like me. Alone. Works too much. Is there when I

need him."

"A convenience?"

"No, a *friend*. Someone I trust. Who doesn't care that I'm this freak who sees dead people all the time."

"You're not a freak, Sarah. I've told you this. God has seen fit to—"

"Give me a gift. I know. I've always wanted to play the piano. Why couldn't He be a pal and give me that?"

"God is not your pal. He is your Father, and—"

"He knows what's best for me." She wiped her tears with a balled-up fist. "I know He does. It's just that sometimes…"

"Well, why don't you make your Confession now? I have another appointment."

She straightened up in her chair, made the Sign of the Cross, and closed her eyes. She could hear the steady ticking of the mantle clock on the bookshelf behind the priest.

"Bless me, Father, for I have sinned. It's been two weeks since my last Confession. These are my sins. I had sex with a man who isn't my husband."

Later, Fr. Donnelly stood outside in the wet cold with Sarah. She dreaded walking past the school again and pretended to look for her car keys.

"I see you're still wearing the medal I gave you," he said.

"And I never go anywhere without it."

"Oh, I almost forgot. We're having a Catholic singles' dance in two weeks. I'd like you to come."

"Why?"

"Because from what I gather, you're lonely. And call me old-fashioned, but I think you need to meet someone and get married again. Maybe have a couple of kids. You know, a *normal* life."

"Where do I sign up?"

"I'm being serious. You need to move on, Sarah."

"Why does everyone keep telling me that?"

"Maybe because it's true. You'll never be happy doing what you're doing. And remember. Ultimately, that's what God wants, for us to be happy."

"I'll think about it, okay?" She looked down at her medal. "Do you think St. Michael could find me a date?"

"Tickets are seventy-five dollars."

"Seventy-five bucks? Sounds like someone's trying to buy a new furnace."

"There's another gift God gave you," he said. "You're funny."

"Not according to some people."

He opened his arms and gave her a hug. "Take care, Sarah. Pray for God's grace."

"I do, Father. All the time."

She was grateful he hadn't brought up the annulment. It was true, she couldn't receive Communion. But she wasn't ready to accept that her marriage had never been valid in the first place. As she turned to leave, she did pray, though. This time, it was a silent plea that she wouldn't see any more dead people between the parish office and her car.

Greene Realty was quiet as Sarah walked in through the front door. Blanca, their receptionist, was on the phone, speaking to someone in Spanish. From what Sarah could gather, it was a family matter concerning one of her grown sons.

Joe was nowhere in sight, and Sarah assumed he was at the mystery house—or maybe the bank. She could see

Rachel sitting in her office, working. Joe's organizational skills were nonexistent, and as part of her agreement to come back, she required that he hire her sister to handle all the paperwork and run the office. He didn't put up a fight. Sarah loved seeing Rachel every day and took pains to make her happy.

The office was conveniently located next to The Cracked Pot, where Sarah had stopped to grab three cappuccinos and something for Blanca. Setting down the tray, she left a hot chocolate on the receptionist's desk. The middle-aged woman with the short, wiry brown hair mouthed *Gracias* and continued her phone conversation. On her way to her office, Sarah stopped to see Rachel and placed one of the coffees on her desk.

"Thought you could use this."

"Thanks," her sister said.

"My pleasure."

Rachel looked nothing like Sarah. Her skin was much fairer, and her straight, shoulder-length hair had these wonderful blonde streaks in it that Sarah happened to know were real. Not like her own dark, wavy hair. And though Sarah had hazel eyes, Rachel's were green.

When they were little, Sarah was convinced there had been a mix-up at the hospital and her parents had brought home the wrong baby. She used to tease Rachel about it, making her cry, until her father warned her to lay off or he would send Sarah to military school. Rachel's daughter, Katy, got her mother's looks. They were both beautiful women, Sarah felt.

"So, where've you been?" Rachel said. "A potential client stopped by earlier. A real looker, if you ask me."

Sarah had been lingering in the doorway and stepped in, closed the door, and took a seat.

"Joe came over last night."

"Oh, no, honey. Not again."

"Afraid so."

"Well, was it at least…"

"Rachel, it's always good. That's the problem."

"I'm sorry, but I don't see why you two ever got divorced. I mean, you apparently love each other. And he seems to be okay with all your paranormal shenanigans. Most men I know wouldn't put up with that."

"We're friends."

"You're having sex."

"Again, as friends."

"Friends with benefits? No, I'm not buying it."

"Rache, I want to have kids someday, and Joe has made it very clear he doesn't. And even if he did, I doubt he would want to convert."

"Why would he have to?"

"Because when you have children, everything changes. Especially when it comes to religion."

"Well, I don't know about that. But as far as kids, you've got Katy."

"And I love her to pieces but, you know, I want my own."

"No, I understand."

Sarah shook her head . "It's impossible. And now, Fr. Brian wants me to go to some stupid singles' dance."

"It's actually not a terrible idea."

"Oh my G— You, too?"

"Look, if you want to have kids, you *should* get married. And if you're not marrying Joe again, you need to meet someone. That's all I'm saying."

Sarah got to her feet. "Glad we had this talk."

"Anytime. You still coming by for dinner? Eddie's been looking forward to it."

"I'm his daughter. Why *wouldn't* he look forward to it?

Besides, what else have I got to do? Apparently, I'm not having sex ever again."

"There are worse things." There was a sharpness to Rachel's voice, and her sister reddened as she headed for her office to make phone calls.

Nice one, Sarah. What an insensitive bitch.

Instead of turning into her office, she continued out toward the rear exit and dumped the remaining two cappuccinos in the trash. She wanted to spend the rest of the day with Joe—she needed his company. It was a powerful urge, and as she retrieved her car keys, it hit her.

It was that dream. And she was scared.

On her way to her dad's house in Santa Barbara, Sarah thought about her last conversation with Rachel and again regretted that stupid crack about not having sex. Her sister was a widow. Her husband, Paul, was a Marine and had deployed to Afghanistan twice. On his third tour of duty, he went to Iraq. In Mosul, his unit was attacked by ISIS forces. They managed to overpower the enemy, forcing them to retreat. But on the way back, the Humvee he was riding in hit an IED, and Paul was killed instantly. Katy had just turned three.

Sarah pulled up to her dad's modest Westside home and parked in the driveway. Rachel and Katy had moved in with their father after Paul died. It turned out to be a good decision. Eddie was getting on in years and, though he still taught at Santa Barbara City College, both his girls felt that, being a widower himself, he could use the company. Besides, he loved his granddaughter, and she was crazy about him, especially since she no longer had a father.

Though Sarah and Rachel preferred wine, Eddie liked beer, so she had picked up a six-pack of Modelo along with a bottle of pinot noir. Whenever she came back to "the old house," Sarah's head filled with memories. Not of ghosts or poltergeists or other phenomena. Usually, she would remember the silly things.

Her old bedroom, which Katy now occupied, was on the second floor and faced the street. Approaching the house, Sarah smiled, recalling the time she tried to sneak out through her window after curfew to meet a boy—what was his name?—in the park so they could make out. She was thirteen and had gone to the trouble of using pillows to make it appear she was in bed. Eddie caught her, though, and grounded her for a month. Good times.

As soon as Sarah walked in the door, Katy greeted her. Sarah set down her purse and plastic bags and gave her niece a hug.

"Aunt Sarah, what's in the bag?"

"Oh, beer and wine. And…"

"Something for me?"

"Maybe."

"Can I look?"

Katy went through the bags and pulled out a fifty-piece set of Art-I-San gel pens in neon, glitter, and pastel colors.

"Oh wow, I've been wanting these! Thank you!"

Rachel walked in, wearing an apron. Folding her arms, she shook her head as Katy ran off with the pens, saying *thank you* repeatedly as she disappeared around a corner.

"You spoil her," Rachel said. "Truly."

"And you." Sarah pulled out the wine and showed it to her sister.

"And me. Come on, the food's ready."

"Hey, hang on a sec. Rache, I'm sorry about what I said earlier. That was thoughtless."

"No, I get it. You get horny. A lot."

"Okay, I guess we're even now."

Dinner was simple: salad, chicken enchiladas, rice, and beans. Rachel was the first to admit she didn't cook as well as Sarah. But the food was good, and the company even better.

"Aunt Sarah?" Katy said.

"Yes, my love?"

"Why do you think God wants you to see ghosts?"

"Katy, for crying out loud," Rachel said.

"The other day, our teacher was telling us about Padre Pio and how he had seen apparitions most of his life. But he's a saint. Are you—"

Sarah laughed. "A *saint*? No, honey. You see, it's the gift I was given."

"But aren't those things, like, dangerous? I was watching this show about ghost hunters and—"

"Sometimes, they are. And, look, Katy, I'm no expert. But I think they're mostly sad."

"Oh. I never thought of that." For a moment, Sarah's niece looked dejected. Then, she brightened. "I drew something for you today."

Katy picked up the drawing pad she always kept with her, tore out a page, and handed her aunt a pen-and-ink drawing of a comical-looking ghost trying to order coffee.

"Oh my gosh, this is fantastic!"

"And don't forget," Rachel said, "your aunt was an art history major in college, so her opinion counts."

Sarah gave her niece a hug. "Thank you."

She adored her niece, who was extremely talented. Katy looked almost exactly like Rachel when she was eleven.

"Can we please not have any more talk about ghosts?" Eddie said.

She turned to her father and noticed his irritated expression. He seemed smaller somehow, his once dark hair streaked with white and skin that was soft—almost baby-like. And those kind hazel eyes she'd gotten from him. She liked that he had kept his moustache.

"Not a problem," Sarah said. "So, what's going on with you, Eddie?"

"The same. Doctor keeps telling me to cut down on bad fats."

"You should listen to him."

"When I'm dead I'll cut down. Which reminds me, don't even think about canceling my pork tamales this Christmas."

"We'll see."

He took another swallow of beer. "How's the car running?"

"Fine. Although it could use an oil change."

"Bring it over on Saturday."

"Thanks, Eddie."

He finished his beer and set the bottle down. "I haven't seen Joe in a while."

"He works a lot."

"He's been promising to take me to a Lakers game."

Rachel laughed. "That will only happen if they're playing the Knicks."

The conversation moved on to Katy and school. Sarah took a slow swallow of wine and gazed out the front window. A low, pale fog had settled on the street. Something inside it was moving. She looked closer. That's when she saw her. Alyssa. She was floating in the mist in the middle of the street, translucent in the amber glow of the streetlights.

She seemed to be watching Sarah.

Three

HE LOOKS SO VULNERABLE. Sarah was standing across from a man wearing a gray Italian wool sweater and Ralph Lauren sport coat with, what, Rag & Bone jeans? Just a tad on-the-nose, she felt. Still, he was handsome. Mid-forties maybe? Her antique English oak pedestal desk stood between them as they shook hands. Joe had found it for Sarah on eBay and decided to buy it when she agreed to rejoin the firm. It was the only expensive thing she owned, other than her car, which her father had restored to factory specs.

"Why don't you take a seat?" she said, sneaking a glance at his left hand. She took note of the line where a wedding band used to be. "I'm sorry, what did you say your name is?"

"Michael Peterson."

"Sarah—"

"Greene, I know. It's on your desk sign," he said, pointing.

She stifled a cackle with her hand. "I'm such an idiot." Then, clearing her throat, "Okay. I understand you dropped by the other day. Can I ask how you heard about us?"

"Well, to be honest, I started with a couple of realtors in Santa Barbara. I didn't really connect with them, though—I have very particular tastes. I happened to attend Mass at Our Lady of Sorrows and saw your ad in the bulletin." He smiled warmly. "And here I am."

"Wow, I didn't think anyone read those ads," she said, laughing. *This guy's Catholic? Is God trying to tell me something?* "Anyway. So why Dos Santos? You look like you could afford a more expensive neighborhood. Montecito, maybe?"

He blushed, which made him all the more attractive. "Well, I'm not what you'd call rich. And besides, I like the quiet. It's been...a bad year. I took a drive up into the forest before coming over here. You know, to get a sense of the place."

"And the verdict?"

"Dos Santos is exactly what I'm looking for."

The "bad year" comment got Sarah's attention. She had an urge to dig into the matter. And he might've told her, too. In two minutes, this guy had said more than Joe did in a week. In a way, it was refreshing.

"Well," she said. "I've got some time this afternoon if you want me to show you a few properties."

"That would be fantastic."

"May I ask what you do, Michael?"

"I'm between jobs at the moment. But don't worry—I have money set aside. I'm from New York. Used to be in banking."

"I see. Well, what's your price range?"

They spent the next half-hour in front of Sarah's large computer monitor looking at properties. The only fragrance she could detect coming off him was the faint smell of deodorant. As they looked at the screen together, she could feel his warm breath on her neck and wondered if he was intentionally staying close.

"Sorry, too close?" he said.

"You're fine."

When they had narrowed the list down to six properties based on Michael's preferences, she printed the listings. She gathered everything up and escorted her new client out toward the front entrance.

"Blanca, I'm on the road!"

But the receptionist was on the phone again, probably giving one of her sons hell.

"My car's in the back," Sarah said when they'd gotten outside. "I need to grab a coffee. Can I get you something?"

"Sure."

The Cracked Pot was bursting with the tail end of the lunch crowd, and Sarah and Michael had to fight their way to the counter to order. While they waited, Michael appeared to be sizing up the place. He seemed to be amused by the employee uniform. Everyone, except for the cooks, wore crisp white cotton shirts, black pants, and red bowties.

"Reminds me a lot of New York," he said.

"The food's good here, FYI."

"Wonderful. So, the agency. You started it?"

"No, that was my business partner, Joe Greene. I joined later. Well, *re*-joined. Long story."

"Okay, and he made you change your name to Greene?"

She looked at him askance and saw that he was smiling. "Joe's my ex-husband."

"Ahh, got it. And you kept his name? Interesting."

She had told this story a million times. What was one

more go-around? Besides, Michael seemed like a good listener.

"I thought about changing it. But it would cost too much, what with all the business cards and the advertising on bus benches. Oh, and the supermarket shopping carts."

"Don't forget the pens."

"Right. Speaking of which." She dug into her purse and handed him a Greene Realty pen.

"Thanks. I guess that makes sense. So, what's your maiden name?"

"Cruz."

This guy asks a lot of questions. Does that mean he's interested?

Finally, their coffees came, and they were on the road in Sarah's Galaxie. The sky was clear—a good day for looking at properties. They started on a street off the main drag—a spacious two-bedroom townhome Joe had reno-vated and put back on the market two weeks ago. After that, they worked their way to other single-family homes scattered around town. The entire time they kept the conversation light and impersonal. Twice Sarah thought they'd found the right house. But each time Michael balked.

It was after five and getting dark when Sarah pulled up in front of the agency. They got out and stood on the side-walk, watching as the streetlights came on. It was a charming street, filled with trendy little clothing and antique shops. A new tapas bar had opened recently, and Sarah had toyed with the idea of inviting Michael for a drink. But in the end, she didn't feel comfortable.

"I appreciate you doing this, Sarah," he said. "Sorry I wasn't more enthusiastic. I warned you, I'm a tough customer. You guys did some amazing work with those renovations, though."

"Thanks. You know, Michael, I was sure one of those

properties would've appealed to you. So, what exactly *are* you looking for?"

"Agents probably hate hearing this, but I'll know it when I see it. After my wife died, I wasn't thinking about much of anything. Certainly not buying a house."

"I'm sorry. If you'd rather not—"

"No, it's okay. I don't mind talking about it. She was killed by a drunk driver on the Long Island Expressway. She was driving back from visiting friends in the Hamptons."

Sarah touched his hand, and he immediately withdrew it. *Shit, do I repulse him?*

"Sorry, I need to go," he said. "I'll let you know if I decide on something. By the way, I love your car. Not every day you meet a woman willing to put up with manual steering. Boy, I hope that didn't sound *too* sexist."

"Not at all. The car is a small price to pay," she said, flexing both biceps. "Get a load of these guns."

"Impressive."

"Okay, um, you have my cell. If you want to do this again…" But he was already walking away. "I'm available." Then, to herself, "Twenty-four-seven. Like 911. God, I am so pathetic."

As Michael headed down the sidewalk toward a red rental car parked on the street, she felt stupid for pulling the Wonder Woman routine, though he seemed happy to play along.

The wind had kicked up, and it was getting colder. She continued watching as he got in without looking back, started the engine, and made a U-turn into traffic. There was something about him. And it was more than the sadness of losing a loved one. Though it was vague, she had the distinct sense he had lost so much more.

"Should I be jealous?" someone behind her said.

Sarah turned to find her ex-husband smiling at her.

"Where've you been all day?"

She worried he'd witnessed her earlier awkwardness with her new client. Joe was wearing fresh clothes, including a leather bomber jacket she didn't recognize, and she knew he'd showered and changed after doing construction work. Was he planning something for the two of them?

"I thought we could grab a drink," he said.

"That sounds good."

"Want to try that new place?"

"Since when do you like tapas?"

"I heard it's good. And for your information, my tastes go beyond bagels and brisket."

"We'll see. But first, I need to move my car. How about I meet you over there?"

By this time, all thoughts of Michael Peterson had evaporated like steam from a kettle. As Joe jaywalked across the street, Sarah thought about how much she loved the way he moved. It was masculine and all kinds of sexy. But there was a real confidence there, too. He seemed to always know where he was going. Literally. Unlike her. In high school, she'd read a book on the life of Hildegard von Bingen, a twelfth-century saint and mystic who had famously described herself as "a feather on the breath of God." *If she's a feather,* Sarah had thought at the time, *then I must be a ball of lint on God's cardigan.*

Her appetite sharpened by thoughts of tasty Spanish food, Sarah pulled around back. As she cut through the office to the front door, she fantasized about drinks and appetizers turning into dinner somewhere, then "dessert" at her house. *Cut it out, Sarah. What would Fr. Brian say?*

Good thing they'd decided to come early because by the time their food and drinks arrived, the tiny venue was packed. El 600, after the street address, was owned by two gay gentlemen named Nicky and Fahim. Nicky was African-American and Sarah was pretty sure Fahim was Persian. Both were in their early thirties, impossibly thin, and loved everything Spanish. They had vacationed together in Barcelona numerous times and, after their last trip, decided to open a tapas bar. Sarah had meant to ask the inevitable *Why Dos Santos?* but had not yet had the chance.

"So you look like you want to tell me something," she said to Joe after taking a sip of her Priorat.

The smells coming off the tiny plates of the food they'd ordered were intoxicating: Patatas Alioli, Canelon de Atun, Jamon con Pan de Tomate—it was all too much, and she was grateful she'd gotten in her run that morning. She made the Sign of the Cross, said a quick blessing, and tried the tuna. Heaven.

"What?" she said, noticing Joe smiling at her.

"Nice to see you have your appetite. I mean, what with the ghosties and all."

"Shut up. Come on, dig in. This stuff is amazing."

He tried the potatoes. "Mm. Sarah, I wanted to talk to you about the new project."

Finally! And I didn't have to threaten to chop off a finger.

"It's our biggest one yet, and it's going to be a lot of work."

"Okay. I take it, you got it at auction?"

"That's just it. It sort of fell into our laps. The bank approached *me*."

"Why?"

"They said they didn't want to lose any more money and knew I would pay a fair price."

"Does that happen often?"

"Not really. I took a ride out there and called them on the spot with an offer."

"Have you got a pic?"

"Hang on." He pulled his phone from his pocket. "This is it."

She studied the photos of the two-story Spanish-revival with the white stucco walls and red terracotta roof tiles. It wasn't anything unusual, Sarah felt. There were lots of homes in the area that looked similar.

"Where's it located again?" she said.

"It's way up in the forest off San Marcos Pass Road."

"I didn't think there were any homes up there."

"It *is* pretty isolated. The original owners bought the lot and built a custom home on it. Wait till you see it in person. It's pretty magnificent."

He's awfully chatty today. "What do you think we'll be able to get for it?"

Joe sat back and folded his arms across his chest. She felt as if there was joke here, but she wasn't getting it and scrunched her nose.

"Joe?"

"A mil-and-a-quarter," he said. "Maybe more."

"Are you *serious*? How much did you pay?"

"Just under four. I figure with labor and materials, we're going to have to put in another three-to-four."

"That only leaves a profit of—"

"Two-and-a-quarter, I know. But it puts us into a whole new luxury market."

She wiped her lips with her napkin. "That's incredible."

"It is." He twirled his fork in the air. "And with places like this opening up all over town, we'll be able to attract a more elite clientele."

"Are you sure you never went to B-school?" she said.

"I'm very excited."

"And here I thought you were keeping secrets from me."

"I wanted it to be a surprise."

"So, when do I get to see the place?"

"Tomorrow morning. I'd like you to walk the property and look at every inch of the place before Manny and the guys start knocking out walls."

Manny Ortiz was Joe's construction foreman and Blanca's long-suffering husband. There was nobody in the business better than Manny.

"I'll be there."

Doing a quick dance move with her arms, Sarah leapt out of her chair and hugged her business partner.

"You did good, Mr. Greene."

But when she leaned in to kiss him, he awkwardly avoided her lips, causing her to freeze mid-hug.

"Sorry," she said. "I was excited about the— What's with the pull-back?"

"Well, there *is* one other thing I need to talk to you about."

"Uh-oh."

Shoulders slumped, she returned to her chair and slugged the entire glass of wine, bracing herself for the worst.

"Okay," he said. "This is going to sound a little weird because… I never thought I would… I mean, it sort of… Happened."

"Joe, can you please tell me already?"

He leaned forward and spoke in a low voice. "I met someone."

"Oh." She blinked hard. "Okay. For a second, I thought you wanted to dissolve the partnership."

"Sarah, come on. This is *our* business."

"Right. I knew that. So, this is why you've been mysteriously absent a lot. Who is she?"

"Her name is Gail."

She felt her body stiffen. Could this be happening?

"Where did you meet her?" she said.

"At the County Recorder's office."

"How romantic."

"She's a paralegal. We hit it off, I guess."

Sarah dismissed the image of her stabbing Joe in the eye with her olive fork. She felt as though she'd fallen down a deep well head first. As Joe continued to effuse over the mystery lady, everything was moving farther and farther away until her ex-husband sounded like that trapped insect from *The Fly*. She had to will herself back to the surface.

"Well, that's…great," she said, forcing a smile that felt as if it would tear her face. "Will I get a chance to meet her at some point?"

"I guess. You're okay with this, right?"

"It's fine. It's not as if you're supposed to be a monk. Do they have Jewish monks?" She tried imagining Joe in a monk robe, which was followed by another naughtier image. *Jeez, Sarah, really?*

"Okay, that's a relief," he said. "We have to work together, and I don't want this to be awkward."

"No, it's not awkward. Or anything." *Kill me now.* "So, I guess you're seeing her tonight? Hence the…" She pointed at his jacket.

"Yeah, later. We're having dinner in Ojai."

"Well, don't let *me* keep you."

She saw a server and waved her over. Joe was about to hand her his credit card when Sarah put her hand on his, a little too hard.

"Let me get this one."

"Are you sure?"

"Positive."

She handed over her Amex card and finished the last few drops of wine. They'd hardly touched their food. Sarah had walked in starving, and now she felt nauseous. After signing the credit card slip, she and Joe left the bar. Outside, it was raining again. Perfect. She'd get soaked walking back to her car. *There goes my stupid hair.*

Joe smiled at Sarah. "See you in the morning. I'll text you the address."

"Night, Joe." Then as he walked off, "Have fun."

She stood in the rain for a long time, not caring that she was getting drenched to the bone. They had never really discussed seeing other people. It occurred to her, this whole time she'd been clinging to the idea that, even if they were no longer married, they would be together somehow. Stupid Catholic school girl fantasy if there ever was one, she told herself.

"*You* were the one who asked for the divorce, genius," she said. "But only because Joe lied about wanting kids."

The parking lot behind Greene Realty seemed darker than usual. One of the outside floodlights was flickering, causing dramatic shadows to appear, then vanish. Somewhere in the distance she thought she heard the sound of beating wings.

Everyone else had gone home, and Sarah's was the only car in the lot. As the rain fell hard in rivulets on her windshield, she sat behind her steering wheel, gripping it tightly, and cried with a sorrow she hadn't felt since the divorce became final.

Four

THE HOUSE SAT at the top of a rise in a clearing that Sarah estimated to be around half an acre. Beyond that on either side and to the rear stood incredibly tall coast redwoods that loomed like gigantic guardians of the forest. A slow mist had gathered at the base of the cement driveway, which was cracked and weedy. Morning light shone through heavy gray clouds, the rays missing the house and leaving it in shadow like an unpopular child in a school-yard. Sarah had often run in the area, but she'd never come this far. *Why would someone want to live way up here? All alone?*

She and Joe had decided to drive up in his truck. Two coffees sat in the twin cup holders. She grabbed hers to warm herself against the morning chill. On the way, she had wanted to ask him about his date but remembered their conversation about not letting things get awkward and decided it was better to let it lie. Joe volunteered noth-ing, and she wondered if the night had gone badly. Then, she realized she secretly hoped it *had* and tried putting the thought out of her mind.

Manny and his crew would arrive later, and Sarah and Joe had the house to themselves for about an hour. Joe always insisted she check a property before starting any renovations. She asked him why once, and he told her it was because she had taken all those architecture and interior design classes after college. But maybe it was something more. Had she rubbed off on him and he wanted to make sure nothing "otherworldly" was going on?

The latter would make sense because typically you would receive little information from the bank about a property they were unloading. In California, you are only required to disclose "material facts" such as structural concerns and total square footage. The property's history was irrelevant and, short of a mass murder, buyers would end up knowing almost nothing—unless they asked. And anyway, Joe seemed to have an instinct about buying properties that were devoid of the paranormal.

Sarah felt cold as they got out of the truck, and she wished she'd worn a sweater under her short black leather jacket. She grabbed her coffee and stood back, taking in as much of the house as she could. At five-eight, she considered herself tall. And in her Steve Madden boots with the three-inch heels, she was enormous—except when she was with Joe, who was six-three. But standing in front of the imposing two-story Spanish-revival, she felt tiny. She was sure it was because of the angle and proceeded to walk the perimeter. Joe remained in the truck, dialing his phone. She wondered if he was calling Gail.

Weeds sprouted everywhere through the sand surrounded the house. Sarah noticed an enormous raven observing her from the roof. When she looked up at it, the bird croaked threateningly and flew off. So far, she hadn't gotten any strange emanations—not that she was inviting them. The white, roughly textured stucco walls were cracked in places, and they would probably want to replace the windows with double-paned. On the side, she found an ugly row of firethorn bushes growing close to the house.

"Hell naw," she said to the curious squirrel observing her from a nearby Manzanita tree.

The rest of the property was unremarkable. A massive hole dominated the backyard where some previous owner had started to build a pool, then abandoned it. Now, it lay there desolately, filled with black, stagnant water and rotting leaves.

"You ready to look inside?" Joe said, walking toward her.

He put a hand on her shoulder, which surprised her, given the whole Gail situation.

"Yeah. We're filling this in, right?"

"Think so? It wouldn't take much to finish the job. A pool will add a lot of value."

"I guess."

They returned to the front door where Sarah noticed white tiles above the lintel with the words Casa Abrigo emblazoned in blood red.

Joe squinted at the words. "Abrigo?"

"It means 'shelter,'" she said.

"Shelter, huh? From what, I wonder."

He removed the key from the lock box and let them both in. What hit Sarah first was the deadness of the air. Not even dust motes were moving in the thin rays of light that fell like dying angels from the windows.

"How many bedrooms?" she said.

"Four upstairs. And a maid's quarters and laundry room down that way off the kitchen."

"Let's start upstairs."

As they crossed the dusty terra cotta floor, their footsteps echoed in the emptiness of a space that was beginning to unnerve Sarah. Out of the corner of her eye, she thought she noticed something moving. At the foot of the stairs, she turned. That same raven was perched in a tree outside, its head cocked to one side. It was staring at her through a window. *This is how it all started in* The Birds.

Room by room, they made their way through the house. Overall, Sarah's impression was that it was a nice property but needed lots of work. Little things. Scratched window casings, cracked floor tiles, water damage on the ceiling, and bathrooms that sorely needed updating. The usual stuff. If they were lucky, they might be able to get away with putting in under three hundred. Unless Joe insisted on the damned pool.

They had decided to look at the kitchen last. It wasn't in bad shape, except for the outdated appliances and fluorescent lighting that made Sarah shudder. As she scanned the room, she noticed an arched door.

"There's a cellar?"

"Guess I forgot about it." Joe walked over and tried the doorknob. Locked.

"You don't have a key?"

He crouched down and peered at the keyhole. "Nope. Just this one—opens the front and back doors."

Sarah heard the sounds of a vehicle door slamming and guessed Manny and the guys had arrived.

"Maybe Manny can get it open," she said.

Leaving her coffee cup on the kitchen island that was thick with dust, Sarah headed out with Joe as Manny was approaching.

"Where are the boys?" Joe said.

"Be here soon."

The "boys" were Manny's three sons—Nacho, Memo, and Pollito—who were two years apart and all in their twenties. Though they were excellent workers, they tended not to manage the rest of their lives very well. In fact, they still lived at home because they were incapable of saving any money, a situation Manny bore with the silent fortitude of an early Christian martyr. And, according to Blanca, they knew nothing about maintaining healthy romantic relationships. From her tone, it was clear the woman was desperate for grandchildren.

Sarah loved Manny. With his salt-and-pepper hair and dark skin, he reminded her of her dad but without the university education. As a boy, Manny had traveled up from Mexico with his mother and younger sister to join their father in the fields in the Central Valley. He learned English quickly and, by the time he was twelve, was working construction. Eventually, he made his way south toward LA. But on a stopover in Ventura, he met Blanca, who was working as a server at a local Coco's restaurant. He never did make it to LA.

"Can you pick a lock?" Joe said, smiling hopefully.

Manny shrugged. "Can't all Mexicans?"

After grabbing some tools from his truck, Manny worked on the door, which was made of knotty alder. The handle and keyhole cover were wrought iron. Manny inserted a tension wrench and turned it slightly. Using a pick, he worked the pins of the lock one by one. When he'd finished with the last pin, he tilted his head toward Joe, who turned the knob. The door opened easily.

"Nice job, MacGruber," Sarah said.

As Joe pushed the door open, they found a tiled stairway with a wrought-iron railing that led to a cellar. Sarah went last, and as she made her way down the stairs, an intense musty odor assaulted her, making her dizzy. Narrow, grime-covered windows gave off a weak light, and for a second, she thought she felt something brush past her.

"Why is it so cold down here?" When she reached the

bottom, she found racks and racks of dust-covered wine bottles.

"That's why," Joe said.

Manny whistled. "*Hijo.* How much do you think all this is worth?"

"There might be an inventory book down here somewhere."

Joe and Sarah began checking the bottles. She recognized French, Italian, and California labels—all expensive.

"How will we know if they're any good?" she said.

"Only one way."

Joe carefully removed one of the bottles and blew the dust off. He handed it to Sarah, who saw that it was 1961 Chateau Palmer Bordeaux.

She smiled. "Looks like we're having pizza and wine for dinner."

"I'll stick to Miller Lite," Manny said.

"*Pa?*" a voice said from the kitchen.

Manny turned to look. "My boys are here. Time for some real work."

Something crashed. All three turned to find a wine bottle that lay shattered on the tile, the dark red liquid pooling around it like blood.

"Don't look at me," he said, and went upstairs.

Later at The Cracked Pot, Sarah and Joe discussed the new project over a chopped salad and corned beef sandwich.

"I don't understand why you think the renovation will cost more than a couple of hundred," she said.

"Well, I thought we could knock out the wall separating the kitchen and dining room. And I want to go high end on the appliances."

"Still seems like a lot. The house is in great shape. Why didn't the bank want more?"

"That's what I said, but they wouldn't tell me."

"And why didn't the other buyer offer more?"

"It's a mystery. Also, remember. I haven't gotten a plumber or electrician out here yet. Who knows *what* we'll find."

Taking a bite of her salad, Sarah watched Joe digging into his sandwich. Though she was hesitant to ask, she decided she might as well know now how things stood between them, romance-wise.

"So, are you going to split that expensive Bordeaux with Gail?"

"I'll pick out another one for her."

She did her best to suppress a victory grin. "You do realize everything down there might be corked."

"It's a chance I'm willing to take."

He began spinning his empty coffee cup, and she wondered if she should roll the dice again and broach the subject of "the date." To be honest, he looked like he wanted to tell her. Like Sarah, Joe didn't have a lot of close friends to confide in.

"Joe—"

"Sarah, about last night," he said. "I didn't mean to spring it on you like that."

"It's okay. Like you said, we both need to move on." *Like hell.* "So, can you tell me anything about her? Please don't say she has a tiny waist and huge boobs."

"She's nice. Went to UCLA. Wanted to be an attorney."

"But settled for paralegal?"

"Decided she didn't want the pressure."

"And what are her views on marriage?" *Wow, did I say that out loud?*

"Sarah, for Chri— Sorry. Look, we've only started dating. How would I know?"

I'd know. "So, is she Jewish?"

"Yes."

Shit. Well, at least his parents will be happy. "And, um, things went well, did they?"

"Okay, this is getting weird."

"Hey, I'm just trying to be supportive."

"We had a nice time."

So, no sex, then. "Okay, I'm done. Are you heading back out to the house?"

"Yeah." He looked at his watch. "In fact, I should get going. I'll check in with you later. You can decide what kind of pizza we're having with the wine."

"You got it."

He got up and left cash on the table. As he started off, he put his hand on hers. "See you soon. Take care of yourself."

"You know me."

Rather than go back to the office right away, Sarah decided to sit a while, and signaled the server to bring more coffee. For a guy who was hot for another woman, Joe was certainly being affectionate. Maybe he felt guilty and was making an effort? Nevertheless, she decided to enjoy it while it lasted. Soon, this other shrew would get her hooks into him, and the next thing you know, Sarah and Joe would be forced to conduct business exclusively by phone and email.

Whoa. Where did that come from? She'd never met the woman. Maybe she was nice. But Joe was nice, too— nice enough to be taken advantage of. *Stop it, Sarah. Joe is a grown man. He can take care of himself.*

Someone who wasn't her server brought over a fresh coffee and set it down. She was young—early twenties—and wore her almost-black hair in a cute choppy bob. Sarah smiled at the small anime tattoo of a girl she recognized on her neck.

"I love the tattoo. Isn't it from *Spirited Away?*"

"Yeah, Chihiro."

"Chihiro, right. My niece loves anime, and I watched that movie with her one time. Thanks for the refill, um…"

"Carter. And no prob."

"I'm Sarah."

"Good to know."

Interesting girl. After she'd gone, Sarah sipped her coffee and decided to put Gail out of her mind, focusing instead on wood-fired pizza and red wine.

Joe called around three. Sarah was in her office updating listings on their website and was surprised to hear from him. Usually, he, Manny, and the boys would go at it all day without interruption. The key to these renovations was to move as quickly as possible to make up for time spent waiting for inspections.

"S'up?" she said.

"We found something in the cellar. I think you should take a look."

"I'm kind of in the middle of something. Can it wait?"

"Can you get over here?" he said. *"Please?"*

"Okay, calm down. On my way."

She disconnected and grabbed her purse. Strange. Joe almost never ordered her around. Unless it was something serious.

When she arrived at Casa Abrigo, Sarah found three

trucks in the driveway and had to park on the street. As she got out, she noticed the damaged storm drain. More money. Approaching the house, she heard the sounds of men's voices and banging, and guessed they'd started taking down the wall.

"Joe?" she said, stepping into the foyer.

Manny and his sons, each with a sledge hammer, were covered in white dust as they removed the last of the two-by-fours separating the dining room from the kitchen. Pieces of drywall and wood sat in piles on the floor. She had to admit, the dining room did look better with the kitchen exposed.

"He's in the cellar," Manny said.

She made her way past the sweaty men and headed down the cellar stairs. She found Joe holding a flashlight, moving slowly along one of the walls.

"You rang?" Sarah said.

"Hey, glad you're here. I want to show you something."

He took her by the hand and led her to an inner wall. Two large wine racks had been pushed aside, and she could see an arched door standing in the middle, similar to the one off the kitchen.

"A secret room? Joe, how did you find this?"

"It was an accident. I dropped my flashlight, and it rolled behind one of the racks. Then, I felt the cold air and had to take a look."

"What's inside?"

"No idea. I waited for you."

"Oh, how sweet. What am I, Miss Marple?" No answer. "Fine."

Joe took a step back, and Sarah tried the doorknob. Locked.

"Manny!" she said, her singsong voice echoing up the stairs.

It took their foreman longer to unlock this door. When he'd finished, Sarah looked at Joe, and he gestured for her to proceed. The door opened inward and let out a sigh of cold, stale air. She tried seeing into the blackness. Faint light gleamed off bottles that sat on racks along the walls. She could make out piles of storage boxes lying around the room. And there appeared to be something standing in the center. It looked like a figure. Joe shone his flashlight, revealing something tall covered in a dusty white sheet.

"Is there a light?" she said.

Joe felt around and found a switch. A single naked bulb crackled to life, revealing a storage room. Sarah approached the object in the center and, glancing back at Joe, took a breath and pulled the sheet off, revealing a large mahogany mirror—complete with brass candleholders—in perfect condition. Nineteenth century, she guessed.

"A mirror?" Manny said. "Let me know when you find gold." He trotted back up the stairs.

"Wow," she said. "What's this doing in a Spanish revival? And why is it down here?"

"I don't know. Where does it come from?"

"I saw something like it once in a catalog. Holland, maybe?"

Joe ran his hand along the wood. "It's in perfect condition—not a mark on it. What do you think we can get for it?"

"Maybe three or four grand? We'll have to get it appraised."

"That's it, I'm moving everything to the warehouse."

As Joe wandered off to join Manny and the others, Sarah stood before the mirror with her arms folded, studying it. Earlier, she thought she'd seen something out of the corner of her eye. Probably the light playing across the room. Suddenly, the door slammed shut behind her, giving her heart a jolt. The light died out, leaving her in a thick, oppressing blackness.

"Joe?" she said.

No answer. Feeling her way, she found the door and tried the knob. Locked. She began to panic as the temperature in the room plummeted.

"Oh, no. Please, God…"

When she turned to face the mirror again, she could see a luminous, white figure floating toward her behind the glass. Getting her fear in check, Sarah moved closer to get a better look. It was a girl—maybe fourteen or fifteen—with striking blue eyes, straight blonde hair, and pale skin. She seemed to be reaching out to Sarah, her mouth moving silently.

Remembering Alyssa's warning, Sarah tried touching the glass. A piercing shriek broke the heavy silence as the girl turned hideous and decayed, then vanished in a thin wisp of smoke as the light returned. Unable to move, Sarah could hear the door unlock behind her and felt the temperature returning to normal.

"The girl," she said to no one.

Five

"Sarah. Hey, Sarah, come on. Wake up."

When she opened her eyes, Sarah found Joe and Manny looming over her, their faces disproportionately large. Dazed, she glanced to either side of her and realized she was lying on the floor in the storage room at Casa Abrigo, her head resting on Joe's jacket.

"What happened?" she said.

Joe gently brushed the hair from her face and helped her sit up. "We were about to ask you."

"I must've fainted."

"Should we call 911?" Manny said. "Maybe she hit her head."

She felt around for a bump and found nothing. "No, I'm fine."

Joe turned to Manny. "Can you get her a water from the cooler?"

"Sure."

"Well, I feel stupid," she said after Manny had left. "Here, help me up."

Joe slipped an arm around Sarah's waist and with his

free hand held hers. As he got her to her feet, she noticed the mirror was covered up again. Nacho and Memo walked in and, slipping past Sarah, began carrying the mirror out.

"Hey, where are they taking that?"

"It's going in my truck," Joe said.

"Joe, I saw something." Manny returned with a bottle of water. "Tell you later."

"Here you go, Sarah."

"Thanks, Manny."

Joe retrieved his jacket from the floor. "I think you should go home and rest. I'll come by later."

"No, I'm fine."

He took her other hand and stood directly in front of her, a grim look on his face. "Home. Bed. Now."

"You really know how to romance a girl. Have you tried using that line on Gail?"

"I'm serious." Then, to Manny, "I'll drive her home in her car and you follow, okay?"

"Sí, señor."

She folded her arms. "Don't *I* get a say in this?"

Joe ignored her. "And make sure your sons don't break anything. I want all those bottles carefully packed and stored properly at the warehouse."

As Joe made the short drive to Sarah's house, she sat on the passenger side with her eyes closed and her arms folded. She'd never fainted before, not even that time when Alyssa's ghost first appeared to her. Maybe taking the afternoon off was a good idea after all. She didn't want to think about what falling might have done to her leather jacket. Good thing she hadn't fractured her skull. She didn't know why but she felt exhausted, as if the ghostly encounter had sucked the life from her.

"Want to tell me what you saw?" he said.

"Do you remember me mentioning Alyssa?"

"Yeah."

"Well, that girl I'm supposed to help? She's living in the mirror."

"Okay…"

"Joe, I *saw* her. I think she was trying to communicate with me."

"I don't like this, Sarah. Let's get rid of that thing—I don't care about the money."

"Please don't. Joe, promise me you won't." He refused to meet her gaze. "Joe? I mean it. *Promise* me."

"Well, it's going into storage, anyway."

"Thank you."

When they reached her house, a yellow-and-white California Bungalow-style home, Sarah let herself out. Joe had blown the budget restoring the property for Sarah because, he said, he wanted her to be happy in Dos Santos. Only she assumed it had more to do with guilt. He'd never apologized to her for lying about wanting children. Maybe in his mind, the house *was* an apology. Nevertheless, the first time she saw it, she fell in love and began filling the small three-bedroom with Craftsman-style furniture and quirky accessories she'd managed to find on eBay and Etsy.

Joe got out and ran around the Galaxie to help her out. Manny had arrived also and waited in his truck with the engine running.

"You sure are being gentlemanly," she said.

"You scared the shit out of me."

"I'm okay."

To prove her point, she raised her arms above her head and awkwardly did a complete 360 on tiptoes. Smiling falsely, she looked at Joe, and when she saw his expression, slumped her shoulders.

"Fine," she said. "I promise I'll stay home and rest. But

this doesn't mean you're getting out of pizza and wine, Mister."

"I'll stop by later." He turned to go.

"Um, Joe?" He looked at her curiously. "Keys?"

"Oh, right." He handed them over. "I'll call Rachel and let her know what happened."

"Tell her not to worry—and please for the love of all that is good and holy, make sure she doesn't tell Eddie."

"Right."

He gave her shoulder a squeeze and hurried down the steps to Manny's truck. She waved as they drove off and let herself in. Gary greeted her. She picked him up and hugged him like a long-lost friend.

"I know," she said. "Why am I home so early? Long story, buddy."

Sarah's phone rang. She removed it from her purse and stared at the number.

"That was fast."

"Sarah?"

"Rachel, I'm fine. Just a little dizzy spell."

"Maybe you should go to urgent care."

"It's okay. I promise. I'm going to take it easy the rest of the day. Please let Blanca know."

"Sure."

"And remember—"

"Don't tell Eddie, I know."

"Love you. Bye."

It was early, and Sarah felt she should be working instead of lounging around. Though the experience had frightened her, she was curious about the mirror's origins and wanted to learn more. She removed her jacket and boots, and closely inspected the jacket. No nicks from the fall—thank goodness. The tiredness she had felt earlier was overpowering, and she decided to take a nap.

It didn't take long for the dream to come. Sarah felt herself floating in a vast, cloying darkness, a dim light wafting toward her. Soon, she was falling fast. She found herself standing on the cold terra cotta floor of the storage room at Casa Abrigo, the antique mirror looming before her. Though she was afraid to look, she seemed to drift toward it against her will.

When she was close enough, she reached out. But there was no glowing light, only her own reflection. She looked different—the way she had when she was fifteen, with curly hair and braces. She recognized the simple black sheath dress and heels her mother had bought her at Nordstrom for Alyssa's funeral.

A numbing cold surrounded her, and she tried backing away from the mirror. A pale, white wisp of a hand came to rest on her shoulder. When she turned, she found the girl staring at her, her eyes nothing but deep, black holes that seemed to go on forever. She grinned as she yanked Sarah by the hair and, pulling her close, whispered something in her ear.

"He's coming."

Startled, Sarah awoke and noticed Gary on the bed next to her, playing with something on the duvet. She leaned over to see what it was and found a pair of blue eyes, the bloody stalks leaving a dark red smear on the bedding. Terrified, Sarah scrambled out of bed and fell back on the floor, hitting the back of her head on the nightstand.

"Ow!"

Recovering, she scooted forward on her knees up to the bed and, bracing herself, took another look. Everything appeared normal. No eyes, no bloodstains. She heard a maow and turned. Gary was sitting in the doorway, calmly licking something off his paw.

After a long, hot shower and a glass of whiskey, Sarah felt better. Joe had called to tell her something had come up, and he wouldn't be able to keep their date. But he wanted to know how she was. She suspected Gail was the reason and, rather than insist, she decided to let him off the hook. He promised to check in on her in the morning.

It was after seven. Sarah fed the cat and fixed herself a mixed green salad and pasta with a carbonara sauce she'd made from scratch and had frozen the previous weekend. She owned an impressive cookbook collection and always kept plenty of food on hand. She had been looking forward to trying the expensive Bordeaux, but instead of opening a different wine decided to stick to sparkling water.

After she'd cleaned up the kitchen, Sarah took two ibuprofen capsules, put on some jazz, and sat at her laptop in her home office. The dream had been terrifying, and she felt the ghost was trying to warn her. *He's coming.* A person? The Ghost of Christmas Yet To Come?

When she and Alyssa were kids, they liked pretending they were ghost hunters. Often, they would lurk around old, abandoned houses and run-down strip malls. When Eddie found out, he put the kibosh on their activities. As an adult, Sarah had undertaken a few informal para-normal investigations. They consisted mostly of checking people's houses for "ghosties," as Joe liked to call them. Nothing serious, and certainly nothing threatening. One time, she'd tried assisting the police chief on a missing persons case. But that had turned out to be a bust, and she ended up not being any help at all.

The mysterious circumstances surrounding the sale of Casa Abrigo bothered Sarah, and she was determined to learn the house's history. But where to start? She went online and looked up information about the property on the county assessor's website. Not helpful. She could always visit their offices in person, but she might have to involve Joe. And this was something she wanted to do on her own. Gary was sitting on her desk, watching her. As she turned to look at him, the cat cocked his head to one side.

"What's that, Gary? The information I need is at the office?"

Though she'd promised Joe she would stay home, the urge to discover the property's secrets was overwhelming. Ignoring any reservations she might have, she got dressed and headed out, hoping she could remember the alarm code.

———

Sarah arrived at the real estate office around ten and, risking a ticket, parked on the street. The Cracked Pot looked lively, and she could see customers alone or in groups sitting at tables near the windows, some wearing earbuds and looking at their laptops or phone screens.

"*Nighthawks*," she said, reminded of the Edward Hopper painting she had first seen in college while studying the painter and his wonderful anti-narrative symbolism.

Sarah unlocked the front door and entered. She had expected to hear the alarm beeping, but all was quiet. Switching on the lights, she gazed around the office. Everything looked normal. And yet, there was something... Shrugging off the feeling, she headed to Rachel's office to look for the Casa Abrigo file. Rachel always closed her door when she left work; now it was open. Uneasy, Sarah turned on the light and went in. From a distance, she could hear quick footsteps. The rear office door banged open. Her heart racing, she decided to investigate.

Outside, the parking lot was dark. A light wind was blowing dead, wet leaves across the asphalt. She'd forgotten to tell Rachel about having the bad floodlight replaced and was afraid to go outside. There was no movement of any kind. After locking the door and rechecking it, she returned to Rachel's office.

She spent several minutes looking through her sister's file cabinets. Rachel was very organized and liked to organize her properties in color-coded files. Sarah remembered her sister kept the most current files in a metal file organizer on her desk. But when she went through it, she couldn't find Casa Abrigo. Next, she went through all the papers on Rachel's desk. No luck. She got out her phone and dialed.

"Hey, Rache?" Sarah said. It was almost eleven, and she hoped she hadn't awakened her sister.

"Sarah? Is everything okay?"

"Calm down, I'm fine. Listen, I'm at the office—"

"*What?* You're supposed to be home resting."

"Come on, dude, I get enough of that from Joe. Anyway, I'm looking for the Casa Abrigo file. It's not in the file cabinet or on your desk."

"Joe has it."

"Oh, okay. Guess I'll get it from him tomorrow."

"Why do you need it? This isn't about what happened today, is it?"

"I wanted to check something out. Hey, you didn't mention my little adventure to Eddie, did you?"

"No. Sarah, listen. You shouldn't…encourage this."

"What do you mean?"

"Look, there are things out there that are better left alone. That's all I'm saying."

"Hey, this has been great," Sarah said. "We should do lunch."

"You are so lame."

"Love you, too. Bye."

Who breaks into a real estate office? Sarah wondered as she made her way home through the wet streets. She was certain someone had been there and escaped out the rear. The rain was starting up again, and she had to turn on the defroster to de-fog her rear window. Though she loved her car, sometimes when she drove in bad weather, she wished she had anti-lock brakes. As the view from her rear-view mirror cleared, she noticed the same car—a black BMW 328i—had been following her for several blocks. *Am I imagining this?*

She made a right at the next corner, which would take her to the 154. Predictably, the other car turned also. Seeing a parked Dos Santos police cruiser, she slowed and pulled up behind it. The Bimmer sped up and continued on toward Santa Barbara. As it passed, Sarah noticed what looked like a splash of red paint on the front passenger side wheel. She thought she saw a woman driving but couldn't be sure. Ahead of her, a police officer was giving someone a ticket. He motioned to the other driver to take off and trudged back toward Sarah as she lowered her window.

"Problem?" he said. He was young—maybe mid-twenties.

"Sorry. I thought someone was following me."

"Oh." He took a closer look at her. "Hey, you're Sarah Greene."

"Yeah…?"

"I saw you come into the station one time last year. You were, um, helping the chief."

"'Helping' might be an exaggeration."

He extended his hand. "I'm Tim Whatley."

"Like the *Seinfeld* character?"

He laughed. "Yeah, I get that a lot. Lou speaks very highly of you."

"I don't know why. I didn't do anything."

"Did you want me to escort you home, or…?"

"No, the whole thing was probably my imagination. Thanks anyway. Bye, Tim."

"See you."

At home, Sarah sat in the living room with a whiskey in her hand, Miles Davis playing softly on her phone. She had lit the fireplace and was petting Gary, who was purring contentedly on her lap.

"Someone was following me—I didn't imagine it." The cat maowed. "Probably the same person who broke into our office. It makes no sense, Gary."

She fell into a dreamless sleep in the chair. It was after one when she awoke and got ready for bed. She would talk to Joe in the morning about the file. He would put up a fuss about another paranormal investigation, but in the end she would win. After brushing her teeth and washing her face, she fell into bed.

"Tim Whatley," she said. "What a hoot."

Then, she was out.

Six

POLICE CHIEF LOU FIORE knocked back his triple espresso and made a few notes in a small black book as Sarah described the events of the previous night. He was wearing a suit with no tie, and his open white shirt collar revealed a generous tuft of curly black hair that complemented the wavy locks on his head.

Joe had introduced Sarah to Lou when she moved to Dos Santos, and she'd gotten to know him when they worked together. She liked him as a friend but sensed the forty-year-old *like*-liked her, though he'd never tried making a move. She had heard he was divorced, with an ex-wife and son living somewhere in the Bay Area.

Lou was seated in the Greene Realty conference room with Sarah, Joe, and Rachel. There was plenty of coffee. A plate of fresh pastries sat in the middle of the table, untouched.

"I don't see how they could've gotten in," Sarah said.

Joe nodded. "Yeah, no doors or windows were busted."

"I checked everything," Lou said. "I think they came in through the rear door after picking the lock."

"And somehow they turned off the alarm?"

"That's easy. They did it before entering. Probably used a laptop with a program that intercepts signals from the alarm system. This happens a lot, unfortunately. The Wi-Fi traffic is unencrypted—"

"What does that mean?" Rachel said.

"It means with the right software, anyone can read the information going to and from the system, including the password."

Joe shook his head. "So, they disabled it without touching it."

"If I were you, Joe, I'd call your alarm company and see if they can upgrade your equipment."

Rachel raised an index finger. "That's my department. I'll get on it today."

"And what about the locks?" Sarah said.

Lou closed his book and folded his hands on the table. "There's no such thing as an unpickable lock. That said, you could look into investing in smart locks."

"I've heard of those," Joe said. Then, to Sarah and Rachel, "You can unlock them using your phone."

Sarah rolled her eyes. "What could possibly go wrong?"

Lou laughed. "Well, there are other low-tech options. And as long as you're talking to the alarm company, you might as well have them install security cameras."

"No one told me this was a high-crime neighborhood," Joe said.

"Things change, Joe."

"And I don't get what they were looking for. Sarah and Rachel checked everything. Nothing was taken."

Lou stood, drained the last of his coffee, and shook Joe's hand. "Hard to say. Thanks for the coffee."

"Anytime. Thanks for stopping by, Lou."

The police chief shook Rachel's hand politely and turned to Sarah, who was digging through her purse.

"Take care, Sarah."

"What?"

"I was just saying, take care."

"Okeydokey."

He extended both hands and took hers between them. They were warm. She glanced at Rachel, who averted her eyes and tried mightily not to smile.

"I heard about what happened yesterday," he said.

"It was nothing."

"Well, be careful, okay?"

"Thanks, Lou."

"Later."

After Lou had left, Sarah turned to her sister, who she could see was covering her mouth and giggling.

"Okay, what in hell was that?" Sarah said.

"What? He's worried about you."

"Rachel, seriously. I do not have time for this."

"Come on, he's a nice guy."

"If you like former homicide detectives," Joe said.

Sarah turned to her ex-husband, who was grinning. She noticed he was holding the Casa Abrigo file and snatched it from him. Then, she reached over the table, grabbed the biggest sticky bun on the plate, and stormed out.

"I hate my life," she said.

Sarah sat in her office going through the Casa Abrigo file when she saw Joe walk past her door. It was after twelve, and she was starving.

"Joe?"

He stopped in the doorway mid-stride. "Absolutely not. I am not double-dating with you and a cop."

"Can you be serious for one minute? And sit down. You're too…tall."

Sighing, he took a seat across from her desk as she flipped through the thick stack of papers, found what she was looking for, and handed it to Joe.

"Okay, so I think I know why the bank was so anxious to unload Casa Abrigo. There *was* a murder. Two, in fact."

"I knew I shouldn't have let you have that file. I'm hungry. Can we do this after lunch? What am I looking at anyway?"

"The property was originally purchased in 1970 by a Gerald Moody. He paid cash." She handed him another document. "He obtains a loan from Wells Fargo." She tried handing him a third paper, but he waved her off.

"Then, he contracts with a company called Santee Construction to build a custom home. I tried looking them up; they're out of business. In 1971, Gerald moves in with his wife, Vivian."

"Everything sounds kosher to me so far."

"I'm not finished. Before coming to California, the wife had been staying at a psychiatric hospital outside Lawrence, Kansas, where they lived."

"Depression?"

"Who knows? Long story short, ol' Gerald sells his insurance business, buys the property in California, builds a home, and moves his wife into it. In 1973, she gives birth to their first child, Peter. Two years later, they have a girl, Hannah. Then in 1990, everything goes—"

"Tits up?"

"Exactly."

Joe shifted in his chair. "Don't tell me. The wife flips out and shotguns the two kids."

"No. The parents were found brutally murdered on a fire road in the forest. Peter, who was seventeen at the time, is the chief suspect. But he has an alibi. He was home at the time, along with his fifteen-year-old sister."

"Come on, she's lying to protect him."

"Maybe," she said. "But the cops have no motive. Supposedly, the kids adored their parents. And neither had ever been in trouble. Peter tells the cops that a day earlier, there was a road rage incident between his father and a couple of 'rednecks' in a truck.

"He'd been in the car at the time and is able to describe the men and the truck, but doesn't give them a license plate. The cops follow up but find nothing. The case goes unsolved."

"Great, let's eat," Joe said, getting up.

"That's not the most interesting part. A few weeks later, Peter and Hannah go missing."

Sarah walked over to her printer, pulled off the top sheet, and handed it to Joe. He stared at the large, grainy newspaper photo of a family standing in front of Casa Abrigo—father, mother, son, and daughter, looking like they were dressed for church on Easter Sunday. Everyone looked grim, except Hannah. Glancing sideways at her brother, she was beaming. Sarah stood, came around her desk, and pointed at the photo.

"Joe, that girl is the one I saw in the mirror. I think Hannah may have died in 1990."

The Cracked Pot was packed with the usual lunch crowd and a few faces Sarah didn't recognize.

"Want to make the order to go?" Joe said as they scanned the dining room for a table.

"No, let's try to eat here. Look, civilians."

"Maybe they heard about the coffee."

"Good thing we left business cards at the cash register. Hey, over there." She pushed Joe forward. "Hurry!"

Four people were leaving a booth. Joe trotted over and grabbed the table before the busboy had a chance to clear the dishes and wipe everything down. He signaled for Sarah to join him. Seeing Lou Fiore at the counter eating alone, she scooted across and slid in. The busboy tidied everything up and got them fresh menus. Both Sarah and Joe laid them aside without looking as the kid left two glasses of ice water.

"So, you've been busy," Joe said.

She was about to respond when Carter, the server with the anime tattoo, walked up to them. Sarah could see the outlines of other tattoos all up and down the girl's arms, faintly visible through the sleeves of her long-sleeved white shirt.

"Hey. What can I get you guys to drink?"

"Carter, right?" Sarah said.

"Yeah. Sarah?"

"Uh-huh. And this is Joe."

Carter smiled. "We've met. So, ready to order?"

As they gave their orders, Sarah noticed that the girl never wrote anything down. After she left, Sarah looked at Joe and quirked her eyebrows.

"What?" he said.

"Isn't she a little young for you?"

"I rent them rehearsal space. That girl? Carter Wittgenstein. She's their lead singer. Come on, stop looking at me like that. You never asked."

"Hmm. Well, are they any good?"

"No idea."

She and Joe amused themselves with their phones until the food arrived. As they ate, they spoke quietly.

"So, you think whoever murdered the parents killed the daughter?" Joe said.

"Uh-huh."

"And now her ghost is trying to talk to you?"

"Pretty much."

"So, why aren't the parents haunting you?"

"That's all I need." She took a bite of her club sandwich, which had been prepared exactly the way she liked it —half mustard and half mayo.

"And what about the son? Is he dead, too?"

"No. Joe, I think he killed his parents, then his sister." She helped herself to some of Joe's fries. "He's out there somewhere. That must be what Hannah was trying to tell me."

"But how can you be so sure?"

"I can't explain. But I have this feeling."

"So, if he was seventeen in 1990, that would make him—"

"Forty-four."

He watched as she reached for more of his fries. "You could've ordered your own, you know."

"They always taste better coming from your plate."

Joe took a bite of his hamburger. "So, what happened to the property?"

"That's the weird part. It was purchased by someone, but there don't seem to be any records. Somehow, the bank ends up owning it."

"How did you find out all this stuff?"

"Because I'm smart and I'm pretty. I started with Gerald Moody. Next, I looked up newspaper accounts of the murders. It's amazing what you can dig up on the internet. For example, did you ever hear about the Lindley Street poltergeist incident?"

"No. Can we focus here? And I'd appreciate it if you didn't poke your nose into *my* past."

"I'm pretty sure you have no past."

She took a sip of sparkling water and didn't notice when Joe looked away uncomfortably.

"So, what did you find out about Peter?" he said.

Making a face, she set her water down. "This needs more lime. I didn't find anything. He evaporated into thin air—they both did. It's as if Peter Moody and his sister didn't exist after 1990."

"He could've changed his name. Hey, what about the police? Maybe you could go through the old case file."

"Would they let me do that?"

"Lou might," he said, tilting his head toward the cash register.

Sarah turned and saw the police chief paying his check. On his way out, he grabbed a toothpick and stuck it between his lips.

"What is he, a tough guy?" she said.

"He used to smoke. You could ask *him* about the file."

She scrunched her nose, and her voice became whiny. "Nooo, can't you ask?"

"Hey, *I'm* not the ghost hunter. Man up."

"But what if he asks me out on a date or something awkward like that?"

"Tell him you're busy."

"This is a terrible idea."

"You'll be fine."

Sunlight fell through the open blinds of Lou Fiore's office.

It was small, dusty, and cluttered and, Sarah had to admit, was in desperate need of a makeover. The desk was messy, and the floor was littered with piles of manila folders jammed with papers and stacks of books with, what Sarah assumed, were mug shots.

Lou was smiling as he sat behind his desk, looking at Sarah in a way that made her slightly uncomfortable. It wasn't a leer, exactly. It was more of a hopeful will-you-go-to-the-prom-with-me expression. Sarah tried hard to think what she could have possibly done to encourage him. When they worked together on the missing persons case, she had maintained a pleasant and professional demeanor. And she certainly didn't recall ever flirting with Lou. *Oh, crap—the dress.*

One time, Sarah had been on her way to meet Rachel to attend a fundraising dinner for Notre Dame School. She'd purchased a black sequin bodycon dress for the occasion. Though the neckline wasn't particularly low, the push-up bra she was wearing made her stand out. In every way. That and the three-inch black heels spelled trouble.

Lou had called her last-minute, asking if she could review a new piece of evidence. He insisted it was urgent, so she stopped by the police station on her way to the function. Now that she thought about it, he'd been acting more attentive to her ever since that day. Why couldn't she have worn a pantsuit and flats?

"I'm glad you stopped by, Sarah. How can I help?"

"Well," she said, clearing her throat. "Joe and I are renovating a property up on San Marcos Pass Road."

"Oh? Which one."

"Casa Abrigo."

"I know the place. Is that where you…?"

"Yes. Of course, when you buy something from the bank, you don't get much information about a house's past, right? I mean, anything might have happened there—even murder."

"That's true," he said, scratching his cheek. "What does this have to do with Casa Abrigo?"

"I've been doing some research, and I learned the man who built the house was killed, along with his wife."

She reached into her new Kate Spade black leather laptop bag and removed a printout of one of the newspaper articles she'd found on the murders. Then, she handed it to Lou.

"It all happened in 1990. Also, shortly after, the son and daughter disappeared without a trace. At the time, the police believed the son had killed his parents."

He scanned the article. "But there was no motive or evidence, right?"

"Exactly."

"And you want to see the case file."

"Yes," she said, relieved that the hard part was over.

He straightened up, turning his head from side to side as if experiencing a sharp pain in his neck. Sarah thought she heard a crack. This didn't look promising. She tried a smile.

"Okay, normally, we don't share that kind of information with the public."

"Oh."

"*But.* It's a cold case from, what, 1990? I guess it wouldn't do any harm for you to take a look. Who knows? You might uncover something."

"Great."

"One problem, though. Everything prior to 2000 is in storage." He got up and came around the desk. "Follow me."

Dos Santos Police Department was part of a recently completed civic center. The old station, a California historical landmark, had been converted into a trendy Mexican restaurant. The new complex included City Hall and had been architected as a perfect square of limestone-and-glass buildings surrounding a beautifully landscaped inner court with a huge stone fountain and benches.

Lou led Sarah down a long aisle. When they had reached the end, he removed a key and opened a door to what looked like a storage room the size of several class-rooms. He flicked on the lights and let her pass. Racks and racks of storage boxes filled the room, and she wondered how long it would take to find the file.

"I wish I could tell you this would be easy but."

"No, it's fine. How are these organized?"

"Take a look at the upper corners of each rack. Supposedly, they're arranged by year. Other than that, you're on your own."

He lingered in the doorway, and she was afraid he was going to ask her to join him for a drink later.

"Was there something else?" she said.

"I want you to promise me if you get any, you know, 'feelings' about the case, you'll share them with me. Deal?" It annoyed her that he had used air quotes.

"Deal. Thanks, Lou."

"Don't mention it. I'll check on you in a couple hours."

He closed the door and locked her in. Sarah glanced at her phone and saw that it was already after three. She wished Rachel were here to help her and began examining the racks one by one. Lou had been partially right about them. They had been organized by decade, some files going back to the mid-1950s.

Sarah was somewhat familiar with the town's strange history. It was founded in 1917 by a group of ex-soldiers who were given the land as a reward for fighting in the Border War. Led by a man named John Dos Santos, they built homes in the town and, with the blessing of the Diocese of Monterey-Los Angeles, married young women from a local convent school.

When WWI came, the men were again drafted. All of them—except for one—were killed, leaving behind widows and children. Sarah recalled a magazine article she'd come across about the lone survivor, John Dos Santos. His wife had died in 1918 from the Spanish Flu. Back in California, Dos Santos was living on an army pension when, as if by magic, he became rich. There were rumors of parties, drinking, and underage girls. Mysteriously, he died without leaving a will. He had no children.

Eventually, many of the remaining families abandoned the town, and it fell into decay. After WWII, people again started to settle here because of the cheap housing prices. Over the next few decades, the town's reputation grew, but so did the ghost stories surrounding their "haunted cemetery."

Meticulously, Sarah went through each of the record storage boxes, looking at every file and returning it to the box. Though she hadn't yet found the one she wanted, she ran across other homicide and missing persons cases that piqued her interest. She checked her phone and saw it was after five.

"This is going to take forever," she said.

Disgusted, she got to her feet and stretched. Shaking her head, she knelt again and continued searching. The temperature plummeted. Out of the corner of her eye, she caught a glimpse of something gliding between the racks. She thought she heard a faint voice. It sounded like a sigh. Now, the distinct sound of rustling papers.

"Hello?"

Frightened, she closed her eyes and clutched her St. Michael medal until the temperature returned to normal.

Looking past the box she was working on, Sarah noticed a single case file lying open on the concrete floor. She was sure she'd put all of them away. When she examined the label, she realized it was the one she was looking for.

"No way."

Inside, she found typewritten reports on the investigation, which had been led by then-Chief Kyle Jeffers. As she sat there wondering how to get in touch with him, she could hear the sound of keys jingling. A moment later, the door opened, and she saw Officer Whatley smiling at her.

"How's it going?" he said.

"Good. I found what I was looking for. Tim, can you give me a hand putting these boxes away?"

"Sure thing."

As they restacked the boxes, Sarah couldn't wait to go through the file. At first, she thought of returning to the office. But the recent break-in had her spooked, and she would be alone there since everyone would have gone home. When they got outside, Officer Whatley locked the door and walked Sarah back to the police station. She decided to text Joe to see if he was up for pizza and wine. After all, he promised.

Seven

Joe's phone went off as he drove to the Biltmore in Santa Barbara to meet Gail. She'd called last-minute, and he had had to scramble to get home, shower, and change clothes. She was always doing that, he noticed. Lunch. Coffee. Phone calls. Not that she was disorganized. She had struck him as highly efficient. He preferred to think she was spontaneous, and it occurred to him as he approached the hotel driveway that he rather enjoyed her unpredictability. Sarah would be okay, he told himself.

"Hello?" he said.

"Joe? I found the file."

Sarah's voice was breaking up as it came through the truck's sound system. A vague feeling of guilt radiated across his insides, and that irritated him. After all, he'd done nothing wrong.

"That's great," he said.

"I was hoping you had time to meet tonight so we could go over it together. Pizza and wine, remember?"

"Can't. I'm…"

"Let me guess. On a *date*." She sounded angry.

"Sorry." He pulled at the collar of his new dove gray dress shirt.

"Hey, no problem. Don't mind me slaving away over here while you enjoy your new love life."

"Sarah, don't. Hey, I meant to ask. How are you feeling?"

"Fine. Not that you care. So, where are you having dinner?"

"The Biltmore."

"Nice. You never took me there."

"We'll go for your birthday."

"Don't put yourself out. Have a good time, Joe. I'll let you know if I find anything interesting. And stay away from the dessert tray. You're starting to look a little... chunky around the middle."

"Goodbye, Sarah."

Joe disconnected before his ex-wife could drag out the goodbyes, which she tended to do whenever she was upset. He truly loved Sarah, but sometimes she acted as if they were still married. And it didn't help that they continued sleeping together occasionally. He blamed himself. Now that he was seeing someone, he decided he would need to keep their relationship on a strictly friend basis. It was for their own good, he told himself.

Joe had chosen a table by the fire. Though it was cold out on the patio of the Bella Vista Restaurant, the view of the Pacific Ocean was breathtaking, and watching the sunset made him glad once again he'd decided to remain in California instead of returning to New York after college. In fact, for years he'd considered himself a California native. He loved everything about the place—especially the weather.

Joe was eighteen when he arrived in Los Angeles on his way to Santa Barbara. Though he had been accepted to the University of Pennsylvania, he found he was craving adventure and decided on UCSB to do his pre-med studies. In his sophomore year at a World Music Series event, he met a freshman named Sarah Cruz. They hit it off immediately, becoming good friends and going together to basketball games, movies, and concerts.

Toward the end of his four years, Joe decided he didn't want to become a doctor—much to the dismay of his well-meaning parents. After graduating, he got his real estate license and went to work. Eventually, he began flipping houses in and around Santa Barbara and finally ended up settling down in Dos Santos, where most of his business was.

Over the years, Joe's friendship with Sarah deepened. They saw each other through a seemingly endless parade of failed romantic relationships, misguided career choices, and family heartache, the latter being the tragic death of Sarah's brother-in-law Paul. That experience had brought them closer than ever, and soon they found themselves falling in love. Joe never regretted marrying Sarah but was not surprised when she announced she wanted to call it quits. It was all his fault—he shouldn't have misled her about wanting kids. At the time, he had honestly thought he could change. But after they were married, he knew the truth. There were men who were meant to raise families. And there was him.

Taking a swallow of his house Cabernet, Joe looked up and saw Gail Cohen approaching. He noticed she'd removed the couture jaw clip she normally wore, letting her blonde hair loose. Her pink-and-black print shirt was striking, the pattern suggesting a field of eyes. And her short, black pencil skirt and heels stirred something in Joe that surprised him.

He was the last person to rush things but couldn't help wondering if Gail, too, would want children eventually and he would have to end the relationship. Somehow, he couldn't picture her with kids, though. Not that she was cold; just the opposite. Though poised and professional, she exuded a smoldering sexiness you didn't normally see in a paralegal.

"Sorry I'm late," she said. "I wanted to change."

She was about to sit opposite him when he stood and came around the table.

"No, you sit there so you can see the ocean."

"What about you?"

"I've got a pretty nice view."

"Aren't you the charmer?" She took his hand and pulled him down beside her. "There. Isn't this better?"

Her perfume was intoxicating. Joe spotted a server and waved him over. Then, to Gail, "What would you like?"

"A Chardonnay would be great."

Joe looked at his date as she gazed at the ocean, her chin resting in one hand. She was lovely, with shiny, shoulder-length blonde hair, blue eyes, and perfect teeth. *Cohen.* Aware she'd never been married, he couldn't get over the fact that she was Jewish. His parents would love that. Although they'd been crazy about Sarah, they were traditional. He'd dated Jewish girls before, but it was Sarah who had stolen his heart. Sarah. He made an effort to put her out of his mind.

"Were you waiting long?" she said.

"What?"

She laughed. "Mind wandering?"

"I was thinking how much I love that shirt."

"Oh, I'm glad. I picked it up at Top Shop. Doesn't this pattern remind you of—"

"Eyes."

"Exactly. I think that's what attracted me to it."

Her drink arrived, and she reached for the glass. Joe couldn't help notice the perfectly manicured nails. Everything about her seemed...premeditated? He smiled to himself, wondering why he'd landed on that particular word. Sarah would've said *calculated*. Why was he thinking about her again?

"So, Gail," he said, "you know all about me, but I know very little about you."

"What would you like to know?"

"Well, where's your family from?"

"Massachusetts."

He hesitated. "It's funny, I've known Jewish girls all my life and..."

"I don't *look* Jewish."

"No, it's—"

She laughed and stroked his hand. "It's okay, Joe. I get that a lot." She leaned in and whispered conspiratorially, "If you want to know the truth, my parents paid for my nose job as a high school graduation present."

"Okay, that's..."

She took his face in both hands and kissed him full on the lips. It was long and lingering and aroused him immediately. As they ignored everyone around them, she slipped a hand under the table and began stroking his inner thigh. Then, as if nothing at all had happened, she leaned back and drank her wine.

"You were saying?" she said.

The server appeared and handed out two menus. Joe was still flushed and used his menu to hide his face. He felt his heart racing, wondering what just happened.

"Did you want to hear about the specials?"

Joe glanced at Gail, and she nodded. The server began telling them all about the fish, caught fresh that morning.

"'We'll go for your birthday'," Sarah said to Gary. "Don't do me any favors."

The cat was sitting near her on the floor as she maniacally chopped meat and vegetables to the sounds of Benny Goodman's "Sing, Sing, Sing" coming from her phone. The animal was hoping something would find its way down, and when it didn't, he crouched, preparing to leap onto the counter. Unfortunately for him, Sarah caught him in the act.

"Don't you dare, Mister. I've had it with men, and that includes you."

Maowing pathetically, he wandered off in search of his food bowl. Sarah wiped her forehead and took another swallow of a decent Orvieto she'd picked up at Whole Foods.

It wasn't that she was angry with Joe for seeing other people. Per se. Okay, maybe. But what was he supposed to do? They were no longer married, and that was that. Thanks to her. And besides, hadn't they promised each other not to let things get weird between them when she signed on again?

No, this wasn't about Joe. It was the case that was getting to her, she told herself. She needed to discover the truth about Hannah Moody and, hopefully, end the hauntings. But the thing of it was, she didn't like doing it by herself. Joe Greene was her best friend—her confidant. For fifteen years, they'd shared everything together—ups, downs, and everything in between. And now he was *unavailable*?

"Putz," she said, using an expletive she'd learned from Joe.

She tossed handfuls of ingredients into the sizzling peanut oil, adding soy sauce and, to spice things up, a generous splash of garlic chili paste. In a few minutes, she was sitting at her butcher block table, eating with chopsticks and going through the police file.

According to the documentation, Police Chief Jeffers had personally run the investigation; most of the handwritten and typed notes were signed or initialed by him. From what Sarah could tell, he'd been thorough, interviewing Peter and Hannah several times after the murder and following up on every lead.

Apparently, he'd brought in two men for questioning. She found mug shots and a photo of their pickup truck. Based on the description provided by Peter, they must have been the prime suspects. But even with their obviously sketchy past that included petty crime and domestic violence, they had alibis and had been nowhere near the crime scene at the time of the murders, which the coroner had determined to be around 8 p.m.

Sometimes, when Sarah would hold an object or a photograph in her hand, a mental picture of a person or a place would form. The key was to relax and clear her mind of all random thoughts. While at UCSB, she had decided to try meditation to relieve stress during finals week. But the first time she did it, she saw something hideous and immediately stopped.

Last year, Lou asked Sarah to assist him with a high-profile case. He'd been working feverishly on finding an eight-year-old girl who he feared had been abducted. Desperate for any help he could get, he decided to try the so-called local psychic. Joe and Lou were friends, and often Joe would brag about his ex-wife's abilities. That was good enough for Lou.

But Sarah hadn't been able to contribute anything more than sympathy for the missing girl. It was clear to her that she didn't want to work on a case involving a child, because she was afraid of what she might discover. After trying meditation again, she found that her psychic mind was closed for business, and she saw nothing.

Fortunately, Lou never mentioned Sarah to the grieving parents. She saw them occasionally either at the market or The Cracked Pot. A year later, they still looked sad. There were so many times she wanted to go up to them and offer her deep-felt sympathy, but it felt wrong. Especially since she hadn't been able to help find their daughter.

Was this why Sarah was so anxious to solve the Hannah Moody case? To make up for that little girl who, as far as anyone knew, was most likely dead? It frustrated her to think she had to take on a burden like this. On the other hand, as Fr. Brian had pointed out so many times, God had given her a gift. And, she was pretty sure, He expected her to use it to help others, even if it meant her suffering in the process.

After dinner, Sarah cleaned up the kitchen and, sitting by the fire, went through the rest of the file. She lingered over a photograph of Peter Moody. It looked as if it had been taken in one of the smaller bedrooms at Casa Abrigo —most likely Peter's room, judging from the posters of Black Sabbath and the horror movie *The Omen*. Books lined the wall, and Sarah could almost read the titles. Judging by the light, she guessed the photo had been taken in the late afternoon.

Peter was maybe fifteen and sitting in a desk chair near the bed, smiling at the camera in a way that seemed almost hypnotic. There was something about his expression. It wasn't malevolent exactly, but Sarah could feel a cold dread she wasn't able to put her finger on. It was as if the answer to the secret of this boy lay just out of reach.

Without warning, a powerful light flash tore through her head like Uriel's flaming sword, and in her mind's eye, she could see the scene coming alive in front of her. Peter was leaving the chair and moving toward the camera. As Sarah's heartbeat quickened, she could see what *he* was seeing. It was his sister. She'd been the one behind the camera.

And she was naked.

Sarah shook herself awake and realized she was still holding the photograph. She didn't want to wait for morning to speak with Lou. She searched through her phone for his number. Though it was after ten, she needed to see him.

"Hey, it's Sarah."

"Hi." To her relief, he didn't sound annoyed. "I understand you found the file."

"Yeah. Lou, I've been going through it tonight." She scrunched her nose. "Do you think we could meet over at The Cracked Pot? I know it's late but—"

"Sure. I can be there in fifteen minutes."

"I'm going to need a half hour. Sorry, I'm a girl."

"See you there."

Well, that was easy. She didn't know why, but she wanted to look nice. It was part of being a professional, she told herself. After a quick shower and a change of clothes, she headed over, reminding herself she wasn't romantically interested in the Dos Santos police chief in any way, shape, or form.

This was strictly business.

The sparse late-night crowd had settled in, and Sarah walked into the restaurant to find Lou sitting at a booth toward the back. She imagined he didn't want anyone else being privy to their conversation. Smart move. When he saw her, he stood. He'd taken off his black leather jacket, and she could see that he was wearing a form-fitting shirt underneath. She'd never noticed before, but he looked very fit. Not like some sloppy, small-town cop from the movies.

"Thanks for meeting me," she said, sliding into the booth and opening the file.

"No problem. What'cha got?"

Carter walked over and stood at their booth. She smiled at Sarah in a curious way, and Sarah quirked her eyebrows.

"You guys don't normally come in together," the girl said.

Lou smiled professionally. "What's your name?"

"Carter."

"Well, Carter. You're very observant. Sarah, what would you like?"

"Single-shot decaf espresso."

"And I'll have a *full-strength* cappuccino."

As usual, Carter didn't write anything down. "How many shots?"

"Two."

"Okay, then."

"Make it three."

"You got it."

After the server had left, Lou turned to Sarah, smiling. "Nice girl. So, please tell me you have some great insight into my cold case."

"Actually, I do. Peter was having sex with his sister. In fact, he'd been doing it for years."

"Incest? How did you—?"

"Because I saw it." She pointed to her head. "In my mind."

"And you're sure you couldn't have—"

"Imagined it? No. That's not really how this works, Lou. When I experience something in that way, you can bet your ass it's real."

Carter returned with their coffees and, seeing they were deep in conversation, set them down and left immediately.

"Okay," he said.

He drank his coffee, holding the cup with both hands, as if to warm himself. Sarah left hers untouched.

"What about the parents?" he said. "Do you think they knew?"

"If they *had* found out, it would've given Peter the perfect motive to kill them, don't you think?"

"Okay, that might be a stretch. Unless... You didn't happen to see *that*, did you?"

"No. It's a hunch. I do think he killed his parents, though. But I'm not clear yet on why."

She tried her espresso, then added both of the rough-cut brown sugar cubes the server had left for her on the saucer.

"Lou, do you know whatever happened to Police Chief Jeffers?"

"Kyle? As a matter of fact, I do. He's living on a boat in Ventura."

"Great. I think we should go see him."

"'We'?"

"Yeah. Is there a problem?"

He looked at his hands. "I guess not. To be honest, Sarah, I didn't think we'd be reopening the case."

"Oh, I get it. You thought this was going to be like the last time." Angry, she grabbed her purse and stood.

"Not exactly. I— Hey, come on. Sit down. Please?"

She looked around the room and found Carter observing her from across the room. Realizing she'd made an ass of herself, she sank back into her chair.

"Sorry," she said. "Look, I feel bad about not being able to help you find the little girl. Lou, please believe me, not a single day goes by that I don't think about her. But I'm getting close to something here. I can feel it."

He smiled in a way that made her relax.

"Look, Sarah. I know you did what you could to help me before, and I'm grateful. So, it didn't pan out. We gave it our best shot. But that doesn't mean I think any less of you."

"Thanks."

"Now, I'm not sure how this whole paranormal thing works. I mean, I was raised Catholic, and we believe in angels."

"I'm Catholic, too, remember? And *I* believe in angels. But I also happen to believe in ghosts."

Sarah could tell he was getting uncomfortable. He sat there for a long time, holding his coffee. As if settling on a course of action, he drained the cup and set it down.

"Okay," he said. "Tell you what. Let me have the file— unless *you* need it."

"No, take it." She collected the papers and handed them over.

"I'll give Kyle a call and see if he's open to meeting with us. I can't promise anything, though. But if there *is* something, I'll reopen the case. Good enough?"

"Yeah," she said. "I'd better get going. I have an early day tomorrow."

As they got up, he grabbed the check.

"I got this. Police business."

"Thanks for the coffee, Lou. Night."

"Night, Sarah."

Sarah walked out to her car. She had a good feeling about how things were progressing and hoped they would be able to speak with the former police chief. As she started her car, her phone rang. It was Joe.

She let it go to voicemail.

Eight

IT WAS DRIZZLING when Sarah pulled up to Casa Abrigo and parked on the street. She'd gotten a late start and was feeling frustrated that she hadn't had time to get in a run. As usual, three trucks were parked in the driveway, and two of Manny's sons were dragging in a cart filled with heavy bags of plaster. She sat in her car for a time, gazing at the house and wondering why Gerald Moody had decided to uproot his family and move all the way across the country to Dos Santos of all places. She thought about his wife, Vivian. Had living in California been meant as therapy for her?

Finally, Sarah got out and hurried toward the house. It annoyed her that at the slightest hint of moisture, her hair became a frizz ball. Thank goodness for flat irons. Inside, she found Memo standing on an aluminum ladder in the foyer, installing a new iron lantern pendant on the ceiling. The other two were applying fresh plaster to the walls, giving them an attractive terra fresco finish. It seemed that Joe was serious about going high-end with the renovation after all. Waving to them, she crossed to the kitchen and approached the cellar door, wondering how much the add-ons were costing the business.

"Joe?"

"Down here."

Using the rail, she made her way down slowly and found Joe and Manny sanding. Both were wearing particle masks, and their hair was covered in dust. Her heart sank seeing all those racks devoid of wine bottles. She'd planned to negotiate with Joe to keep several for herself once they determined the wine's value. Nervously, she walked past the storage room as she approached her business partner.

"How's it coming?" she said.

"Not too bad."

Joe set down the belt sander, removed his mask, and wiped his forehead with his sleeve. Manny decided to take a break and did likewise. Though it was cold in the cellar, both Joe and Manny were sweating, and Sarah could smell them. Not that she minded.

"You didn't return my call," Joe said.

"Sorry, I got busy."

"Well, I'm glad you're here. I wanted you to look at the master bedroom again. I'm replacing the built-ins in the walk-in closet and could use your expertise."

"No problemo."

She wasn't sure, but things seemed a little stilted between them. Though Joe was smiling, he wasn't making eye contact. He brushed the dust from his shirt.

"I'm going to grab my tape measure from the truck."

After he had bounded up the stairs, Sarah turned to Manny, who had gone back to sanding. She reached over and turned off the belt sander.

"*¿Qué cosa?*"

"I need to ask you something," she said. "What's up with Joe?"

"Pues, no sé."

He turned the equipment back on, but she switched it off again, making him roll his eyes.

"Manny."

Sighing, he set down the belt sander, removed his mask, and pretended to look for something in his tool belt, but he could feel her staring at him.

"How should I know?" he said, not making eye contact.

"He's acting…weird."

"Seems okay to me. Maybe it's that woman he's seeing. Dale."

"Gail."

"Oh yeah, huh. *Pues,* you guys used to be married, and he's not sure how to behave around you, *flaca.*"

Her mouth fell open. "Shit, you're right."

"He's what you call, conflicted."

He put his mask back on, reached down, and picked up the tool.

"Wow, that's a big-boy word," she said. "You wouldn't happen to be a therapist on the side?"

"Blanca likes watching *Dr. Phil* a lot."

"I see. Well, thanks for the insight." She hesitated. "Hey, Manny?"

"Pinche…"

"Why did you call me *flaca*? You think I'm too skinny?"

"Pues…"

"Come on, I've got curves." She used her hands to illustrate.

"If you say so."

Ignoring her, he fired up the noisy belt sander and went back to work.

Joe appeared at the top of the stairs. "You coming?"

"Be right there," she said. Then, to Manny on the way out, "Fascist."

On the first floor, Sarah was about to follow Joe upstairs when she heard the front door open.

"Hello?" a voice said.

She entered the foyer and found Michael Peterson standing there. He was dressed in a suit and looked as if he'd come from the salon.

"Joe, I'll be right up," she said as she strode across the floor, her hand extended.

"What are *you* doing here?"

They shook hands, and Sarah found herself smiling more than usual.

"I stopped by your office and they told me I could find you here. You look very nice. This house is amazing."

"Yeah, we picked it up at a private bank sale and are in the process of making it gorgeous."

"Well, I was hoping you could show me a few more properties. Would it be terrible of me to ask to get a quick tour? You know, as long as I'm here?"

"Um, sure. You'll have to be careful, though. Lots of equipment and supplies. I wouldn't want you to ruin your clothes."

Joe trotted back down the stairs and approached them both, his hand extended.

"Hi, I'm Joe Greene."

"Michael Peterson. I was telling your partner how impressed I am with this house."

"It's a beauty. We were lucky to get it."

"I'll bet. Sarah mentioned you bought it from the bank?"

"Yeah, it was one of those lucky breaks. So, Mike, you in the market?"

"It's Michael. And yes, I guess I am."

"Well, Sarah can show you around the place. I need to get back to work."

As Joe headed for the kitchen, Michael said, "Nice meeting you." Then, to Sarah, "He seems a little...protective?"

"Well, that's because I'm the one who makes all the money around here. Joe spends it. Come on, let's do the grand tour."

Because it was raining, Sarah and her client confined themselves to the interior. He seemed very interested, running his hand along the bannister and lingering in each of the rooms. After they had toured the upstairs, they returned to the foyer.

"Well, that's about it, Michael."

"We haven't seen the kitchen."

"Oh, sorry. I think I was mentally avoiding it because it's our center of operation."

As they walked toward the kitchen, Sarah thought she saw the lantern pendant in the foyer swaying and put it out of her mind. Michael took a quick look around and proceeded toward the cellar door, where they could hear the sounds of power tools.

"There's a wine cellar?" he said, sounding excited.

"Yes, but how did you——? Would you like to see it?"

"Sure."

Instead of waiting, he trotted down first. When she'd reached the bottom, Sarah found Michael casually moving among the wine racks, running his hand along the wood as he walked. Joe and Manny turned off their power tools and waited patiently.

"So, was there any wine," Michael said to Sarah, "or did you guys drink it all?"

Joe had overhead and laughed. "We moved it into storage."

"And what's that room over there?"

Joe saw that Sarah was hesitating and walked over to join them. He led Michael into the storage room as Sarah lingered outside the doorway.

"This room held cognac, brandy, stuff like that," Joe said.

Michael gazed around at the empty racks. "I see. Anything else?"

Joe glanced at Sarah. "No, I don't think so."

"Okay, well, I think I've seen enough."

In the foyer, Michael approached the front door ahead of Sarah. She looked up and saw the lantern pendant swaying again.

"Michael!"

Suddenly, the bolts holding up the fixture shot out violently, and the lantern fell, barely missing Michael and crashing onto the floor behind him.

"Are you okay?" she said.

"Yeah. Got a major shot of adrenalin, though. Give me a second."

"I am so sorry." Hearing footsteps, she turned and saw Memo. "Where's your dad?"

Manny and his sons stood around the remains of the lantern, arguing in Spanish, with Memo insisting he'd done nothing wrong.

Outside, Sarah and Michael stood in the gray overcast next to his rental car. Seeing him inside the house reminded her how vulnerable he had seemed when they first met. She guessed that, after his wife's death, he was lonely and perhaps desperate to make himself a new home.

"Well, I've had my excitement for the day," he said. "Sorry, when it comes to adventure, I'm a real wuss. Thanks for the tour, though."

"Again, I'm very sorry. Did you want to see those other properties?"

He gazed at the house and smiled wistfully. "I don't need to."

"Don't tell me after that near-death experience, you're in love with this place?"

"I might be. When do you think it will go on the market?"

"Two months, maybe three. Depends on the building inspectors. I can keep you posted. Of course, we haven't priced it yet."

"I'm sure it'll be fair. Well, I need to get going."

She stood back as he opened the car door. Then, she surprised herself.

"Hey, Michael? I had a thought. And you can totally tell me if I'm out of order."

"Okay, that sounded mysterious."

She scrunched her nose and dug the toe of her boot in the wet grass near the curb. He smiled at her expectantly.

"I was thinking. I mean, you're Catholic. I'm Catholic. They're having this singles' dance at Our Lady of Sorrows next weekend. Well, it's not *at* the church, of course, but—"

"Sure. Let's do it."

"Really?"

"Yeah, why not? I could use a little fun. And if the conversation gets too awkward, we can always go back to talking about real estate. Or classic cars."

"Great. I'll text you the deets." *Crap, I can't believe I just used that word.*

"Looking forward to it. Bye, Sarah."

As he drove off, she realized her heart was fluttering. She laughed as she imagined Fr. Brian's expression when she walked into the dance with her impressive date. Above her, she could hear a croaking noise. When she looked, she saw a bird flying off into the distance.

It was a raven.

On her way back, Lou had called to say he was planning to meet with Kyle Jeffers and wanted to know if Sarah wanted to tag along. So instead of returning to the office, she drove directly to the police station and parked in the visitor section. Once inside, she headed for Lou's office when Tim Whatley almost ran into her.

"Oh, sorry. I didn't see you, Sarah. What are you doing here?"

"I'm here to see the chief."

"Huh. Another paranormal investigation?"

For some reason, he lingered there, making her a little uncomfortable.

"Well, gotta go," she said. "Lou's expecting me."

"Sure. See you, Sarah."

Sarah found Lou in his office and rapped on the door frame. "Ready when you are."

"Thanks for coming, Sarah. We're meeting Kyle in Santa Barbara. He had some business in town. I hope you're hungry. I promised him lunch."

"Starved."

"Come on, we'll take my car."

It took them only a few minutes to reach La Super-Rica on Milpas Street. On the way over, Lou explained that Kyle was a Mexican food junkie and this was his favorite spot. Growing up, Sarah had always enjoyed the fish tacos, but it had been a while since she'd gone back.

They parked down the street and, as they got closer to the small, nondescript white building with the turquoise trim, she saw the line. Fortunately, it tended to move quickly, she remembered. They stood at the end, and Sarah was grateful the sun had come out. In a few minutes, a man who looked to be nearing eighty, wearing a Rifleman brown leather jacket, western-style shirt, jeans, and cowboy boots, walked up. He was slender and wore dark-framed glasses.

Lou smiled. "Kyle?"

"Hi, Lou. Nice to see you again." His voice was deep and resonant.

"This is my friend Sarah Greene. Sarah, Chief Jeffers."

The old man laughed as he shook Sarah's hand. "Nobody calls me that anymore. Nowadays, it's just Kyle."

"It's great to meet you, Kyle," she said. "What are you doing in Santa Barbara?"

"Meeting with my accountant. Seems I am unable to write off boat repairs."

They kept the conversation light until they'd gotten their food and were sitting inside. Though the tables stood close together, they had managed to find one in a corner. Lou had brought the case file, and they didn't waste any time getting down to business. As Kyle went through the documents, reacquainting himself with the case, Sarah could tell by his serious expression that the old saying was true: once a cop, always a cop.

"And what is your involvement in the case?" the former Dos Santos police chief said to Sarah.

She noticed that he'd dropped the neighborly demeanor. Taken aback, she started to answer when Lou touched her hand and jumped in.

"Kyle, *I* asked Sarah to look into the case."

"Oh?"

"Sarah is, um. Well, I don't know how else to say this. She's psychic."

Sarah thought the old man was going to give her the dressing-down of her life. She knew plenty of people who didn't believe in the supernatural. He lowered his head and rubbed the back of his leathery neck. Then, he looked at her, his piercing gray eyes seeing into her soul. *Shitstorm alert.*

"Smart move," he said. "I wished I had one when I was working the case."

She relaxed. "So, I studied the file, and I know you did everything you could at the time to solve those murders. But I saw something recently—something related to that photo you're holding."

He examined the photograph of Peter in his bedroom. "And by 'saw,' you mean a vision?"

"Precisely."

"And what is your conclusion, Sarah?"

"Incest. Peter had been having intercourse with his younger sister for years."

"Consensual?"

"I'm pretty sure."

"Hm. Well, I always thought that kid was a little off. There was something, I dunno… He seemed cold."

Lou leaned in. "What do you mean, Kyle?"

"I mean, he wasn't at all upset by the death of his parents. I can still picture 'im, sittin' there like he was waitin' for the bus. Impatient-like."

"What about his sister, Hannah?" Sarah said.

"Different story altogether. As I recall, she was blubberin' like there was no tomorra. And they were *real* tears. I had to bring in a policewoman to comfort her. So, unless she was some kinda actress…"

"We think Peter may have had a motive to kill his parents," Lou said.

The old man took a sip of iced tea and flipped through the file again.

"You think they found out what was goin' on with the sister, and they confronted him. And that's why he killed 'em?"

Lou glanced at Sarah for confirmation. "That's my theory."

"I also think he killed Hannah," Sarah said.

The old man raised his scraggly eyebrows. "Why?"

She looked at Lou and cleared her throat. "Well, because... Because I've seen her ghost recently."

"You know, it's funny. There have been ghost stories floatin' around Dos Santos for over two hun'derd years. I was the police chief of that town for thirty-one of 'em, and I don't recall ever seein' a single spirit."

Lou forced a chuckle. "I'm not exactly a convert myself—"

Kyle looked at him, irritated at having been interrupted, which made Lou blush.

"But that doesn't mean I don't believe in 'em. I know only too well there are some things that defy logic." He smiled at Sarah. "I believe you, Sarah."

"Whew! Thank goodness," she said, laughing. "For a second, I thought you might want to have me committed."

"Only if you start seein' unicorns. So, Lou. I assume your plan is to reopen the investigation, find Peter, and bring 'im in for questioning? After all these years?"

"That's my hope."

"Have you spoken to Harlan Covington?"

"He was the Moodys' family attorney, right?"

Sarah recalled seeing that name in the file.

"Yes. Rather a slippery fella, if you ask me. Then again, I've never met a lawyer who wasn't. You might want to look 'im up before goin' off on a wild goose chase, though."

"Can I ask why?" Sarah said.

"I'd hate to see you waste your time, is all. Peter Moody is dead. Buried in Resurrection Cemetery, next to his parents."

As the other two looked on in stunned silence, the old man took a huge bite of his fish taco and wiped his mouth with a paper napkin.

Sarah realized she was no longer hungry.

Nine

SARAH WAS in Peter Moody's bedroom again, barefoot and wearing a long, sheer white nightgown. It was late afternoon. Summer. A warm breeze was blowing in through the open window, rustling the curtains. Sarah could feel its warmth on her face and arms.

The teenager was sitting hunched over in his desk chair, shirtless, his back to Sarah, rocking and repeating a chant she couldn't make out. He was thin, she noticed. And she could see his bony shoulder blades. Though she didn't want to, something compelled her to move closer. As she did, she could see clearly the books on the shelves: *Encyclopedia Britannica*, *Great Expectations*, *Jane Eyre*, and *Catcher in the Rye*. And comics like *Watchmen* and *Fiends of the Eastern Front*.

Now, she was standing behind him, and as she looked over his shoulder, she saw him carving cryptic markings into his forearm with a penknife, the dark blood dripping into a black bowl decorated with strange symbols in red paint and whose inside was hammered metal. As if sensing her presence, the boy stopped and spun around.

Sarah was standing across the room now, looking toward the bed, where Hannah lay naked under a sheet, trembling with anticipation. Peter was saying something to her, but his voice sounded muffled, as if he were underwater. She looked apprehensive as he gave Hannah the bowl and made her drink.

When she'd finished, she swooned, her mouth ruby red. Carefully, he set the bowl down, peeled back the sheet, and climbed on top of her, moving his hips rhythmically. Holding back her arms, he kissed her on the mouth as dark blood ran from her lips onto the stark, white pillowcase.

Sarah woke up screaming, startling Gary, who'd been sleeping next to her. Her hand on her chest, she could feel her heart pounding and the blood pulsing in her head. It had all been so real, and she was terrified of the evil she had witnessed. Calming herself with careful breaths, she gradually recovered as the remnants of the dream began to dissipate. She prayed fervently.

"Saint Michael, the Archangel, defend us in battle. Be our protection against the wickedness and snares of the devil…"

Turning sideways, she placed her feet on the floor and stood, realizing she was wearing the nightgown from her dream. Had she actually gone to that horrible place in the past? She checked her phone and saw that it wasn't even eleven yet.

She'd had such a full day, first at Casa Abrigo with Joe and Michael, then meeting Kyle Jeffers in Santa Barbara with Lou, and finally returning to her office to take a new client house-hunting. She'd gotten home quite late, and not having the strength to cook for herself, microwaved a frozen dinner of chicken parmigiana that had probably been the worst Italian food she ever ate. She had fallen into bed, too exhausted to read, thinking about what the retired police chief had said.

Peter Moody was dead.

Standing in the kitchen, she poured herself a whiskey and, closing her eyes, took a hurried drink. It felt good going down, warm and soothing. On the way back to town, Lou had expressed an interest in meeting with Harlan Covington and promised to invite Sarah. But what was the point? The attorney would simply confirm what they already knew: the boy had died, the body having been buried in Dos Santos.

Then, a fresh thought. If she wanted to learn the truth, she might need to go to Resurrection Cemetery and visit Peter's grave. Surely, she would pick up some kind of emanation. But she knew in her heart she didn't have the strength to set foot in that place. It was too frightening—even for someone who'd been experiencing the paranormal for much of her life. What if she saw something more horrific than what she'd experienced in her nightmare? She might go insane.

Sarah tried putting the idea out of her mind, but it was no use. When she moved to Dos Santos, Joe had joked about having a picnic at the cemetery. And now, it seemed as if she might need to go there. *No, not yet.* First things first. Better to wait and see what the lawyer said. Maybe there was another way.

Instead of dwelling on the problem, she concentrated on her upcoming date with Michael Peterson. She would buy a new dress and maybe visit the salon. Though she knew she was getting ahead of herself, she tried imagining a possible future with Michael. He seemed nice, and though he was more than ten years older, she wondered if he was at all interested in having children. He'd never mentioned any from his first marriage.

Then, another thought. If somehow things did work out between them, he could very well be the proud new owner of Casa Abrigo. And Sarah would have to come to terms with living there. Even with the remodel, she knew she would never be comfortable. *Really, Sarah? You haven't even danced with the guy yet.*

Sarah felt a sudden chill. Draining her glass and setting it down, she looked out her kitchen window into the backyard, where she noticed something tall floating above the ground, shrouded in mist. Looking closer, she could see it more clearly.

It was the mirror.

"It can't be. Not here."

She made herself look away. But as she turned, she found Hannah's ghost in the kitchen, less than a foot in front of her.

"Not dead," she said with lifeless eyes.

Then, the ghost screamed in a way that suggested the whole world had lost its ability to hear.

Harlan Covington was not a tall man, though he seemed larger than life sitting in his wood-paneled office filled with leather-bound legal books and antiques mostly from Europe. Recently, he had purchased the pricey building on State Street and rented office space to other attorneys at higher than market prices. Sarah knew this because she'd shown a nearby condo recently, and the owner—a family law attorney and no fan of his new landlord—had readily given her all the "juicy" details.

Dressed in an expensive-looking custom-tailored suit, Covington appeared to be in his early seventies—impossibly thin with straight, snow-white hair he combed forward, presumably to hide a receding hairline, Sarah suspected. His tanned face was lined, his teeth even, though a little too pointy for her taste. He wore no wedding ring, but on his right hand she noticed an unusual, wide silver ring with a flat onyx face depicting something she couldn't make out.

"I see you're admiring my ring, Ms. Greene," the lawyer said, smiling. His voice was pleasant but with a force that belied his age.

She and Lou were sitting across from him, separated by a large antique walnut desk Sarah recognized as Italian and hand-carved with full relief foliate motifs. There were two ornate male figures, one at each corner. They seemed almost to be watching Sarah, which made her uncomfortable.

"Sorry, I didn't mean to stare," she said. "It's beautiful."

Getting to his feet, Covington reached over and presented his hand to her. She detected a subtle odor of soap. She saw what was etched into the onyx was a depiction of what appeared to be an old man, slightly bent and holding a staff. She'd never seen anything like it.

"I found it on a trip to Venice some years back," he said, not bothering to show it to Lou.

Leaning forward, the police chief squinted at it. "What does it represent?"

Stiffly, Covington took his hand back and sat, the tufted leather chair squealing to the touch as he settled in. For no reason at all, Sarah thought of pigs in a slaughterhouse.

"I have no idea," he said.

Sarah turned to look at the objets d'art. Several things caught her eye instantly. The first was a magnificent Fardouelle à Paris clock featuring a carved dial with Roman and Arab numerals in enamel. And on a different shelf, an authentic Meissen ewer and octagonal basin, each decorated with polychrome Watteauesque figures against a gray monochrome park setting. *Who in the world can afford these kinds of pieces?*

"I see you appreciate the finer things," Covington said, almost startling Sarah.

"Your collection is very impressive."

"My family was originally from the north of England. In those days, we couldn't afford meat. Strange how things turn out. My assistant told me you're here to discuss a former client?"

Sarah took a sip of coffee from the bone china coffee mug she was holding and glanced at Lou as he opened the manila folder and referred to his case file.

"That's right, Peter Moody," Lou said. "We understand you were the family's attorney?"

"Yes, that's right."

"We're looking into the 1990 murder of his parents, Gerald and Vivian."

"Whatever for?"

Sarah hoped Lou would be discreet about her involvement in the case. She'd gotten lucky with Kyle Jeffers, but she sensed Harlan Covington was the kind of man who would be less than impressed by input from a psychic.

"We've uncovered some additional evidence we think might point to Peter's involvement in his parents' deaths."

Sarah was surprised at Covington's reaction which, in fact, was no reaction at all. As he smiled professionally, she had a strong feeling the attorney knew something but wasn't telling. He leaned forward, as if trying to peek at the file.

"And the fact that Peter Moody is dead?"

"Is irrelevant," Lou said, his tone becoming authoritative. "Look, Mr. Covington, I've been a cop for a long time."

"Chief Fiore, I seem to recall you used to be with homicide here in Santa Barbara."

"Correct. And I don't like cold cases. If I can prove Peter Moody had something to do with his parents' deaths, it doesn't matter to me whether or not he's alive to stand trial. All I want is to solve the case."

The attorney studied him, his hands steepled together in front of his face. An image of him pressing a secret button and them falling through a trapdoor flashed through Sarah's mind.

"I see," Covington said at last. "Well, as you know, anything my client may have told me is covered under attorney-client privilege."

"But—"

"*And* survives the death of the client. Don't believe me? Ask the Supreme Court."

"How did Peter Moody die?" Lou said, changing course.

"I'm sorry to report he committed suicide."

"Do you recall when that was?" Sarah said. "And was that here or…"

"1993, if memory serves. He was living in Lawrence, Kansas. Now, if that's all, I have other appointments."

"One more question," Lou said. "Please. Do you know if his sister, Hannah, is alive?"

Sarah looked at him sharply. Why would Lou ask that? He knew as well as she that the girl was dead. *Hello? I've been seeing her ghost?*

The attorney smiled cryptically. "That's an odd question. Sounds to me as if you think something may have happened to her, too?"

"We're looking into that possibility."

"Well, I'm not sure how helpful I can be. After her brother's death, I lost touch. As far as I know, she's living in Lawrence. I have the address of her aunt and uncle. You can get that from my assistant."

"Thanks."

"I understand Peter is buried in Resurrection Cemetery?" Sarah said.

"Yes, that's right. Along with his parents. Now, I must conclude this meeting."

Covington stood. Lou glanced at Sarah, and they got to their feet as well. Carefully, she returned her mug to the coaster sitting on the desk. As she and Lou gathered their things together to leave, Covington stepped around his desk and offered his hand.

"May I ask what *your* involvement is in all this, Ms. Greene?" the lawyer said as he shook Sarah's hand.

She blushed as Lou answered for her. "She and her business partner are renovating the old Moody house. They found something we think might be relevant to the case."

"I see. And what might that be?"

Lou smiled. "Sorry, that's covered under *police* privilege."

Covington looked at him darkly and almost said something. When they were at the door, the attorney spoke.

"I can tell you with confidence, Chief, that my client had nothing whatsoever to do with those murders. I do hope you can find the real perpetrators, though. This tragedy has been weighing on me for many years."

"We'll do our best. Thanks for your time, Mr. Covington."

After Sarah and Lou had left, the lawyer returned to his desk and made a call.

"It's me," he said. "Fine. As I predicted, their questions

were routine. No, nothing to be concerned about. No, I *don't* know where the mirror is. Look, you do your part and I'll do mine."

He disconnected before the other person could respond. Although the police chief hadn't said so, Harlan knew that Sarah and her business partner had indeed discovered the mirror. And he also knew that, surprisingly, Sarah had made a connection with it. That was unfortunate.

Glancing down at his phone, he noticed a text from his assistant. *Bradleys r here to discuss will.*

He texted her back. *Send them in.*

Ten

WHEN THEY REACHED THE STREET, Sarah looked up to find dark clouds that seemed to surround the neighborhood like reapers closing in. Perfect, considering how she felt after having met the prince of darkness himself, Harlan Covington.

"Hungry?" Lou said.

"Always." They started walking. "Hey, Lou, why did you ask Covington if Hannah is alive?"

"Because I wanted to see his reaction."

"Ahh. Smart. Only, it didn't work."

"Yeah, unfortunately. He's good, I'll give him that."

They decided on Jane Restaurant, which was within walking distance. It was after eleven, and Sarah and Lou were able to get a table before the traditional lunch crowd arrived. After the server had delivered their drinks and taken their orders, Lou went into debrief mode.

"So, did you get any sense of this guy back there?"

"You mean, other than the fact that he scares the shit out of me? No. He's a riddle wrapped in a mystery inside a dick."

Lou laughed out loud. "I'll have to remember that. Seriously, though, I think he's hiding something. When I get back to my office, I plan to call the aunt and uncle. Maybe *they* know where Hannah is."

"Well, you already know what I think."

"And I'm pretty much in agreement with you, but I need to consider every possibility."

Lou had ordered a triple espresso and drained the cup in one swallow.

Sarah laughed. "And I thought *I* was a caffeine junkie. Hey, maybe you should fly out to Lawrence and interview the relatives in person."

"I don't have budget for that."

"Well, I've got airline miles up the wing-wang, so I could go. But I'm not a cop."

"It's okay, Sarah. I'm a professional. I can do this all by phone, email, and fax."

"Me, I prefer the personal touch. But, hey, you know best."

Their food arrived. The server presented Sarah with the Fettuccine & Homemade Lamb Sausage pasta bowl. Lou was having the El Macho Burger. Both were starving, and things went quiet for a few minutes as they ate.

"I didn't tell you about my latest dream," Sarah said. "And what happened after."

"Do I want to know?"

"Okay, so Peter was into some kind of devil worship, I'm sure of it. He made his sister drink his blood."

Lou had been ready to take a huge bite of his burger when he noticed the red meat juice dripping onto his plate. Making a face, he set the burger down.

"Sorry," she said. "Then later in my kitchen, I saw Hannah again. And that damned mirror. Lou, this time, she said something curious. 'Not dead.'"

"Huh. Does she mean her brother?"

"That's what I'd like to know. I need to take another look at that mirror."

"Are you sure? Didn't you pass out last time?"

"I wasn't prepared. This time, I will be."

"Because I don't want you going all loopy on me. I need you on this case."

"Oh, how sweet."

He picked up his burger again. "Where's the mirror now?"

"At our warehouse, why?"

"Call it a hunch. I think maybe you should move it."

"Why?"

"Well, look at what we've got so far. Both Kyle and that lawyer confirm Peter Moody's death. Then, you're visited by some ghost wailing 'Not dead' or whatever. What if Peter is *alive* and knows about the mirror?"

"Okay, sold. I'll talk to Joe when we get back. How's your appetite, by the way? I would've thought a homicide detective would have a cast-iron stomach."

"We do. Normally. Do me a favor, though. No more dream talk until I finish, okay?"

"Lightweight," she said, and took another bite of her sausage.

It was almost dark when Sarah and Joe arrived at the public storage facility. And it was starting to rain again. It had pained Joe to shell out on a separate storage unit when they already owned their own warehouse in Goleta. Joe had bought it for pennies on the dollar during the last downturn. Sarah had convinced him this was important, though, and he and Manny had dutifully moved the mirror earlier in the day. When they arrived, he climbed out and used his circular key to open the gate. He drove through and cruised slowly toward the last aisle.

"Thank you for coming with me," Sarah said as they got out in front of their unit.

Lately, she had felt awkward around Joe, almost as if they were becoming strangers. Maybe it was her imagination. Or her Catholic guilt over attending a dance with another man. But why should *she* feel guilty? He was seeing that Gail person. And that was another thing; so far, he didn't seem all that smitten.

"No worries," he said as he unlocked the padlock and raised the roll-up door.

The inside was cold, barren, and full of shadows. Sarah felt apprehensive and wanted Joe close by. So, as she approached the mirror, which was covered in a sheet and stood in the middle of the unit, she took his hand. Despite the cold, it felt warm.

"Sure you want to do this?" he said.

"You'll catch me if I faint, right?"

"Always." He gave her hand a squeeze and took hold of the sheet. "Ready?"

She nodded and waited for him to uncover the mirror. She stared at it again, wondering if Hannah would appear. She thought about the possibility of Joe seeing what Sarah saw. But that was crazy—he was tone deaf when it came to things like that.

Closing her eyes, Sarah moved closer and touched the frame. She felt a surge of energy and was tempted to pull her hand away. But she also wanted Hannah to explain what had happened to her and whether her brother might be alive. Spirits weren't very good storytellers, she noticed. They seemed to always be distracted. Nothing. Not even a glimmer of an image. Disappointed, she stepped back and looked at Joe.

"Anything?" he said.

"No."

"Maybe I should leave you alone."

She didn't want that. Not now. Not ever. But she knew she needed to try and, giving him a look of desperation and letting go of his hand, waited for Joe to leave. As he walked out, she watched him, wishing with all her heart she'd never seen the damned mirror in the first place. She looked into its milky darkness and waited.

After twenty minutes, Sarah shook her head.

"Elvis has left the building."

She re-covered the mirror with the sheet and walked outside.

"Joe?"

It was dark and deathly quiet, except for the sound of rain. The silence unnerved her as she lowered the roll-up door and locked it.

"Joe?"

Something—an owl?—stirred in a nearby pine tree. She heard the sound of flapping wings. Joe's truck was still parked outside. He wasn't one for practical jokes and would never have left her alone this way. She could hear the sound of approaching footsteps and recognized Joe walking toward her from around the corner.

"Sorry," he said. "I got a call and didn't want to disturb you. You weren't scared, were you?"

"Oh, no. *Terrified* maybe, but not scared."

"How about a drink?"

"That's the most sensible thing you've said all day."

"So…nothing?"

"*Nada*. Time for Plan B."

"Which is?"

"A visit to Resurrection Cemetery."

Sighing, she pretended her finger was a gun and, putting it to her head, pulled the trigger.

Eleven

THE SUN WAS RISING over a distant line of trees, its jagged rays tearing through a blanket of gray clouds, when Sarah locked her front door and started her run, which would take her north toward the cemetery. Her earbuds firmly in place, she selected Dizzy Gillespie—one of Eddie's favorite musicians—and began stretching.

Her father had turned her on to jazz when she was eleven. At first, she considered it "old timey." But each weekday as he dutifully drove Rachel and her to and from school in his beloved black Galaxie with the red vinyl interior, she began to understand the magic that was jazz and eventually asked to hear more.

Mile One. Though she hadn't been plagued with any more nightmares, she had spent most of the night worrying about what would happen if she entered Resurrection Cemetery and encountered a vengeful spirit. The frail ones—the elderly or children—who wandered about lost in a fog of memories and clinging to their earthly lives didn't concern her. No, it was the angry ones she feared most. And having researched the cemetery's history, she thought it likely she would in fact see such things lurking among the moss-covered gravestones.

Mile Two. In Santa Barbara, the Spanish had reserved the mission's cemetery for priests, notable Native Americans who had been baptized, and members of certain prominent Catholic families. And they chose a remote plot of land in what eventually would become Dos Santos to bury common criminals and the poor. John Dos Santos, the town's founder, along with the other men who had marched off to fight the Germans during WWI, were buried there as well. And now, Gerald and Vivian Moody and their son, Peter, had taken up residence.

Mile Three. Huffing as she took the hill leading to the cemetery gates, Sarah thought of that iconic scene in the mayor's office in the original *Ghostbusters* movie: "The dead rising from the grave! Human sacrifice, dogs and cats living together...mass hysteria!" But as she got closer, she saw something she never expected in a ghost-fueled, paranormal apocalypse where, literally, all hell might break loose at any moment.

Breathing hard and checking her pulse, she watched as men and women exited a series of white trucks parked in front of the gates. Next to them was a van with a logo Sarah recognized, accompanied by a single word in bright, blood-red letters: DUBIOUS.

"Oh, hell," she said.

Dubious was a reality television show broadcast on the Discovery Channel. It featured the husband-and-wife team of Donnie and Debbie Fisk who, every week, spent an hour "debunking" the paranormal all across the country. The ratings must have been high, because they were picked up for a fifth season. Sarah despised the show's smarmy hosts, who looked to be in their late twenties, were blond and pale, and hailed from Orange County where, according to Wikipedia, they attended Orange Coast College, majoring in Visual & Performing Arts.

What Sarah hated most, though, was not the fact that these two posers were making a living on television. No, it was that they were such obvious hucksters. Unlike their colleagues on shows like *Ghost Hunters* and *Ghost Adventures*, who at least acknowledged that there are things out there we can't explain, these two geniuses figured out a way to make money with the genre by going the *other* way—attempting to prove once and for all that the whole of the spirit realm was horseshit. Never mind the occasional background noise which sounded suspiciously like something otherworldly and was always dismissed as "static," or the ghostly images on video which Donnie and Debbie referred to with a nervous laugh as "some kind of light distortion." Oh, and that stupid catchphrase. Puleeze. "Welcome to the *real* world, boys and girls!"

And as if this wasn't bad enough, after marrying Joe, Sarah learned to her never-ending horror that he was a *fan*. Now that she thought about it, this was probably one of the things that had contributed to her wanting a divorce in the first place. As impossible as it seemed, the man was devoted to the show and watched it regularly.

One time, she grudgingly watched an episode with him, scoffing the whole time at Donnie and Debbie's so-called "proof" that neither ghosts, spirits, or demons existed in this or in any other dimension. Finally, exasperated, she went off on him.

"Joe, how can you sit here and watch this crap?"

"What? They make me laugh."

Great. Why were these two idiots in Dos Santos? Maybe she would find a way for La Llorona to pay them a midnight visit.

Sarah didn't know what she was more upset about: not

being able to explore Resurrection Cemetery when she had finally worked up the nerve or seeing the Opposite Twins about to tramp through a haunted graveyard with their fancy equipment, making wisecracks and mugging for the camera. Calming herself, she decided to check things out.

As she approached the vehicles, where crew members were unloading camera and lighting equipment and heavy cables, she noticed Joe's truck parked up the road. She saw her ex-husband standing off to the side, drinking coffee from a Cracked Pot to-go cup. Was he hoping for an autograph? Perfect.

"Figures I'd find you here," she said.

"Heard about it this morning when I was getting coffee."

"So, have the prima donnas arrived yet?"

"No, only the crew. I guess you won't be checking out Peter Moody's grave today, though."

"Looks that way. Hang on."

Sarah flagged down one of the crew members, a woman in jeans and a ski vest who looked to be in her mid-thirties.

"Excuse me. How long are you guys planning to be here?"

"All day. We're setting up now and shooting the episode tonight."

"Okay, thanks."

Sarah shook her head and returned to Joe, who seemed sympathetic.

"Looks like you'll have to come back tomorrow," he said.

Joe's phone rang. Handing Sarah his coffee, he grabbed it from his jeans pocket and, taking back the cup, answered.

"Yo. What? Okay, I'll be right there."

"What happened?" Sarah said.

"Someone broke into our warehouse. One of Manny's sons was hurt."

"Which one?"

"Pollito."

"I'm coming with."

Though it was less than ten miles to the warehouse, heavy traffic clogged the northbound 101, making Joe uncharacteristically angry as he inched his way forward.

"Take it easy," Sarah said. "How about some music?"

She fiddled with the stereo until she found the jazz station. As Count Basie's "April in Paris" filled the cab, she kept thinking about Lou and his hunch regarding the mirror. Had the break-in at their office been a prelude? And did this mean Peter Moody *was* alive? *Don't get ahead of yourself, Sarah.* In any case, it was a good thing they'd followed Lou's advice and moved the haunted object.

When they finally arrived at the building on Calle Real, Joe found Manny's and his son's trucks, as well as a Goleta police cruiser and an emergency vehicle parked out front. As they approached the emergency vehicle, Sarah saw Pollito sitting in the back. His head was bandaged, and he was wearing a gray patient blanket. Manny stood before him, his hand on his son's shoulder.

"Manny," Joe said, approaching the men.

A Goleta cop intercepted him. "Sir, are you the owner of this property?"

"Yes. I'm Joe Greene. This is my wi— This is Sarah, my business partner."

Sarah watched as Joe walked off with the police officer, smiling like the Cheshire Cat. Interesting. He'd almost called her his wife. *Guess things must not be going all that great with ol' Gail the Whale.* She would have to do some investigating later. She approached Manny and Pollito, the youngest of the three boys and a heartbreaker when it came to looks.

"I'm so sorry," she said to Manny's son.

"It's okay, I'm fine. And I don't need this *pinche cobija*, Pa."

Manny removed the blanket from around his son's shoulders and tossed it into the vehicle.

"So, what happened?" she said to Pollito.

"I was here early, picking up supplies on my way to work and saw the front door was open. It was dark inside, and when I went to turn on the lights, somebody hit me hard."

Manny rubbed his eyes. "He was out cold. When he woke up, he called me."

"Does Blanca know?"

Before Manny could answer, one of the EMTs appeared, ready to strap Pollito onto a gurney for the trip to the hospital.

"I don't need no hospital," Pollito said, his voice testy.

Sarah touched his hand. "You should let them check you out. You might have a concussion."

Manny turned to the EMT. "I'll take him to urgent care. We'll be fine."

"Okay," the EMT said, handing Manny a clipboard with a form on it and a pen. "Your son needs to sign this."

"I'm going to look for Joe," Sarah said and headed toward the entrance. "Take care, Pollito."

The small warehouse was bursting with construction supplies and piles of booty Joe had recovered from dozens of homes he'd purchased. An entire section was devoted to furniture, fixtures, and artwork he used regularly to "stage" properties he and Sarah had put on the market. He always attached price tags to them, and when a buyer expressed an interest, he worked the item into the purchase agreement.

Manny's sons had moved the wine from Casa Abrigo here, and Sarah wondered where they'd stored it. Things were packed so tightly, Sarah wondered how Joe was able to find anything. As she made her way past aisles of lumber, drywall, and huge white plastic pails of paint, she could see her ex-husband in the distance speaking with the cop, who was taking notes.

"Hey," she said, joining them. "So, do we know if anything was stolen?"

Joe shook his head. "We'll have to do an inventory, but from what I've seen, I don't think so."

The cop took a quick glance around. "I'll be surprised if nothing is missing."

"Pollito probably interrupted them," Sarah said.

The cop closed his notepad. "I'll file a report. But the chances of catching whoever broke in are pretty slim. The victim didn't report seeing another vehicle. You should think about installing some security cameras."

"You're right," Joe said. "Okay, thanks."

As the cop left them, Joe found Sarah grinning at him, her arms folded across her chest.

"What?" he said.

"'My *wife*'?"

He started walking away, pretending to inspect merchandise. "What are you talking about?"

"Don't you remember?" she said, following him. "You almost called me your wife back there. I *knew* you missed me, ya big lug."

"You're crazy. I was upset." He handed her a random table lamp.

"Uh-huh."

"Can we please change the subject? And since you're here, I need you to help me do a quick inventory."

"Okay…*honey*."

"Shut up," he said, unable to keep himself from smiling.

The inventory had taken several hours. By the time Sarah and Joe arrived back at the office, she was starving. As Joe had predicted, nothing was missing, which in Sarah's mind proved that Lou's hunch had been right. Someone *was* looking for the mirror and most likely wouldn't stop until they found it.

As they entered through the rear door, they heard the sounds of men's voices and power drills. Two guys wearing alarm company uniforms were standing on ladders, installing new sensors, as well as video cameras. A third man was at the front door, down on one knee, installing a new deadbolt system.

"Wow, Rachel moves fast," Sarah said.

She went to look for her sister. When she didn't find her, Sarah walked up to the front to check in with Blanca. The receptionist was in the middle of typing an email.

"Blanca? Is Pollito okay?"

"*Gracias a Dios.*"

Rachel appeared at the front door, waiting for the locksmith to stand and let her in. She was carrying two large takeout bags from The Cracked Pot. When she saw her sister, she smiled.

"Just in time. I brought lunch."

"*Gracias a Dios,*" Sarah said and helped her with the bags.

Sarah, Joe, and Rachel sat in the conference room, eating their lunch.

"Where's Blanca?" Joe said, taking a huge bite of his sandwich.

Rachel shook her head. "I put hers in the fridge. She says she's too upset to eat."

"Poor thing," Sarah said, taking another bite of her Cobb salad. "Pollito is her baby. Hey, Joe? Is there any way I can talk you into skipping the dating scene for one night and come with me?"

"Where?"

"Resurrection Cemetery."

"Won't the TV crew be there?"

"Yeah, so?"

"You're not planning something crazy?"

"Like what?" Rachel said.

"Like getting into it with Donnie and Debbie." Then, to Rachel, "She hates those guys."

Sarah pretended to be surprised. "Joe, I am shocked —*shocked*—that you would suggest such a thing. To think that I, Sarah Greene, the, the…"

"Beautiful and talented?" her sister said.

Sarah pointed at Rachel. "Local psychic would think of—"

"Fine, I'll come."

Joe threw the remains of his lunch into one of the bags and placed his hands on the table, trying to give Sarah a serious look but breaking into a smile.

I still got it. Sarah grinned and popped a piece of avocado into her mouth. "Mm, great salad, Rache."

Harlan Covington stepped out onto State Street and began

walking in a northerly direction. The sidewalk was filled with pedestrians, and Harlan had to maneuver carefully. A family of tourists was approaching, struggling with a toddler apparently in the throes of a titanic tantrum. The young parents seemed exasperated.

The elderly attorney smiled. He didn't dislike children. On the contrary, perhaps if he had chosen a different path, he might've married and raised a family. There *was* a girl once. Marie Legrande. French Catholic. Her father was a wealthy banker, he remembered, and not opposed to his daughter marrying Harlan. She would've made an excellent wife for a young attorney. But as often happens, fate stepped in. And with it the promise of unimaginable power.

Absently, he fingered the silver ring with the onyx face. He felt his phone vibrate and removed it from his coat pocket. Recognizing the number, he slipped into a nearby alley and walked all the way to the back, where it dead-ended in a brick wall.

"How did it go? What?"

He could hear the sound of an approaching siren. He pressed the phone against his ear and covered the other ear with his free hand.

"So, it wasn't there? Well, I was sure— What? Yes, I'll make some inquiries. Don't worry. We'll find it. In the meantime, don't do anything stupid."

The voice at the other end must have said something insulting, because Covington pulled the phone away from his ear, stared at it in disgust, and ended the call. When Harlan looked up again, he saw a stranger approaching. He was a man of around fifty, wearing baggy jeans and a windbreaker. But it was his eyes.

They were completely black.

Harlan raised his hand, showing the man the ring. The

stranger stopped mid-stride. Wearing a snarl, his entire being filled with rage. As he continued toward the old man, he grabbed his head and began moaning, the intense pain blinding him and making him fall onto his knees. He lay on his side, convulsing on the ground as a putrid, yellowish bile poured from his lips.

When Harlan was certain the man was no longer a threat, he walked out of the alley onto the sidewalk, where once again, he saw the young couple and their other children huddled around the toddler—a boy with beautiful blond locks. He was lying prostrate on the sidewalk, his arms and legs extended, crying inconsolably. The old man strode toward them.

"What's all this?" His voice was filled with concern.

The frantic mother's eyes pleaded with him. Smiling, he patted her hand and crouched down on his haunches— not an easy feat at his age.

"So, you've decided to take a nap, have you? Out here in the street?"

The boy had stopped bawling and was looking at the old man in fascination. He noticed the unusual ring and silently pointed at it.

"This? Want to see?"

The boy nodded, having forgotten all about whatever it was that was bothering him. Covington looked up at the parents for permission; they smiled gratefully. He reached out his hand and allowed the little one to touch the ring. As if by magic, the boy smiled and sat up. Babbled something to his mother and reached out his arms to her. She picked him up and held him, kissing his ear.

"Thank you so much," she said. "He gets this way sometimes."

"Probably tired," Covington said. "I'm sure he'll be fine once he's had a nap."

The family watched as the stranger with the unusual ring moved into the flow of foot traffic. As he got farther away, Harlan thought of what lay ahead. Sometimes, he felt *he* was that boy, fighting and screaming against everything he was meant to do. Perhaps one day, he could rest. In the meantime, he had work to do, especially now that the mirror had been discovered.

A shadow in the sky passed over him, accompanied by the faint sound of beating wings. Looking up, the old man shielded his eyes as a flock of crows passed overhead, cawing. Crows, not ravens. But he knew the ravens weren't far off. They were waiting in Dos Santos.

"Soon," he said to no one. *Soon.*

Twelve

IF WAS after eight when Sarah and Joe arrived in her car. Heavy, rain-filled clouds obscured the moon, and the only illumination came from the lighting equipment the television crew had set up, all powered by a huge white portable generator sitting on a trailer parked outside the gates on the street. As Sarah approached it, careful to step over the heavy black cables, she was surprised at how quietly it ran.

Fans had gathered there, hoping for a glimpse of the show's stars. Sarah noticed Carter, the server from The Cracked Pot, standing off to one side with a small group of other twenty-somethings.

"Is that her band?" Sarah said.

Joe glanced over. "I think so."

As Sarah continued watching Carter, she noticed a dark, viscous form moving rapidly toward the group. Her pulse quickened as she realized it was something malevolent. Concerned, she started toward the girl to warn her. The others standing with her were oblivious. Sarah stopped when she saw Carter turn and appear to react to the entity. *She can see it?* The girl said something to her friends and walked away as the thing vanished. Touching her chest, Sarah let out a sigh. She decided she would need to speak to the girl first chance she got.

"Hey, look," Joe said.

Sarah turned to where he was pointing. A black Escalade had pulled up, and the fans began cheering and shouting.

She shook her head. "Here we go."

The two minor celebrities exited the vehicle to the cheers of "Welcome to the *real* world, boys and girls!" Before the fans could mob Donnie and Debbie, several security guards wearing *Dubious* windbreakers intervened. Each of those guys could have easily weighed three hundred pounds, Sarah guessed.

After the stars had entered the cemetery, Sarah nudged Joe and began walking toward the gates.

"You're not trying to get backstage?" he said.

"Watch and learn, my friend."

She removed her wallet from her purse and, getting out her driver's license, approached one of the security guards, who was holding a clipboard.

"I'm Sarah Greene," she said.

He glanced at the ID, referred to his clipboard, and waved her through. As Sarah walked in, he put a hand up to Joe's face.

"Who are you?"

Sarah turned casually. "It's okay. He's with me."

The cemetery looked eerie in the white glow coming from the bright lights that had been set up around several of the gravestones. To play it safe, Sarah had said a Rosary earlier. Though she was secretly terrified, she wanted to prove to herself she could handle being in such a haunted place. As she made her way over slowly, she took in as much of the atmosphere as she could handle.

"Okay, are you going to explain how you did that?" Joe said.

"Did what?"

"Get us past Andre the Giant."

"I'm not completely helpless, you know." Joe said nothing. "Okay, fine. Lou arranged it."

"You could've waited till tomorrow."

"And have you miss meeting your two favorite celebs? I hope you brought a Sharpie for the autographs. Hey, maybe they can sign your butt."

Up ahead, Sarah could see Donnie and Debbie conversing with the woman she'd met that morning. Apparently, they were going over the script. *They use scripts for reality TV?*

"Joe, can you wait here a sec?" she said.

Sarah walked confidently up to Donnie and Debbie and waited politely for them to finish their conversation. She'd learned the crew member's name was Gillian. Recognizing Sarah, she smiled.

"Hey, Gillian."

"Guys? This is Sarah Greene."

The husband and wife team turned to Sarah. She introduced Joe, and everyone shook hands.

Donnie and Debbie appeared older in person, and Sarah realized they were probably her age. She also noticed neither was naturally blond. And Donnie wore thick glasses when he wasn't on camera.

"We were able to locate Peter Moody's grave," Gillian said.

Sarah smiled. "Great. I appreciate this."

Holding Joe's hand, Sarah approached a gravestone

that had been lit. A camera sat on a tripod nearby, pointed toward it. Donnie, Debbie, and Gillian had accompanied them while the rest of the crew was off somewhere else setting things up for the actual shoot.

"You really think you'll see something?" Debbie said.

Sarah was staring at the gravestone, which filled her with dread, and didn't appear to have heard. Joe nudged her, and she turned.

"Not sure. But if there *is* anything, maybe your equipment will pick it up?"

"You never know," Donnie said. "It'd be a first on our show. Well, let's do this."

Gillian walked over to the camera and focused on Sarah as she drifted slowly between the gravestones of Peter Moody and his parents. Another crew member with a boom mic had appeared next to the camera, and someone else wearing headphones—a sound man?—took a seat near a cart with expensive-looking electronic equipment.

A kid who looked as if he could have been in high school stepped in front of the camera, holding a clapperboard, and someone shouted for everyone to be quiet. Gillian started recording and the kid created a slate. Joe hung back behind the camera with the show's hosts.

Attempting to shut out all distractions, Sarah closed her eyes and slowed her breathing, expelling air to make room for the supernatural. Nothing. She concentrated on Gerald and Vivian, then on Peter. She tried picturing Peter as he might have looked in 1993. A little taller maybe, with the downy beginnings of a young man's beard. Still nothing.

A memory of seeing him in his room on top of Hannah flashed across her mind; she dismissed it. She opened her eyes and began moving slowly toward Peter's gravestone. This was the part that terrified her most—touching the cold granite—not knowing what to expect. But when she did, she felt nothing but the rough, wet stone. Not even a glimmer of the paranormal.

Sighing, she turned around and faced everyone as Gillian said, "Cut!"

The kid returned and created another slate.

"So, nothing?" Donnie said. "What a surprise." He turned to the sound man. "You get anything?"

"Zip-a-dee-doo-dah."

"Oh," Debbie said, her voice dripping with fake sincerity. "Maybe next time, huh?"

Donnie touched Sarah's arm, smiling disingenuously. "We'll review the video and sound later and let Chief Fiore know if we uncover anything, 'kay?"

"Thanks," she said, avoiding eye contact.

Joe came around and took her hand, giving it a gentle squeeze. He expected her to be disappointed. But when he saw her face, he noticed she was wearing a huge grin.

"What?"

"Oh, nothing."

She looked over again at the two hosts, who were discussing the scene they were about to shoot. Next to them floated three rotting, mutilated corpses dressed in WWI army uniforms, practically breathing down the necks of the two clueless unbelievers. One of them tried touching Donnie's ear, and he absently brushed it away.

"Nothing at all," she said.

"I don't understand," Lou said, chewing furiously on a toothpick. "You got *nothing*?"

He and Sarah were sitting in his office, fingers of soft

morning light pushing stealthily through the blinds. Sarah had returned home after her little adventure, had a whiskey, and gone to bed. She'd hoped Joe would ask to stay over. But lately, he was being "proper." After he kissed her on the cheek and left, she grudgingly told herself it was probably for the best.

Having been in the place she feared most, Sarah thought her night would have been filled with the sights and sounds of decaying bodies and wailing voices of the damned. But not even those WWI dudes had made an appearance, and she'd slept like a rock. She couldn't remember a single dream when she awoke the next morning and found Gary on her stomach, kneading his paws and purring like a toy motorboat.

She was dreading giving Lou the bad news and dawdled at the office until right before nine. It was Saturday, and she had decided to dress down, wearing a gray cashmere pullover, jeans, and her Frye black leather riding boots, which played havoc with the clutch whenever they got wet in the rain. She forced herself to get into her car and head over, hoping the police chief was in a good mood. *Another failure, Sarah.*

Lou was looking at the case file and, for a brief time, acted as though Sarah was not in the room. She noticed the more focused he got, the harder he chewed on his toothpick. Was *she* the toothpick? Sighing, he closed the file and looked at her with irritation she hoped wasn't directed at her.

"The parents are murdered," he said, "and a couple years later, their kid commits suicide. I mean, come on. This has got Stephen King written all over it."

"I know, Lou. But I didn't touch the parents' gravestones. And, strange as it sounds, I got absolutely nothing from Peter's. Did you speak to the aunt and uncle?"

"No luck there either. Morris Moody passed away two years ago and his wife, Colleen, is in some retirement facility."

"So, did you speak with *her*?"

"As a matter of fact, I did. Unfortunately, she wasn't much help. I think she might be a little, you know, forgetful. When I asked about Peter, she told me he and his family were living out in California."

"Oh, boy."

Lou tossed his toothpick and grabbed a fresh one. "Sarah, I'm beginning to think you're right about visiting the aunt in person."

"Makes sense. And you might dig up more relatives to interview."

"Interesting choice of words."

Leaning back, he rubbed his eyes with the heels of his hands. When he looked at her again, she noticed it wasn't with stars in his eyes. Maybe his little crush was over? *Thank goodness.*

Tim Whatley poked his head in. "I've got those traffic reports you requested. Oh, hey, Sarah."

"Hi, Tim."

He entered and handed a manila folder to Lou, who set it on top of a pile of folders. Sarah noticed that, as he did, he was surreptitiously scanning Lou's desk.

"Thanks for the file, Tim. Could you close the door on your way out?"

"Oh. Um, sure."

When they were alone again, Sarah said, "Is it my imagination, or is Tim a little—"

"Nosey? Now that you mention it. You know, it bugs me that you didn't sense anything at the cemetery. I mean, how is that possible, what with your other experiences?"

"Seriously. The whole area around the Moody

gravesite was like one big dead zone—no pun intended. Wait a second…"

"What?"

"Whenever I'm around the dead—especially in places that are haunted—I always get *something*. I saw the ghosts of three WWI veterans without breaking a sweat. Doesn't it strike you as odd that I…"

Lou leaned forward, a concerned look on his face. "Sarah?"

Chewing her lip, she looked at him intently. "Unless someone—or something—was *blocking* me."

"What do you mean?"

"I mean, somebody might have prevented me from experiencing anything. But whoever it was clearly couldn't control the whole damn cemetery, which would explain why I was able to see those other dead guys."

"Is that possible?" he said.

"Sure. If they performed a spell."

"Whoa." Lou got to his feet and began pacing. "Okay, I was willing to accept that you have these powers to see… weird shit. And now, you're telling me witches are real?"

"They don't have to be witches, Lou. Just someone who knows how to cast spells."

"So, who do you suspect?"

She scratched her head and thought for a moment. "Well, let me see. I was with Donnie and Debbie the whole time. Those two idiots couldn't have done it. And why would they? They don't believe in any of that stuff."

"What about the crew?"

"I guess."

"But they'd have no reason to…"

"Right."

"Is this mojo something someone can do from far away? You know, remotely?" he said.

"Sure."

Lou stopped pacing and sat on the edge of his desk. "Okay, the way I see it, there are two reasons why someone wouldn't want you to get any information about Peter Moody. One: he's guilty as hell and they don't want him being blamed for his parents' deaths for whatever reason. And two—"

"The person in that grave is *not* Peter Moody."

"That's what I was thinking." He walked back around the desk and took a seat. "I need to make a few calls."

"Lou, what are you planning to do?"

"Going to dig up a corpse."

Sarah entered the garage from the kitchen, carrying two beers. Her car was already up on the scissor lift, and she could see Eddie's legs, clad in faded blue overalls, sticking out from underneath. She and her father had been working on the Galaxie for sixteen or seventeen years—she couldn't recall exactly—and, like her father, Sarah knew every bolt, wire, and hose. She was perfectly capable of changing the oil herself, but she and Eddie both knew he loved the car like a son and always enjoyed getting his hands dirty.

"I'm setting your beer on the workbench," she said, taking a swallow of hers.

This was the only time she enjoyed drinking beer. She had tried ordering one at a baseball game once in college and found it disappointing. She was in Los Angeles with Joe, who was twenty-one at the time. The Dodgers were playing the Mets. In addition to the beer, he'd bought her a hot dog and peanuts, but nothing helped. A few days after she turned twenty-one, she drove her car into the garage because it was "making a funny noise." Instead of getting right to work, Eddie went into the house and brought back two Modelos. Then, he toasted his daughter.

"I've been waiting years to do this," he said, clinking bottles with her.

And that was when beer at the old homestead was the best thing in the world.

"So, where is everybody?" she said as Eddie used his heels to roll the car creeper back out with him on it.

"Katy is hanging out with friends and your sister is at Costco."

He stood, walked over, and took a long swallow of beer. Then, he returned to the car, popping the hood to take a look at the engine while the oil drained. He continued working as they talked. Shaking his head, he turned around and showed her a frayed spark plug wire.

"When's the last time you changed these?"

She smiled. "I think what you meant to say was, when's the last time *you* changed them."

"Right." He went back to work. "So, what's happening with that case?"

"Oh, Eddie... I asked Rachel not to tell you."

"She didn't. *You* just did. You can't outsmart your old man."

"No shit. Hey, I've been meaning to ask. How in the world did you know I'd sneaked out of the house that time in middle school?"

"I heard you on the phone with Alyssa. You might as well have broadcasted it on the nightly news."

"Whew! And all these years, I thought you had this sixth sense. You know, like Grandma."

"Nope, just the five."

"Look, I'm helping the police chief out with one of his cold cases."

"That involves ghosts."

"Yeah. But I'm fine. Nothing to worry about." She took another swallow of beer and burped.

"You always were a good burper."

"Eddie, I know you don't like me talking about super-natural stuff. For whatever reason. Which is why I didn't tell you."

"Well, don't forget. I grew up around that kind of stuff. And my opinion is, nothing good can come from it. I don't want anything to happen to you, Sarah." He stopped and turned to her, looking serious. "You and Rachel and Katy are my world. *¿Sabes?*"

"Yeah, I get it. But don't forget, I have St. Michael."

"I'd feel better if you invested in a good aluminum baseball bat."

"I'll think about it," she said, and finished her beer.

"So, you and Joe. No chance you guys are going to—"

She looked away. "He's seeing someone at the moment."

"Oh." He sounded disappointed. "And you?"

"Well, if you must know, I have a date tonight."

"Not a ghost, I hope."

"Nope, a normal guy. We're going to the singles' dance."

He came over to get his beer. "That's great, *mija*. Make sure you don't scare him off with all that crazy supernat-ural talk. And your hair could use—"

"Hey. As a matter of fact, I'm going to the salon right after this."

She kissed him on the cheek. He set his beer down and returned to the car.

"Not every girl gets to kiss her mechanic," she said.

"And not every mechanic will work for free beer."

She watched as his upper body disappeared under the

car and wondered why he was so afraid of the supernatural. Did something happen? But instead of analyzing it further, she decided to get herself another beer.

The nursing aide whose name was Hildy knocked softly and slowly opened the door to Colleen Moody's room. As usual, she found the old woman seated by the window that looked out over the small garden at the retirement facility. It was after sunset in Lawrence, Kansas, and Hildy had come to help Colleen change into her nightgown, brush her teeth, and comb her hair.

She had grown fond of the old woman, patiently listening to her ramble on about family members long departed, and her daughter, Nicole. Nowadays, her only visitor was her younger brother, Owen. To the aide, he seemed to be an impatient man with a lot on his mind. But, to his credit, he passed the time conversing with his sister about the old days, which Colleen had safely retreated to. Also, he read to her from the newspaper until she fell asleep.

Colleen was unaware that the aide was in the room. She imagined her clothes were floating away from her body, as if she were lying in a deep pool with no bottom. Magically, her nightgown would descend on her—the one with the little daisies around the collar. It reminded her of the one her daughter loved when she was little and wore to bed every night until the fabric thinned and tore at the seams. Colleen was forever repairing that nightgown with the old Singer sewing machine, she remembered.

The old woman had been thinking a lot about her daughter lately. And she wondered why it was she never came to visit. She had recalled Owen saying something about it once, but she couldn't remember the details. That happened a lot. To her, details were like grains of sand forever slipping through her fingers. She missed Nicole. And she missed her husband, though she was still angry with him.

Despite her mental condition, she knew Morris was gone. She'd gotten it into her head that he'd run off with the cashier at the Golden Corral, where they used to eat dinner on Sundays. The woman—what was her name? Jessie! She was half Morris's age, and she had always had her eye on him. It was shameful. When he didn't come home that day in November before Thanksgiving, Colleen knew. Her husband had given in to temptation and gone off with the dirty schemer and paid off her brother to sell their home and move her to this strange place.

"I hope they're both very happy," the old woman said as Hildy helped her into bed.

"Who, dear?"

"Morris and that… Why, I can't even say it. *Jessie.*"

The aide knew the truth, though. "I'm sure he feels terrible about it."

"Well, he should. Leaving me here like this. Shameful."

"Why don't you close your eyes, Colleen? Would you like me to read to you?"

The old woman looked at the aide sharply, as if seeing her for the first time.

"Can you please try again? Please can you call my daughter?"

Hildy fluffed her pillow. "I'll try."

It was always the same question. Every night. And each evening, the aide promised to try. Sometimes, she wondered if the old woman dreamt of Nicole and Morris and everyone else in her life who was lost to her.

"Goodnight, Colleen," the aide said. "Don't forget to say your prayers."

Thirteen

THERE WERE dozens of hair salons in Santa Barbara, and Sarah felt as though she'd tried every one. She was still looking for that "magical" stylist who would make her hair look stunning *every time*. As she sat waiting up front at one of the more trendy establishments on State Street, her legs were crossed, and she was absently pumping her right foot up and down.

She'd been reviewing her listings on her phone, something she often did to reassure herself she *was* a successful realtor. At the top of the screen there was a banner with Sarah's name and photo. She'd gotten lucky the day they took the headshot, having found a stylist who hadn't felt the need to "experiment" on her hair. Unfortunately, that woman had moved to Idaho.

As she scrolled down, she saw a crisp photo of each property followed by the house's details and price. She smiled, remembering how awful her pictures had looked when she was starting out. It was Joe who had taught her about camera angles, lighting, and the million and one other details that went into making her listings "pop."

Joe. Sarah tried imagining him married to someone else, an exercise she'd gone through hundreds of times since the divorce. What kind of woman *was* he looking for? She had known the man for most of her adult life, and as far as she knew, *she* was everything he ever needed. Well, except for the part about becoming Catholic and wanting kids.

And as long as she was performing a forensic autopsy on the rotting corpse of their former married life, what in the world did *she* want in a man? Well, that was easy: Joe. But a different Joe—one who would convert and have sex with her every night until she got pregnant. Okay, if push came to shove, maybe she *could* let the conversion part slide. But he would have to agree absolutely to the children —Liesl, Louisa, Brigitta, Marta, Gretl, and Joe Jr.—being raised Catholic. Was that too much to ask? Sarah realized she was doing it again—praying. Begging God to make an exception in her case and perform a miracle. *Fat chance, Sarah.*

"Sarah?" She looked up to find a stylist whose name was Dante smiling at her. "Are you ready?"

"Oh, yeah. Sorry."

Dante seemed nice, though she suspected that wasn't his real name. From what Sarah could glean, he had served in the military and decided he liked cutting hair better. His fiancée was still serving, and they were hoping to eventually move to Portland where she had family. Sarah had been very specific, and after he shampooed her, she asked Dante to trim no more than a quarter inch. She also wanted him to flat-iron her hair and put it up in a bun.

As the stylist prattled on about his life, Sarah thought about Michael Peterson. Being the suspicious person she was, she wondered why he had agreed so readily to go out with her. Trying not to be conceited, Sarah was aware she was attractive. So, why not? But since discovering her abilities, she always felt a little self-conscious. Then again, why couldn't God have put someone in her path to distract her from the now-canceled Joe & Sarah Show?

Dante had worked fast, and before Sarah knew it, he was ready to try out some bun styles. Having long hair, Sarah had lots of options. They tried a top knot bun, ballet, twisted, angular, and several others. Nothing seemed to satisfy her, though. Dante stepped away and looked at Sarah like someone observing an abstract painting in a gallery.

"I think I've got it. We'll go with a low-side chignon."

She scrunched her nose. "Are you sure? I don't even know what that is."

"Trust me."

When he was finished, Sarah looked at herself in the hand mirror. "Wow, you were right."

He walked her to the front desk and peered out at the sky which, so far, looked clear. "Make sure not to let it get wet."

"Roger that."

Thrilled with her hair, Sarah left her stylist a generous tip. Before walking out, she lingered at the front desk. People who pay good money for their hair also need good realtors. Smiling engagingly at the receptionist, she pulled out a few business cards.

"Okay if I leave these on the counter?"

Sarah realized she was nervous as she and Michael walked into the Santa Barbara Woman's Club, which was located near the mission. She had been lucky and found a biscuit-colored strapless evening dress and matching shoes for the occasion. The dress was modest by most standards. She knew from experience that though this was a singles' dance, it was sponsored by her parish, and Fr. Brian would be there for sure, if not judging, then proctoring. As she looked around at the other women, many of them in their twenties, she realized they must not have gotten the memo. *Skin City.*

Fortunately, the rain had stayed away, and Sarah's hair looked perfect. Michael helped her remove her gray wool dress coat and handed it to the check girl.

"So, what do you think of the place?" Sarah said as she and her date walked toward the ballroom.

"Nicer than I expected."

"They do a lot of weddings here." She noticed his horrified expression and tried to recover. "Not that I was implying…"

"Gotcha," he said and walked on ahead of her.

When she saw the cash bar in the corner of the ballroom, she sighed. *Thank God.* She'd had only sparkling water at dinner and felt she needed to loosen things up. Not that dinner wasn't good. They had laughed together at all kinds of things—books, movies, reality shows. Somewhere during dessert, Sarah had the impression that Michael "got" her. And she began toying with the idea that a life without Joe might be possible.

The DJ was blasting soft rock hits from the nineties, most of which Sarah remembered from her childhood and wished she could forget. When they segued into "I Want It That Way" by the Backstreet Boys, she burst out laughing.

"What?" Michael said.

"Sorry, it's that music. I mean seriously, Weezer not good enough?"

"Maybe I can bribe the DJ."

"It's fine."

They stood that way for a few moments. Then, "I Will Always Love You" by Whitney Houston came on.

"So, what do you think?" Michael said. "Want to dance?"

"Why not?" *This was promising.*

He took her hand and led her to the dance floor. They both stuck to the traditional box step, and he made sure his hands were where they should be. She felt herself settling into his arms and had to concentrate on where she was stepping. Then, Michael tensed, and they stopped moving. She noticed he was staring at the ballroom entrance. When she turned to look, she noticed Fr. Brian entering the room, sharing a laugh with a couple she recognized from church.

"Looks like the cavalry has arrived," she said. "Better watch your step tonight."

But Michael wasn't amused. He kept looking at the priest, and Sarah tried to comprehend what was going on.

"Do you know Fr. Donnelly?" she said.

"I've seen him." He turned back to her, trying to smile. "Sorry, I was a little surprised a priest would be attending this kind of function."

"He always does. One time, he told me he was scouting for future couples he could marry. Michael, is something wrong?"

"I…" He winced and touched his stomach. "Sorry, that fish I had at dinner isn't sitting too well. I'm going to visit the restroom. If you'll excuse me."

"Sure."

She watched as he headed toward the entrance, making a wide circle around the priest, who had seen Sarah and was making his way through the crowd toward her.

"Sarah," Fr. Donnelly said as he gave her a hug. Then, looking around, "Don't tell me you came stag?"

"No, I— Actually, my *date* stepped away."

"Wonderful. Can't wait to meet him. In the meantime, can I buy you a drink?"

"Hm. An old tightwad like you buying a girl a drink? Must be the dress."

"It's very becoming. No, I'm encouraged. I'm betting on your happiness, Sarah."

As they walked toward the bar, she thought about Michael's odd behavior and said, "You might want to save your money, Father."

"Nonsense. Now, what'll you have?"

No sooner had Fr. Donnelly bought Sarah a glass of wine than someone cornered him, asking to speak in private about some urgent parish matter. He made his apologies to Sarah and left her standing at the bar. She moved off to one side, holding her unmemorable cabernet and watching the entrance. Ten minutes had gone by, and she was getting worried about Michael, hoping the problem wasn't serious, when she heard something.

She set her glass down on a nearby tray and took her phone from her black leather crossbody bag. "Hello?"

"It's Michael."

She moved farther away from the crowd and covered one ear with her free hand.

"Where are you?"

"I can't tell you how embarrassed I am. I think I might have gotten food poisoning."

"Oh, no. Do you need me to drive you somewhere?"

"No. Look, I'm a mess. I…threw up on myself."

"Michael, I don't care about that. Let me drive you to urgent care."

"I've already left. I'm at a pharmacy. Going to grab a few things and head home. Can you Uber it?"

"I guess."

"Again, I'm sorry, Sarah. I'll call you in a few days when I'm feeling better."

"Okay."

She returned the phone to her purse and picked up her wine. She was about to put it to her lips when she noticed a bloated black fly floating on its back, furiously working its wings. Disgusted, she set the polluted drink down, retrieved her coat, and walked outside. It had started raining again, and she could feel her hair transforming into something out of a nature documentary.

"So much for happiness," she said.

The thought of ordering an Uber and slinking back to her empty house was more than she should bear.

It took Rachel only a few minutes to arrive. Sarah was standing near the entrance out of the rain, watching absently as happy couples came and went. She could hear the band playing "Island in the Sun" and smirked. *Great, now you decide to play Weezer?*

"Need a ride, little girl?" her sister said from the rolled-down passenger window.

Smiling gratefully, Sarah got in and rolled up the window to shut out the rain. "Thanks so much, Rache. This date couldn't have gone any worse. No, I take that back. The guy could've puked on my shoes instead of himself."

"Wow, good times. So, where to? Your place?"

"Can you take me to your house? I feel like I could use some company."

"Sure thing."

In another few minutes, Rachel was pulling into her driveway. She opened the garage and drove inside. As

Sarah and Rachel walked into the kitchen, they found Eddie sitting at the table, trying for the bazillionth time to teach his granddaughter how to play Texas hold 'em, his stacks of chips towering over Katy's.

"Oh, hey, Aunt Sarah." Sarah's niece put her cards down. Then, to Eddie, "Fold."

"Real nice, Eddie," Sarah said. "Taking money from an innocent girl."

"How else am I supposed to save for my retirement?" He collected the cards and began shuffling. "Another lousy date? Well, there's always the convent."

Sarah gave him the stink eye. "Not funny."

Katy jumped up and grabbed a water from the refrigerator. Then, after giving her aunt a hug, she walked out.

Eddie craned his neck, his eyes following her. "Hey, what about our game?"

"Cards are boring. Going to my room."

"That kid'll never make me rich." He sighed and put the cards away. Then, to Sarah, "You staying over?"

"I thought I might," she said, taking a seat and helping her father gather up the chips.

"What about your cat?"

"He has a clean litter box and a full food dish, so I think he'll survive."

She held up a one-hundred-dollar black chip and pretended it was a monocle as her father rolled his eyes.

"I remember when you tried teaching Rachel and me. To this day, I have no idea what a 'boat' is."

"Full house, set, and a pair," Rachel said, putting down two wine glasses.

"At least someone around here listens," Eddie said, getting up to get a beer. Then, to Rachel, "Want to play?"

"No, thank you."

"So, what happened?" Eddie said to Sarah as he sat.

She ignored him and instead watched as Rachel poured out two glasses of a pinot noir from Los Olivos.

"Aren't *we* getting fancy?" Sarah said.

"I like to splurge once in a while."

For a few minutes, the three of them sat quietly. Sarah sighed and, dipping her forefinger in wine, circled the lip of the glass until it sang.

"You used to do that when you were five," Eddie said. "Drove your mother and me nuts."

"Joe wasn't a fan either. When we were married…" Sarah looked at her father. "Tell me something. If a guy wants to get out of a date, does he go to all the trouble of faking an illness?"

"Depends. Are we talking blind date?"

"No. He's a client. Everything seemed all right. Dinner was fine. But at the dance, he said he felt sick. Too sick to drive me home, apparently."

Rachel touched her sister's hand. "It is possible he was telling the truth."

"I guess. Only…"

"What?"

Sarah took a swallow of wine. "It's the strangest thing. He seemed fine until Fr. Brian showed up."

"Maybe he'd had one of those bad Catholic school experiences."

"No. It was something else. I can't put my finger on it." Sarah refilled their glasses. "Anyhoo."

She gazed at the old Westclox Coffee Time wall clock that had been in the kitchen for as long as she could remember. She had always loved the numbers on its face and used to describe them to her parents as being "melty." It was only nine. Some big night on the town. Rachel seemed to know what her sister was thinking.

"Want to borrow a pair of my jammies and watch a

chick flick? I can make popcorn, and I think we might have some M&Ms."

"You read my mind," Sarah said, and finished her wine.

The women rose and, as Rachel went off to get things ready, Sarah tidied up the kitchen. Eddie sat back, drumming his fingers on the table.

"You guys wouldn't consider *John Wick*?"

"Nope."

"Fine. I'm going to *my* room. And listen to Charlie Parker."

They kissed each other, and Eddie wandered off. Sarah drifted into the living room, knelt in front of the bookcase under the TV, and began going through the movies. *While You Were Sleeping*, no. *You've Got Mail*, no. *The Notebook*, hell naw. *Notting Hill*... Maybe.

Rachel walked in carrying a folded pair of cotton Tweety Bird pajamas. She noticed the look on her sister's face.

"Hey, it's this or Yosemite Sam."

"Fine." Pouting, Sarah grabbed the PJs and went to the guest room to change. "But just for that, we're watching *When Harry Met Sally*."

"You can't beat the classics," Rachel said and teed up the movie.

Fourteen

A KNOCK at the door woke Sarah. As she opened her eyes, she was momentarily disoriented, then remembered where she was.

"Yeah?"

Her voice was hoarse and sounded noticeably lower. What was in that wine, anyway? A muffled voice spoke through the door.

"It's me, Katy. You have a phone call."

"What time is it?"

"Seven-thirty."

Sarah tried focusing, but her field of vision was filled with little, floating, squiggly things. She could hear her niece telling someone to hold please. She patted her hand around the nightstand, looking for her phone, and realized she didn't have it with her.

"Okay, come on in."

The door swung open, and Katy, wearing Bugs Bunny pajamas, ran in and handed Sarah her phone. As she took the call, her niece plopped herself on the bed.

"Hello?"

"Sarah?"

"Yeah."

"It's Lou. Sorry, didn't sound like you. How soon can you get over here?"

"What's up?"

Katy was swinging one leg up and down, up and down. Sarah placed a hand on her knee to get her to stop, wondering if the girl had picked up that habit from her.

"Time to test out your theory," he said. "Meet me in my office as soon as you can."

"I do have an actual job, you know."

He ignored the comment. "So, I'll see you in, what, an hour?"

Sarah sighed dramatically, causing Katy to sigh in sympathy.

"Fine. See you soon."

After Sarah had disconnected, she continued staring at the phone. Katy leaned over and pulled on her sleeve.

"Who was that?"

"What? Oh, the police chief."

"Does he like you?"

"I guess."

Katy picked a microscopic piece of lint off her aunt's sleeve. "Do you like him?"

"Come here, you."

She grabbed her niece and began tickling her, which set off a fit of uncontrollable giggling.

At the kitchen table, Sarah sat drinking coffee and eating the scrambled eggs with machaca Eddie had cooked for everyone. Wearing her Notre Dame uniform, Katy finished her milk and let out a loud burp. Rachel appeared in the doorway, adjusting one of her earrings.

"I heard that. Come on, kiddo. Time for school."

"Just have to brush my teeth," she said, running out of the room.

"No breakfast?" Eddie said to Rachel.

"I'll grab something later."

After a few moments, Katy appeared at the door, wearing a JanSport backpack, and they left.

"Okay, we're outta here," Rachel said. "I'll be back in a couple of minutes to take you home, Sarah."

Sarah watched as the two went out to the garage through the kitchen. She was wearing her outfit from the night before, including the heels. She'd borrowed her sister's flatiron and was wearing her hair in a French braid courtesy of Rachel.

"I feel stupid dressed like this," Sarah said.

Eddie shook his head. "You look nice. So, what's up with the police chief?"

"Katy told you, huh? He wants to see me. Probably something to do with the case."

"Or maybe he likes you," he said.

Getting to her feet, Sarah groaned. "Honestly, you people need to get a life."

"Watch yourself, *mija*."

When she looked into her father's eyes, she saw concern. She hugged him and kissed his cheek.

"I will," she said. Then, smiling, "Is there something on your mind?"

"I'm a father. It's my job to worry."

"Well, I'm a big girl."

Eddie left the room, and she began clearing the table. Recalling her recent dreams, she wondered if she *would be* fine. Touching her St. Michael medal, she said a prayer.

It was after nine-thirty when Sarah arrived at the police station. She had gone home to change and look after Gary. She wore a black skirt and matching matador jacket. The sun had come out as she walked into the building. *Always a good sign.*

Lou was on the phone when she entered his office. Three empty paper coffee cups lay on their sides among the rest of the clutter on the desk. He signaled for her to take a seat.

"Okay, tell them to get started. We're headed over there now. Yeah. See you soon."

When he disconnected, he looked up and smiled broadly at Sarah.

"Why are *you* so cheery?" she said.

"I convinced the judge to sign the disinterment order."

"Are you kidding? Why would he do that?"

"He's an old friend. Also, I happened to catch the guy who was threatening him and his family over a murder trial. Want to know something funny? Harlan Covington heard about the order and tried using some obscure legal challenge to stop it."

"And?"

"It didn't work. Anyway, we need to get over to the cemetery. The coroner is already there."

Sarah felt anxious and wished she hadn't suggested that anything might be amiss in the first place.

"Why do *I* need to be there?"

"Because this time, no amount of mojo is going to stop you from seeing whatever it is they don't *want* you to see."

Lou came around the desk and waited by the door. Feeling a deep dread that seemed to leach out of her bones, Sarah got up and followed.

"Good thing I keep a rosary in my purse," she said. *Something tells me I'm going to need it.*

It would only take a few minutes to get to the cemetery, and Sarah convinced Lou to stop at The Cracked Pot so she could fortify herself with an extra large macchiato. He took the opportunity to order himself a triple espresso, and they were on their way. She felt she drank a fair amount of coffee, but she was a lightweight compared to this guy and wondered why his heart rate wasn't through the roof.

The cemetery was quiet. Dapples of sunlight played among the redwoods. Birds were singing. If Sarah hadn't known better, she might have expected to see frolicking children instead of ghosts. Fortunately, the spirits must have all been asleep because she didn't sense anything. As they got closer, she noticed a Santa Barbara Coroner's Office vehicle and an unmarked truck parked along the road.

Lou pulled up close to the gate, and they got out and walked in. Warily, Sarah looked from side to side as they made their way toward a large area marked off by barricade tape. She could see several figures standing around a grave as a backhoe dug into the earth. When they reached the site, Sarah found a genial-looking fifty-something African-American man overseeing the operation, accompanied by another man in a suit—an assistant?—and two cemetery workers, one of whom was operating the machinery. Lou and the man in charge exchanged a greeting, speaking loudly over the sound of the backhoe, which had already removed more than two feet of earth.

"Sarah, this is Dr. Franklin Chestnut, Santa Barbara Sheriff-Coroner. Frank, Sarah Greene."

"Pleasure to meet you, Ms. Greene. Lou, I hope you're right about this. To be honest, we have more pressing cases."

"I know, Frank. And if I'm wrong, I'll buy you and your wife dinner anywhere you like."

"Well, Bev and I do have a favorite bistro off the Boulevard Saint-Michel."

"Paris?" Lou said. Then, to Sarah, "There goes my pension."

"I thought you knew what you were doing."

Everyone else was watching as the backhoe operator drove the bucket deeper into the cold ground. Sarah closed her eyes, took a deep breath, and joined them, cringing each time the shovel hit the ground with a loud thunk. After a half-hour, she heard a scraping noise.

"Stop!" Lou said to the operator.

The backhoe pulled away, and one of the cemetery workers, who was carrying a shovel, jumped into the hole and carefully began exposing the burial vault. After another ten minutes, he had finished securing straps attached to the backhoe's boom to eye hooks embedded into the sides of the concrete container.

Slowly, the backhoe operator began raising the heavy box out of the ground. At first, it looked to Sarah as if the straps would break from the strain. Eventually, the burial vault came up, and the second cemetery worker guided it up and out of the hole.

"Please don't let there be a pile of rocks inside," Lou said to Sarah.

"No. There's a body in there."

Though the sun was warm, Sarah felt ice-cold. Her mouth was dry, and her head ached. The dust floating in the air assaulted her, and she felt her throat closing up. Covering her mouth, she turned away and coughed. *Why did I choose to wear black today?*

When the vault was sitting on the grass, the second worker got into a nearby pickup truck and backed it up. The backhoe operator was about to lift the container when Sarah stepped forward, her hand raised.

"I want to see the body."

Franklin glanced at Lou. "Normally, we'd have you come down to the morgue." Then, to the cemetery workers, "Open her up."

The two cemetery workers carefully lifted the heavy concrete lid and laid it on the grass. Using a crowbar, one of them pried open the casket lid. Sarah gritted her teeth against the loud squealing noise. When they'd gotten it open, they stepped back. All eyes were on Sarah. Terrified, she stood there without looking. Saying a silent prayer, she forced herself to approach the vault and gaze down into the casket. The smell of decay made her dizzy, and she worried she might vomit.

A man's desiccated body lay in the open coffin, dressed in a dark suit. What remained of the hair looked like it might be Peter Moody's. Though she knew better, the corpse seemed to be staring at her. She touched the coffin, and immediately, she felt as if she were falling.

An image of a long, bright corridor flashed across the backs of her eyes, and she could hear the faint sounds of a PA system. She could see a young man wearing pajamas sitting on a simple bed in a sterile-looking room, rocking back and forth. He was facing a window with bars, and she couldn't make out his features. Then, the image was gone, and Sarah was back in the cemetery. She reached out to Lou, and he helped her off the flatbed.

They watched as one of the cemetery workers drove off with the burial vault, followed by the crane operator.

"You'll let me know if I need to take out a loan to pay for your trip?" Lou said to Franklin, resting a hand on his shoulder.

"I'll get to work on this right away." As the coroner turned to leave, he said, "Nice meeting you, Sarah."

"Yeah, same here."

Sarah felt light-headed and didn't want to spend another second in the cemetery. As they walked toward the gate, Lou touched her arm.

"So, did you see anything?"

"He was in an institution."

"Peter?"

"Yes. We have to find out where." She stared at Lou with haunted eyes.

"Come on. I'll drive you back." Then, leaning in, "I thought you were very brave, by the way."

"Apparently, you didn't hear my knees knocking together like coconuts."

As they made their way along the main path, Sarah happened to look up. In the distance, she could see Hannah floating near a stand of tanbark oaks. Her arms were outstretched.

Blood was running from her eyes, like tears.

Sarah entered Greene Realty through the rear entrance. As she passed Joe's office, she was surprised to see him sitting at his desk with the door closed, on the phone. The conversation looked tense, and on an impulse, she decided to hang back. Though his voice was muffled, she managed to catch a few words here and there. "Sorry…" "Not true…" "Maybe if…" *It's not you, it's me.*

Rachel appeared in the hallway, a huge smile on her face, startling Sarah.

"Want some good news?" Rachel said. "Two of your properties closed escrow. You're forty-eight thousand dollars richer."

"That's great."

Rachel's face fell when she saw her sister's expression,

and she followed her into Sarah's office. Sarah could hear Joe's door opening and quick footsteps as he exited silently through the rear. Sighing, she went behind her desk and plopped down. Rachel took a seat opposite her and watched as her sister opened and slammed shut various desk drawers.

"What exactly are you looking for?"

Sarah stared at her, her face the picture of anger and frustration.

"You know those old movies where the grizzled newspaper editor pulls open a drawer and takes out a bottle and a glass?"

"You need a drink?"

"I need you to buy me a bottle and a glass."

"Well, don't get mad at me."

"I'm sorry, Rache. It's that stupid business at the cemetery."

"I'm guessing you didn't find rocks in the coffin?"

"No."

"Can I ask? What exactly *did* you find?"

"Peter Moody's remains."

"Well, that's good news, right? Now Lou can close the case, and you can get on with your life."

"Not quite. There's the little problem of the ghost that's plaguing me."

"Well, maybe she'll move on."

"Yeah, maybe. Still…"

Rachel stood and went to the door. "Hey, it's after twelve. Want to grab lunch? Celebrate your newfound wealth?" Sarah didn't answer. "Come on, it'll do you good."

"Maybe you're right."

Sarah got up and, grabbing her purse, followed her sister out. As they headed toward the front door, Sarah noticed Blanca repeatedly poking one of the keys on her computer keyboard. She seemed upset.

"Everything okay, Blanca? How's Pollito?"

"He's fine. Got himself a girlfriend—the urgent care nurse. *¡Me saca de quicio!*"

"Well, he may drive you crazy, but he's your *mijo* and you love him, right?"

"Excuse me."

They watched as she got up and stomped toward the restrooms, muttering in Spanish.

Outside, the sky was bright blue with large white clouds that reminded Sarah of the gigantic Mardi Gras heads she'd seen once on a college trip to New Orleans. She immediately turned toward The Cracked Pot when her sister grabbed her arm.

"Where are you going?" Rachel said. "This way. I thought we'd try that new sushi place."

"There's a sushi place?"

"You know, for a big-time realtor, you are seriously out of touch with your community."

"Shut up. I've been distracted."

"Yeah, yeah. This way, Sherlock."

Sarah had to admit that spending time with her sister had been just what the doctor ordered. Though the Japanese place was small, it was beautifully decorated. The bar and tables were made of bleached eucalyptus and the floor was slate tile. Sarah was admiring the lighting fixtures when a server directed them to a table for two, past a group of business people apparently celebrating a birthday with copious amounts of alcohol. Rachel noticed the drinks and smiled.

"Want me to order some sake? she said. "You know, to take the edge off."

"There's an edge?" Sarah tried a smile. "I'd better not. It'll make me sad. How's Katy, by the way?"

"She's fine. Why do you ask?"

"I feel like I don't spend enough time with her."

"Well, you're rich now. Why don't you two have a spa day or something?"

"You know, that's a great idea."

"Sarah, I was totally joking. You don't need to spend that kind of money."

"No, I want to. We'll go to the Four Seasons."

"Wow. How will you top that when her birthday rolls around?"

"I have plenty of time to think of something."

Soon, they were eating. As Sarah bit into her raw tuna, she noticed her sister looking at her.

"What? Is there something on my face?"

"No. I was thinking. Katy idolizes you."

"But I'm a mess."

"Well, she thinks you're amazing. And so do I."

Sarah put her chopsticks down. "Are we breaking up?"

Rachel laughed. "No. I'm… I guess what I'm trying to say is… Do you remember when we were little? You picked on me a lot. I mean, a *lot*."

"Rache, I'm sorry—"

"Let me finish. I used to spend hours a day being mad at you, wondering what I'd done to deserve it. But now that we're grown, I can see that you were a kid. And I was your annoying little sister. I mean, that's what kids do, right?"

"Rachel…"

"Sarah, I can't think of anyone I'd rather have in my life. I mean, you were there for me when Paul died. And your relationship with Katy is…"

Rachel brushed away her tears. Sarah reached over and touched her sister's arm.

"Hey, what's wrong, honey?"

Rachel took Sarah's right hand in both of hers. "I don't want anything to happen to you, that's all."

"I'm not going anywhere, Rache. And you can take that to the bank. What do you say we enjoy our lunch, and after, you and I get our nails done?"

"I should get back to work."

"Hey, I'm your big sister and I'm still allowed to boss you around sometimes. So, no more arguments."

"Yes, ma'am."

"That's more like it."

Fifteen

FRANKLIN CHESTNUT WAITED PATIENTLY outside Lou Fiore's office door as the police chief finished up a call. He and Lou had become friends when Lou was working homicide in Santa Barbara. They'd spent hours together looking at the gruesome outcome of people's enflamed, misdirected passions. Estranged husbands going after ex-wives with power tools, meth heads attacking strangers at bus stops with claw hammers, assorted gang-related stabbings and shootings. It was endless. But through it all, the men had kept their sense of humor. And that was why the coroner decided not to call in his dinner marker.

As soon as Lou hung up the phone, Franklin entered and took a seat.

"Frank, it's nice to see you, but couldn't we have done this over the phone?"

"You know what a people person I am."

"Yeah, *dead* people. So, what have you got for me?"

"You're not going to like it."

"Meaning, Paris here we come?"

The coroner laid his black attaché on the disorganized

desk, pushed aside a few empty coffee cups, and removed a folder containing a file and several color photographs, all of which he handed to Lou.

"The body is definitely that of Peter Moody."

Lou examined one of the photos more closely. This was going to look bad on his record. Never mind the dinner. Exhuming the body, transporting it, and reburying it in a new coffin would cost the city upwards of ten thousand dollars. And that didn't include the Coroner's Bureau charges. He'd been so sure.

"So, how'd he die?"

"Slit throat. Self-inflicted. Look closely at the cervical vertebrae in that photo you're holding. You'll see a small nick made by a sharp instrument. And the angle? This is consistent with the report from the original autopsy."

"Which was performed in Lawrence?"

"Yes. I called the coroner's office there to confirm my findings. I'm sorry, Lou, but everything checks out. Dental records, DNA—the whole shebang."

Lou exhaled loudly. "Guess the judge won't be too pleased that we wasted taxpayer money on this."

"I'll write up something in my report expressing my confidence that you made the right call, given the circumstances."

"I appreciate it, Frank. Okay if I keep the file?"

"Of course. That's your copy." Grabbing his attaché, Franklin rose. "Oh, I almost forgot. The pathologist who performed the postmortem wrote something in the report that, to be honest, has me stumped."

"What's that?"

"He said that, according to medical records, Peter Moody was suffering from cardiomyopathy. It's a heart condition usually caused by an infection, or alcohol or drug abuse."

"Drugs, maybe?"

"No, the tox screen didn't show anything. It's all in the report."

"Okay, I'll take a look."

"And don't worry about dinner. Feel free to buy me lunch sometime." He headed for the door.

"Thanks again," Lou said. "Hey, Frank?"

"Yeah?"

"You believe in ghosts?"

"Not sure. Never actually seen one."

"Me neither. And I pray to God I never do."

After Franklin had left, Lou Fiore remained in his office chewing toothpicks like a beaver and mulling over the Peter Moody file. He'd been over the documents several times and was re-examining the autopsy photos the coroner had given him. The fact that Peter Moody was dead didn't do much to cheer him up. He didn't know for sure who had murdered the kid's parents, and he worried that, given ghosts *were* real apparently, Sarah might be haunted by some creepy dead girl for the rest of her life.

Sarah. Since meeting her, he admittedly had entertained vague notions of a romantic relationship. Nothing untoward. He was Catholic, so was she. They were both divorced, and the only complication Lou could see was his son who, at some point, would have to meet her. How would she take to him? Louis Jr. was eight, still young enough to adjust, he supposed. But there was Joe. Lou could tell those two loved each other, and he was the last person to create an awkward situation. No, better they all stayed friends. Right. Until the next time he smelled her perfume and gazed into those smoky hazel eyes.

He decided he'd better walk it off. Some nice strong coffee would distract him. By the time he'd gone to the kitchenette and pulled two shots from the espresso machine he'd purchased with his own money, he found he was already thinking about the case again.

Lou had hoped to find answers in Lawrence. He wanted to speak to the elderly aunt in person to see if he could get through to her. If he was lucky, she would have a moment of clarity and provide some insight into what happened all those years ago. But he had to get travel approval from the mayor's office. And that was unlikely since this was not an active case. Not to mention the fact that the police chief had given himself a black eye by exhuming that body.

Better call Sarah with the news. Somehow, he felt she already knew the truth.

Sarah sat in her car, staring at the stark, flat image of Casa Abrigo against the wet, gray sky. The house looked as if it had been cut out of a magazine and pasted onto a dull cardboard backdrop that lacked depth. And after getting the call from Lou, it had somehow taken on a more sinister aspect, becoming something brooding and threatening.

She wasn't surprised the body was that of Peter Moody. She'd known it the moment she touched the coffin, faint echoes of his spirit rising like spirals of invisible noxious mist. It bothered her, though, that the police chief would probably not be making the trip to Lawrence. Answers lay there, she felt. Truths the girl in the mirror wanted Sarah to uncover. Someone needed to go.

Grabbing her purse, she got out and made her way up the soggy driveway toward the house. Joe, Manny, and the boys were all inside, and she could hear the familiar sounds of professional renovation. She used to enjoy seeing a house coming together, being made ready for a new family to enjoy. But there was something about this house that made Sarah think the project was doomed. She recalled the light fixture falling without warning, almost striking Michael in the head. And she didn't want to think about the lawsuit, had there *been* an accident.

Sarah had tried calling Michael Peterson twice, but each time she was taken directly to voicemail. For some reason, he was avoiding her—probably out of sheer embarrassment for having abandoned her the other night. Not that she was harboring any kind of grudge. She had called simply to find out if he was feeling any better. *Give him some freaking space, Sarah.*

When she opened the front door, she found Manny standing on a ladder, adjusting the lantern pendant. She could see shallow gouges in the hardwood floor where it had fallen. Those planks would have to be replaced. More expense.

"So, what happened?" she said as Manny climbed down.

He bent over and picked up a chain. *"Mira."*

She took it from him and examined the tip, which looked as if someone had taken an acetylene torch to it. But how was that possible?

"I don't get it," she said.

"My son did nothing wrong, that's what I'm saying. Someone made this fixture fall."

"Or some-*thing*."

"Ghosts? *Madre...*"

"Has anything else weird happened?"

Joe stepped out from the kitchen and came toward them. He touched Sarah's arm and kissed her cheek, which surprised her. She glanced at Manny, but he was avoiding eye contact.

"What was that for?" she said.

"I heard about your date."

"Oh, that. Nothing lets a girl feel special like making the guy she's with puke himself. I hope you're having better luck with Dale."

"Gail," Manny said.

Joe scratched his ear. "We haven't spoken in a few days."

She knew he was lying but decided to play along. "You try calling?"

"Yeah."

She put her hands on her hips. "Okay, what did you do?"

"Nothing. It's all good."

"Well, not to take advantage, but maybe we can finally have that pizza and wine."

"Let's do it. You free tonight?"

"Sure."

Out of the corner of her eye, she caught Manny rolling his eyes and bared her teeth at him like a feral cat.

"So, Joe. I was asking Manny about that pendant. Anything else strange going on around here I should know about?"

"The usual, I guess. Only, the boys seem to be misplacing more tools than usual."

"Hm. Well, how about a quick tour? I'm starting to work on some ideas for the listing."

"A little premature, don't you think?"

"I don't like waiting until the last minute."

"I taught you well. Okay, let's start upstairs. We've added those new built-ins I was telling you about."

"Great. See you, Manny."

Taking Joe's arm, she left the foreman with a final scowl to remember her by. But Manny didn't acknowledge her. He was looking at the chain in his rough hands, trying to understand what powerful, unseen force could have caused it to break like that.

Sarah had finished giving the cat fresh water when the doorbell rang. She pretended to ignore her heart skipping a beat and walked into the foyer to answer it, smoothing her already pressed jeans and adjusting her bra strap under the white cashmere sweater.

When she opened the door, she found Joe smiling and proffering a large sausage and mushroom pizza from Papa Pepito's.

"Where's your striped shirt and cap?" she said, taking the box. "I thought we might set up the video camera later and…"

"Funny."

As she stepped back, he walked in, smelling of citrus and sandalwood. The cologne was intoxicating, and she had the urge to throw the box aside and drag him feet-first into the bedroom. But then, she remembered their lives were "complicated" now. Though she suspected Joe and Gail were over, she decided she'd better behave. At least until they got to the scotch. *Sarah!*

He led the way into the kitchen, and as she followed, she noticed his hair was wet from a shower. He had on a new pair of jeans and a gray knit V-neck sweater that looked incredibly soft. *Pace yourself, Sarah.*

As Joe set the pizza down on the counter, he noticed the Chateau Palmer Bordeaux standing near the sink, uncorked. She followed his gaze.

"I thought I should let it breathe."

"So, have you tried it?" he said, walking over and picking up the cork.

"I wanted you to have the honor."

He sniffed the cork as she got down two wine glasses. "Mm. Promising." He held up the bottle to the light, squinting. "Lots of sediment, though."

"Do you think we should aerate it?"

"Definitely."

Wine was another thing Sarah had learned about from Joe. Like a professional, she got out an aerator she had picked up at Williams-Sonoma as Joe positioned the wine glasses. His scent was driving her crazy, and it was all she could do to concentrate as she held the aerator over one of the glasses and carefully poured the wine. When she'd finished filling the first glass, Joe took it, swirled it under his nose, and tried it.

"Well?" she said.

"Amazing."

"Whew."

She repeated the process with the second glass. Then, she set the aerator aside and took a sip of hers.

"Oh. My. Gosh."

"Yep."

"That settles it. We're eating in the dining room tonight."

Sarah had made a mixed green salad to accompany dinner. Inspired, she'd made croutons rather than using packaged ones.

Dinner with Joe was like old times when they were married. She had always felt comfortable around him, and as she gazed at him through a filmy curtain of wine-induced lightheadedness, she wondered again if somehow they could make it work. So far, she'd been encouraged because Joe hadn't mentioned Gail once. It was as if she had never existed, and it was just the two of them again.

They had been talking for more than an hour, and when she got up to refill their glasses, she found the wine bottle empty.

"Uh-oh."

"What?"

Looks like we killed the bottle."

"Time for the Talisker?"

"Only if you promise to take advantage of me." She broke into uncontrollable wine giggles. "I meant *not* take advantage. Wow."

"Freud would be proud," Joe said, entering the kitchen with the dishes.

He set them on the counter and watched as Sarah stood on tiptoes to reach the bottle of scotch. He couldn't help looking at her luscious curves, how the sweater hugged her in all the right places. When she had retrieved the bottle, he was standing directly behind her. He took in the fragrance of her hair. She could feel his hands gently touching her waist and permitted them to turn her around to face him.

"Why, Mr. Greene. What *are* you doing? This is highly irregular."

He took the bottle and set it on the counter. But as he was about to kiss her full on the lips, she shimmied downward and, clearing her throat, escaped his grasp as if they had stolen a moment in the office copier room and someone walked in.

"What's wrong?"

"Nothing's wrong," she said, avoiding his gaze.

All business, she took two whiskey glasses from the cupboard and headed for the living room. He followed, carrying the bottle. She set the glasses down and, touching his shoulders with her index fingers, gently pushed him into a sitting position on the sofa. Uncomfortable, he removed his phone from his pocket and placed it on the floor.

Humming "Peel Me A Grape," she filled two glasses and handed him one. The whole time, he was looking at her curiously. When Gary trotted in, he gave the cat a questioning look, as if waiting for the animal to clear things up for him.

Sarah was about to sit when she remembered something. Wagging a playful, warning finger at Joe, she turned and raced—a little wobbly from the wine—into the kitchen. When she returned, she was carrying her phone. She put on some jazz and set it down on the end table. Curling up next to Joe, she placed his arm around her shoulders, and retrieved her glass.

"There," she said. "Isn't this nice?"

"I guess?"

"Two old friends spending a relaxing evening together."

"Uh-huh."

"All very innocent."

They were quiet for a long time. As she leaned her head against his chest, she could hear the beating of his heart. The sound comforted her, and for no reason, she felt weepy. Pretending she had something in her throat, she coughed and patted her chest until the moment passed.

"You okay?"

"Yeah, just a tickle. Joe, can I ask you something?"

"Anything."

"Are you and Gail still together?"

He didn't respond right away, which was a good thing in Sarah's book, since she wanted him to think before answering. She found a few chest hairs poking out of the top of his sweater and, using her pinky, made a swirling pattern on his skin. After a moment, he took her hand and shrugged so she would sit up.

"No," he said. "I broke it off."

She sat up straight and looked him in the eye. "Can I ask why?"

"I don't want to talk about it."

She ignored him. "But I thought things were going so well for you guys."

He sighed. "They were. At first."

He drained his scotch and reached for the bottle. Sarah took the glass from him and refilled it. When she handed it back, she noticed his pained expression.

"If you don't want to talk about it," she said, "it's fine."

"No, I do. I need to tell someone."

"My gosh, what happened?"

"I'm not sure. I mean, when we first met, she was nice. You know, funny. And sexy. *Really* sexy."

"Okay, I get the picture."

"We had coffee a few times, lunch, stuff like that. Then, I took her to dinner."

"At the Biltmore, I remember."

"And she suddenly came on to me. I was a little embarrassed—no, a *lot*."

"I'm guessing you had sex?"

"No. To be honest, I was a little put off. She called the next day and apologized. Said it was the wine. But she'd barely had any.

"Anyway, we saw each other again. And later, we ended up at her apartment in Santa Barbara."

"Nice place?"

"Yeah. Well, one thing led to another, and next thing I know, we're in bed. Are you sure you're okay with this?"

"Yeah, please continue."

"She, um…"

"Gave you a hickey?"

"No." He looked at her, his expression grim. "She wanted me to… To *hurt* her."

"You mean, like Fifty Shades kind of—"

"I'm pretty sure."

"Oh my God."

"So, I got out of there. And that was the last time I saw her."

"Joe, I'm so sorry. That's creepy. By the way, you never told me exactly how you two met."

"Yeah, I did. It was at the County Recorder's office. Don't you remember?"

"But you never said *how* exactly. Women *live* for the details—I thought you knew that."

"Well, I was waiting in line, and she was standing behind me. She asked me to save her spot while she went to the restroom."

"That was it?"

"No. When she got back, she took a phone call. Whoever was speaking to her was making her upset. When she hung up, she was muttering about some asshole attorney. I asked if she was okay, and we started talking."

"Hmm."

"What 'hmm'?"

"It's just that… I mean, doesn't it all sound a little *contrived*?"

"Sure. And inviting your client to a dance is *not* contrived?"

"Exactly."

"Huh?"

"I've said it before, and I'll say it again. Men. Are. *Clueless.*"

She emptied her glass, set it aside, tucked her feet under her, and faced him.

"Don't you see? It's *women* who call the shots. Gail gets you to take her out, and I get Michael to go with me to a stupid dance."

"Hang on." She could see he was getting steamed. "Are you saying men are incapable of being proactive?"

She scrunched her nose. "Well?"

"I see. Huh."

He set his glass on the coffee table, then reached over, and with both hands on her face, kissed her before she knew what was coming. The feel of his lips on hers made her melt, and she let her hands find his neck. Somewhere, Gary was maowing. Sarah scooted down until she was lying on her back. She smiled dreamily as Joe hovered over her. As he lowered himself, he kissed her warm neck, sending her into orbit.

Her head was spinning from the wine and the scotch, and she couldn't tell whether the cat was caterwauling or a phone was ringing. She didn't want this moment to end and wished everything would go away and leave them alone. Finally, the call went to voicemail, and she relaxed. Then, the phone went off again.

Flushed, Joe sat up and glanced at his phone on the floor. When he recognized the number, he reached for it.

"No…" she said, trying to pull his hand away.

But he took it and answered the call as Sarah sat up, visibly frustrated. As he spoke, she picked Gary up and petted him the way a person would if they were trying to transform their cat into a bald Sphynx.

"Hello? Lou? What's going on?"

Concerned, Sarah pressed her ear to the back of the phone. Though Lou's voice was faint, she could make it out.

"Hey, Joe. Sorry to bother you so late. I'm in Santa Barbara with the police. I'm afraid there's been an accident."

"What?"

"A woman. I thought you'd want to know."

Joe stared at Sarah. "Why? What are you talking about? What woman?"

"I think you know her, Joe. We found your business card in her wallet. Looks like you'd written something personal on the back."

"No, it can't—"

"Joe, it's Gail Cohen. She's dead."

Sixteen

JOE LET the phone slip from his hand, and it slid to the sofa cushion. Somewhere, like a faint radio signal, he could hear Lou describing what they found in Gail's apartment. And what the body looked like.

"Joe, you there?"

When he didn't respond, the connection dropped. Sarah took his hand and rubbed it. She pulled him close and held him, as if he were a child who'd learned his parents had died in a plane crash.

"You're not in this alone," she said.

Though she'd never met Gail Cohen and, in reality, considered her a rival, Sarah was heartbroken that something so tragic could have happened to Joe. He didn't deserve this. She had entertained the idea that, if things *had* worked out with this clearly unworthy woman, she would wish them well and promptly get on with her life. Find someone new. Though, in truth, the only man she could ever see herself growing old with was sitting next to her.

"Did Lou say what happened?" she said

"Something about being attacked in her apartment."

"Joe, I am so sorry."

He reached over, grabbed the whiskey bottle, and refilled both their glasses. For a time, they sat in silence next to each other. He could feel the warmth of her hips next to him, and if this were any other night, he would have made love to her right there on the sofa. But he felt numb. This *thing* had happened—this horrible thing. And sure, he hadn't seen any kind of future in a life with Gail—especially after what happened between them. But her death deserved to be acknowledged.

"Do you think they're going to want you to ID the body?" Sarah said.

"Maybe. She told me she didn't have any family."

"I can go with you, if you want."

He looked at her, and she noticed the tears in his eyes. For as long as she'd known him, Joe had never cried—not even at their wedding. Did Gail mean more to him than he was letting on?

"I'd appreciate it," he said.

He rose and, leaving his drink, reached for her hands. She gulped hers, set the glass down, and stood, too.

"I want to lie down with you," he said. "We don't have to do anything. But I need you, Sarah."

She had never seen Joe so vulnerable. He'd always been the comforter in the relationship—the strong one. And, to be honest, she was a little uncomfortable. But *she* was strong, too. It was simply that she'd never been given the chance to show her strength when she was with him.

She touched his face and, taking his hand, led him to her bedroom. Without words, they lay on top of the bed. She put his head on her breast, and he closed his eyes. Soon, she found herself stroking his hair, the way a mother might do with her child.

In any other circumstance, the fire that consumed them both would have flared into a raging bonfire, and they would have made mad, crazy love into the night. But as the effects of the wine and the whiskey took over, mixed with an overpowering sense of dread, Sarah found herself drifting off to sleep, the sound of Joe's soft, steady snoring accompanying the horrifying dreams she was sure would come.

It was late, and Sarah found herself in the dreaded room in the cellar of Casa Abrigo. She was dressed the same as she had been that evening. Outside, a cold wind was blowing, and Sarah could hear tree branches scraping against the house like fingernails on a chalkboard. She was alone. The feeling of dread was overwhelming; she wished she could wake up.

She heard voices. It sounded like a boy and a girl. They were whispering and giggling. As the talking grew louder, Sarah panicked and turned toward the door where she came face-to-face with the ghost. She was standing in front of Sarah, her skin a deathly gray, her lips a pale pink. Her eyes were closed.

Sarah could feel her heart pounding. The sound was deafening. She tried moving past the girl, but when she stepped to the side, a hand composed of bone and wilted flesh grabbed her wrist and held her firmly. As Sarah struggled to free herself, the hand's skin flaked off and floated away like cinders. The girl's eyes flew open, revealing two pools of oily blackness that led to an endless void. She opened her mouth impossibly wide.

"NOT DEAD!"

When Sarah opened her eyes again, it was morning, and Gary was sitting on Joe's stomach, kneading his paws and purring. Not wanting to disturb Joe, she slipped out of bed and went into the bathroom to take a shower.

She had finished washing her face and was about to step into the steaming jet of water when Joe walked in, naked. Without a word, he entered the shower with her. As the water drenched them both in a hot, luxurious downpour, he stood behind her and pulled her to him in a powerful embrace.

As showers go, this was probably the best Sarah had ever had.

Harlan Covington sat at his desk, rereading a short article in the Local section of the *Santa Barbara News-Press*.

A woman was found dead in her luxury apartment on upper State Street around 10 p.m. last night, the apparent victim of an animal attack. According to police, there were no witnesses. Neighbors had heard someone screaming and called 911. When the officers arrived, they made the grisly discovery.

When asked if there were any signs of foul play, Officer John Dougherty, a spokesperson for the Santa Barbara Police Department, would only say that they were considering the accident "suspicious." The name of the victim has not been released.

He laid the paper down and reached for his coffee. So

far, everything was going according to plan. There had been no witnesses—nothing to connect him to the woman's death. And, though he felt a twinge of guilt, he justified himself with the knowledge that she had willingly chosen her fate. She had, in essence, written her own death sentence. As did the other one.

The lawyer looked down at his aging, liver-spotted hand and considered the ring. He knew he was getting old, like the old man with the staff etched in onyx. He hadn't found the ring in Venice, as he'd told Sarah Greene. No, the ring had found *him*. And its power was undeniable—a force he had served faithfully for nearly fifty years. But he was quite aware that, at some point, he would need to let the ring go to pursue its next owner. He would miss it, though. Even in death.

Sarah Greene. It was only after their meeting Harlan realized that she presented a real problem for him. She was, according to his source, able to see things that were not meant to be seen. She and that buffoon of a policeman had all but admitted she'd found the mirror. And she seemed to know what secrets it held. Why else would they have hidden the wretched thing? And then, that business with the cemetery. He'd succeeded in keeping Sarah from uncovering anything about Peter Moody. Ultimately, though, he'd failed. Now, Chief Fiore had exhumed the body.

His phone had been lying on his desk, silent. When it vibrated, he glanced over and noticed the number. He was expecting the call. He had played many roles in his life, and it was time for him to be the silken-voiced consigliere who brought a sense of calm while controlling the situation. Taking a breath, he answered. The voice at the other end sounded frantic.

"I realize what a shock this is," Harlan said, doing his

best to mollify the caller. "And I'm very sorry. No, I don't have any idea what happened, but I promise to start an investigation. Yes, I will.

"Any luck locating the mirror? It's up to you now. No, I'm not trying to sound— Might I remind you, this whole thing was *your* idea, and you're going to have to see it through. Yes, I already said I would." He softened his tone. "All right, talk to you later."

He disconnected and looked at the paper again. He wondered why the police had hinted that the death was suspicious. It was probably nothing. That cop Dougherty was a nobody with little experience in homicide investigation. Harlan was certain the death would be ruled accidental. But he still had Sarah Greene to contend with. He didn't know the extent of her abilities, and that troubled him. He would have to keep an eye on her.

At some point, she would present a real problem, especially if she learned any more about the mirror. What would he do? Eliminate her? Was the mirror worth that much to him? He already knew the answer. It would be messy, though. He had never taken an innocent life before. Still.

Harlan had always known the risk. It was what happened when you chose to dance with the devil.

Seventeen

SARAH AND JOE sat in the next-of-kin room, waiting to be called. She had let Rachel know they wouldn't be coming into the office for a while but provided few details. Joe had let Manny know to continue working on the house in his absence. He would be along sometime after lunch.

They'd come over together mostly in silence, Joe hardly making eye contact. He said nothing about their "special" morning together, even after Sarah had made a stupid joke about possibly needing a bigger hot water heater. Sarah recalled the last time she and Joe were together after someone died. It was the trip to the church for the funeral of Rachel's husband. Now this. Though she wanted to be supportive, she dreaded the thought of seeing that dead woman.

The door opened, and Dr. Chestnut stepped through, wearing blue scrubs, followed by Lou Fiore and another man in green slacks and a tan sport jacket that spelled cop. Sarah lay down the magazine she was reading and, hesitating, got to her feet. This was a mistake. What was she thinking? The last thing she wanted was to see a mutilated corpse and, possibly, the angry spirit who had occupied it.

"Mr. Greene?" the plainclothes detective said as he approached the couple. "Vic Womble, Santa Barbara PD Homicide."

Catching her deer-in-the-headlights expression, Joe squeezed Sarah's hand.

"I believe you know Police Chief Fiore."

"Yes. And this is my business partner, Sarah Greene."

"Your business partner has the same last name?"

"I'm also Joe's ex-wife," Sarah said, barely able to get the words out.

Sensing she had not made a favorable impression, she stepped forward to shake the detective's hand when Lou moved in.

"Sarah's been helping our department out on a case."

"I see," the detective said, utterly disinterested.

Womble seemed irritated about something and, forgetting her nervousness, Sarah decided she didn't like him. He had the air of a mansplainer. She pictured him in his brown shoes dishing it out to the women on the force who could only suffer in silence. And what was with that name? *Womble?* It sounded like something squirrels did as a prelude to vigorous sex. And that pencil moustache. Who did he think he was—John Waters?

Sarah felt herself getting upset. This asshat had a helluva nerve acting superior. Here they were cooperating like any good citizen, and this short man in cheap, off-the-rack clothes was giving them attitude? She was about to make a sharp remark when Dr. Chestnut cleared his throat.

"Shall we go in? I'm sure Joe and Sarah have a busy schedule."

"Right," the detective said, and led them back into the autopsy room without saying anything further.

As Sarah passed Dr. Chestnut, she mouthed the words *thank you*. Suppressing a grin, he followed.

The room was clean and well lit, with a row of gleaming, stainless steel autopsy tables standing in a single row down the length of the room, the last of which had a body lying on it covered by a sheet. So far, Sarah had only seen such a place in movies and on television shows. She expected it to reek of death, but surprisingly, the only thing she could smell was a strong combination of detergent and bleach.

The detective approached the body and looked pointedly at the assistant standing nearby as if she'd just insulted his green polyester tie. As they gathered around the table, Sarah braced herself. She detected a sweet, putrid odor, and before she could stop herself, she whirled around and vomited on the floor, barely missing Dr. Chestnut's shoes.

"God, I am so sorry," she said as Joe grabbed her arm to steady her.

"It's all right," Dr. Chestnut said and signaled for the assistant to clean up the mess. "Happens all the time."

"You okay?" Joe said.

Embarrassed, Sarah wiped her mouth with the back of her hand. "Maybe I'd better wait outside."

"I'll be out as soon as I can," Joe said.

It surprised her that the smell hadn't turned his stomach as well. Joe was notorious for complaining about the odor of garbage and urine outside some of the sketchier properties they had visited over the years. Why hadn't *this* affected him?

She made her way to the door, her heels clacking on the polished cement floor, and exited without looking back. The last thing she wanted was to make eye contact with

Womble, who was probably gloating over the skirt with the weak stomach.

Joe watched Sarah and wished he could have gone with her. He wasn't sure he could go through with it, not without his best friend. Lou touched his arm.

"Joe, you don't need to do this. Fingerprints and ondontology will give us what we need."

"I want to. Out of respect."

"Are you ready, Mr. Greene?" the detective said, his voice subdued.

"I think so."

"I'm afraid there's a lot of...damage."

Dr. Chestnut pulled the sheet down as far as the shoulders, revealing a cold and pale monstrosity Joe hadn't expected. The woman's face was barely recognizable—covered in lacerations. The once-beautiful blonde hair was caked with brown, dried blood, slivers of glass visible among the strands. Both eyes were missing, the flesh around the sockets picked clean to the bone.

"Oh, God," Joe said. "What... What could've done this?"

"Birds. Ravens, to be exact."

"What?"

"Apparently, a huge flock of them crashed through the glass sliding door and attacked Ms. Cohen inside her apartment."

"How do you know they were ravens?"

The coroner retrieved a plastic evidence bag and showed it to Joe, who stood there staring at the body of a huge black bird.

"We found dozens of those things inside," Womble said. "All dead."

Tasting bile, Joe swallowed hard and turned back to the body. Angrily, he yanked the sheet all the way off, exposing the Y-incision that had been sewn closed with heavy twine. The face, neck, and scalp were covered in slash marks and bruises. And so were her hands as, presumably, she tried warding off her attackers. Joe noticed the swollen, bloody tongue sticking out between her lips, and he could see purple swelling on her knees. Altogether, she had the appearance of a demented doll that had been hacked to pieces.

"What happened to her knees?"

"Those bruises probably occurred when she fell," Franklin said. There were carpet fibers all over the front of her clothing. She may have been trying to crawl away."

"How... How exactly did she die?"

Dr. Chestnut glanced at the two cops. "Blood loss. One or more of those birds punctured a carotid artery. There." He pointed to the left side of the neck.

Joe stepped back and turned around, covering his eyes with a trembling hand. Womble seemed impatient and was about to say something.

Lou placed a hand on Joe's shoulder. "Joe, for the record, any identifying marks you can recall?"

"We didn't have sex, if that's what you're suggesting."

Lou could tell Joe was getting upset and didn't see any point in continuing.

"Vic, I think we're good, don't you?"

The assistant was about to cover up the body when Joe spoke.

"She wore a toe ring. On her left foot."

"Yes," Franklin said.

He walked over to a desk and retrieved a clear plastic bag. When he returned, he handed the bag to Womble. The detective peered inside at the small, silver ring deco-rated with black scrollwork.

"Toe ring," the cop said. "Okay. Thanks, Mr. Greene. We'll let you know if we have any other questions."

Joe didn't answer, but turned and headed for the door.

In the women's restroom, Sarah rinsed her mouth again, cupping her hands and pouring in water, swishing it around and spitting it out. She grabbed a few paper towels and patted her mouth dry. She felt hot—especially the back of her neck—and a little light-headed. Digging into her purse, she found her Starbucks mints and popped four in. When she exited the restroom, she found Joe waiting for her.

"Well, that could've gone better," she said. "Any comment from Dapper Dan?"

He came closer and kissed her cheek. "Let's get the hell out of here."

Thankfully, Sarah and Joe had missed the breakfast crowd at The Cracked Pot. As they took their seats in a booth near the rear, Carter walked over, smiling and handing each a menu.

"Hey, Carter," Sarah said. "How's tricks?"

"Sarah, right? Excuse me for saying, but you don't look so hot."

"Nothing that a strong cup of Peruvian won't fix."

"Coming right up."

"Same for me," Joe said.

Sarah watched as the server left them, recalling the incident at the cemetery when she saw that dark presence hovering near the girl and her friends. She wanted to ask her about it, but needed to find the right opportunity.

Joe reached across the table and took Sarah's hands. "Thanks for coming with me."

"And?" she said.

"And for this morning. It was, well, you know." He rubbed his eyes. "I can't believe Gail is dead. It's just so…odd."

"How did she look?"

"Dead."

"No, I mean…"

"I can't."

"Must have been terrible for you."

Carter had set down the coffees when Lou walked in. Spotting them, he headed over.

"I thought I'd find you two here. Can I join you?"

"Sure," Joe said and slid over.

"Double espresso," Lou said to Carter as he took a seat. Then, to Sarah, "Feeling better?"

"Sorry about that, Lou."

"Don't be. I remember my first homicide. When I arrived at the crime scene, I heaved up everything I'd ever had, including a hot dog I'd eaten at the church fiesta when I was twelve."

"Thanks for the visual."

"No charge."

Sarah raised her cup and took a sip. *Heaven.* "Hey, Lou? What's with that surly detective, anyway?"

Lou held up his hand. "I know, I know. Vic has issues. Never really got along with him when we worked Homicide together. He's a bit of an oddball, to be honest."

"Putting it mildly. I certainly hope *you* didn't dress like that back in the day."

"Vic's divorced. I guess he doesn't have anyone giving him fashion tips."

"Or lessons on manners."

Joe had been quietly drinking his coffee. He set his cup

down and looked at Lou. "Any clue as to what the hell happened? I mean, come on. *Birds?*"

Sarah turned to Lou. "What's he talking about?"

"Well, I'm not supposed to discuss the case. But seeing you knew her, Joe. We got nothing. So far, we're considering it an animal attack."

"I don't understand," Sarah said.

"We think Gail Cohen was killed in her apartment by a flock of ravens."

Sarah had been about to take another swallow of coffee, when she dropped the cup, spilling the hot liquid on the table.

"Shit."

Getting up quickly, she stood back as a busboy ran over with a wet cloth and wiped the table clean. A moment later, Carter appeared with a fresh cup.

"Thanks," Sarah said, embarrassed, and sat.

"You okay?" Joe said.

"Fine." Then, to Lou, "Why would a bunch of birds suddenly decide to go after someone? That only ever happened in a Hitchcock movie."

"Actually, that's not true. Crows, for example, have been known to viciously attack humans. Usually in the spring. There have been thousands of reports over the years."

"So, Lou, how did you get involved, anyway? I mean, this is Santa Barbara police business, right?"

"True. Vic called me when he discovered Joe's business card."

"I seem to remember you saying Joe had written something on the back of the card."

Joe looked down and drank his coffee. "Never mind, it was stupid."

Sarah smiled. "Come on, what did you write?"

"'You had me at hello,'" Lou said, almost choking on his espresso.

"Oh, no, not *Jerry Maguire*."

Joe looked at her, his eyes pleading. "I told you it was stupid. And anyway, that was before—"

"Oh, before the…"

"Yeah."

"I have no idea what you two are talking about," Lou said. "Anyway, before calling Joe, I decided to check it out and met Vic at the crime scene."

"I wish this was *your* investigation," Joe said.

"Me, too. In a way, though, I'm glad it's not. I mean, you're my friend, and I wouldn't want there to be any appearance of…"

"A bromance?" Sarah said.

Both men looked at Sarah, expressionless.

Sarah got up. "Excuse me a second."

She walked back past the kitchen and down a long corridor toward the restrooms, the background voices in the kitchen and restaurant fading away. When she had finished, she walked out and happened to notice that the rear door was open. Carter was standing outside, alone, smoking. On an impulse, Sarah walked out and joined her.

"Taking a break?"

"Yeah. Did you need something?" the girl said.

"No, we're fine. I'm Sarah Greene, by the way." She extended her hand.

"I know." The girl shook it.

"Just making it official. Hey. This is going to sound weird—and I totally get it if you think I'm nuts and should mind my own beeswax."

"Whoa, sounds serious."

"It is, kind of. Do you remember the other day when that TV crew was out at the cemetery?"

"Yeah…?"

"Well, I saw you there with your friends." Sarah looked away. "And…I saw something else, too."

Carter tensed, tossed the cigarette butt, and crushed it violently with the toe of her black high-top Converse.

"Like what?" she said.

"A dark entity. It was hovering near you. I think you saw it, too, and that's why you left." The girl refused to make eye contact. "I only bring it up because… Look, if you ever want to talk about it, I'll listen. I'm in tune with those things, too. Just thought I'd offer."

Carter was silent for a long time. Composed, she looked up at Sarah and gave her a plastic smile.

"I think what you probably saw was a shadow from the trees. I left because I was late for my shift. Speaking of which, I'd better get back inside." Then, at the door, "You coming?"

"Yeah, sure."

Disappointed, Sarah followed the girl into the corridor and made her way back to her table. She decided to leave her alone. But there was one thing she knew for sure. Behind the fake smile, she had detected an unmistakable fear in Carter's eyes.

Joe was sitting alone, drinking his coffee and looking at his phone.

"Where's Lou?" she said, taking a seat, her back to the restaurant.

"Got a call from one of his officers."

"Don't tell me, Tim Whatley."

Joe laughed. "How did you know? Anyway, he promised to keep me in the loop."

"Joe, I'm sorry. And I didn't mean to laugh at that thing you wrote. I thought it was sweet."

He smiled in a way that broke Sarah's heart, as if he were about to say goodbye.

"It's funny. I was sort of in a fog when Lou told me over the phone. When I saw the body, that's when it became real to me. Gail was dead. Laid out there on that table like… And you know what I thought? The very first thing?"

"No."

"I thought, it could've been *you*. And I got scared. I wondered, what I would do? If it *was* you lying there, I mean. What in God's name would I *do*?"

"It *wasn't* me, though. Look, I'm fine." She showed him her medal. And I've got St. Michael to protect me."

A tear fell onto his hand and, embarrassed, he wiped it away. Surprised and moved, she reached over and took his free hand in hers.

"Look," Joe said, recovering. "This isn't some play to try to get us back together or anything. I get that we have issues, but—"

"You don't have to say anything, Joe. Let's leave it at I love you too. Okay?"

Suddenly, a crash. Sarah turned around to look. Carter was standing near the counter frozen, looking off somewhere. She was deathly pale, and her hands were trembling. The ceramic coffee cups she'd been carrying lay shattered on the floor in the middle of a dark brownish pool. Snapping out of it, Carter hurried out of the restaurant.

Without thinking, Sarah got up and followed. Outside, she found Carter leaning against a lamppost, looking as if she were trying to catch her breath. Sarah took the girl's wrists in her hands and looked directly into her eyes.

"Carter, what did you see?"

"I… I didn't see anything. It was an accident."

"Shh. It's okay. Tell me what you saw."

Carter bit back her tears and looked at Sarah, her eyes imploring. The curious were passing them on the street. Sarah ignored them. Joe walked out, a concerned look on his face. Sarah waved him away. Turning back to the frightened girl, she smiled encouragingly.

"It's okay," Sarah said.

"It was a darkness. Something...so *evil*."

"Was it moving?"

"Yes. Toward *you*." Sarah bit her lip and glanced at Joe. "The thing is," Carter said, "I've seen it before."

"At the cemetery?"

"Uh-huh. It wants to hurt you, Sarah."

"Why do you think that?"

Carter looked around her, as if afraid someone might overhear. Leaning in close, she whispered something that chilled Sarah to her soul.

"Because it spoke to me."

Eighteen

It was after eight when the doorbell rang. Sarah had been busy in the kitchen preparing an hors d'ouevre and wiped her hands on her apron as she hurried to answer the door. Joe had asked if he could join, but Sarah had thought it better if she did this alone. Part of the reason, of course, was the fact that he was a *guy* and, by design, clueless. The other reason was, he didn't understand the paranormal and would only get in the way, however good his intentions.

Sarah opened the front door and found Carter Wittgenstein standing in the faint light from the porch light, wearing an expensive jeans jacket Sarah recognized from Barneys New York over a printed T-shirt, a short black cotton skirt, and a pair of black Church's ankle boots. For a second, she wondered how someone working in a restaurant could afford clothes like that, but decided not to pursue it.

Sarah noticed how pretty the girl was, though she felt Carter wore too much makeup and not enough jewelry. She looked shy—vulnerable—as she proffered a white cardboard box. Sarah recalled Joe had told her that Carter was in a band. She tried to imagine the girl on stage belting out grunge-era classics like "Come As You Are" and "Hunger Strike," but couldn't reconcile the image with the person standing before her.

"Thanks for coming," Sarah said.

"I almost didn't."

As Sarah stepped back, Carter walked past.

"I'm finishing up in the kitchen," Sarah said. "Follow me."

"I brought chocolate cake from the restaurant."

"Perfect. Would you like some wine?"

"God, yes," Carter said, laughing.

Sarah leaned in conspiratorially. "You *are* twenty-one?"

Sarah motioned toward a bar stool, and the girl sat. She poured two glasses of Orvieto, chilled to fifty degrees, and handed one to her guest.

"Thanks."

As if on cue, Gary trotted into the room, maowing. Seeing Carter, he began purring and rubbing his back against the toe of her boot.

"Hey, kitty." She bent down and scratched the cat's ear.

"Careful," Sarah said. "He'll never leave you in peace."

"What's his name?"

"Gary."

"Hey, Gary."

Carter picked the cat up and placed him on her lap. The animal began kneading his paws on her skirt, and his purr machine was cranked up to eleven.

"I love your house," she said.

"Thanks. It's a work-in-progress. Hey, you're going to be covered in cat fur."

"I don't mind."

Sarah poured more wine for herself and sat next to Carter. "So, this is kind of weird, right?"

"Oh, yeah."

"Joe tells me you're in a band. You're the singer?"

"*Was*, actually."

"Oh?"

"I quit recently. Relationship troubles."

"I'm sorry. I'll bet it was the bass player."

"How'd you know?" Carter said, laughing.

"I've known a few 'bass players' in my time." The air quotes weren't lost on the girl.

"So, what about you and Joe?"

"Well, he's no bass player, that's for sure. Joe's a sweet guy. We used to be married. Now, it's strictly business. Well, mostly. Boy, I talk too much."

"Can I ask what happened?"

"We wanted different things, I guess. Anyhoo." Sarah raised her glass. "Here's to musicians."

The girl clinked glasses with her and tried the wine. "This is good. Just the right sweetness."

"Whole Foods to the rescue."

They were quiet for a time as Carter took in the kitchen. She noticed that among the eclectic knickknacks and doodads, Sarah appeared to favor things Italian. Somehow, the décor was a comfort to her. She smiled at a platter mounted on the wall decorated with a colorful rooster. It reminded Carter of a trip she took to Italy with her parents when she was in middle school.

Sarah cleared her throat. "Carter, I want to talk about what happened. But I don't want to push you."

"No, it's okay. As they say in prison, this isn't my first rodeo."

As Sarah laughed, the oven dinged.

"Hold that thought."

She got up to check on the puffed pastry. Seeing the food was done, she put on mitts and removed a tray from the oven.

"You can wash your hands in the guest bathroom. It's around that corner."

The girl carefully placed the cat on the floor and went to wash up. By the time she returned, Sarah had transferred the appetizers to a pretty platter decorated with brightly painted fruit and honeybees in the center.

"Those look amazing," Carter said.

"Something I threw together. Wild mushroom puffed pastry. I like to cook. When I have the time. We can eat at the table, if you like."

"Here's fine."

Sarah took down small white appetizer plates from the cabinet and tongs, which she handed to her guest. Carter took two and, instead of using her fork, picked one up with her fingers. The pastry was hot, and she blew on it before taking a bite.

"Aw, man."

"Good, right? I added a dash of Swiss Gruyere."

"Delicious."

The women ate in silence for a few minutes. Carter pushed her plate aside and drained her glass.

"I'll get us more wine," Sarah said. "But first, let's have the next course."

"There's *more*?"

Sarah brought out a large bowl from the refrigerator and set it on the counter as Carter's eyes got huge.

"Wild salmon salad with a dill vinaigrette. Oh, and crusty bread."

"I am seriously gonna get fat."

"Not on my watch." Sarah served her guest. "Carter,

you said earlier that thing you saw spoke to you. Do you remember what it said?"

"Oh my God, I'll never forget. It said, 'She's mine.' Really creeped me out."

"No shit. And you knew it was talking about me?"

"I felt it. It's hard to explain."

"No, I get it."

Sarah grabbed the wine bottle and refilled their glasses. For a time, the women talked and laughed about nothing in particular. When they had had enough of the salad and bread, Sarah cleared the counter. Carter rose.

"I'm gonna pop out for a smoke."

"Sure."

In the meantime, Sarah made coffee and brought out the chocolate cake. On an impulse, she took down the bottle of Talisker and poured two glasses to go with the coffee and dessert.

When Carter returned, she said, "I think you missed your calling, Sarah. You are an incredible cook."

"Thanks. Try the Talisker. I think you'll like it."

The girl took a drink, closing her eyes and letting its warmth create a gentle fire inside her. She frowned, as if mulling something over in her mind.

"I'm glad you invited me. I told you I almost didn't come. But after what you said to me this afternoon, I felt like I needed to.

"You see, I can't talk to anyone else about… I, um, I have this gift. Yeah, we'll call it a gift. I can see things most people can't."

"Join the club," Sarah said, putting a huge bite of chocolate cake in her mouth.

"Okay, I *knew* you weren't just being sympathetic before. There was something—"

"Different?"

"Yeah. And a little sad."

"That's the word for it," Sarah said. "So, how long have you been able to see through the veil?"

"Since I was little—I forget how old. My grandma used to live with us. And one night, she died. I remember the man from the mortuary coming out in the middle of the night. He said she'd probably had a stroke and died in bed.

"Anyways, after the funeral, I started seeing my grandma in the house. She'd be in the kitchen and in my room. I told my parents, but they said it wasn't real; it was just that I missed her so much. And I did miss her. Both my parents worked, so she was like my mom. You know, always there for me."

"I'm sorry, Carter."

"It's okay."

"So, I guess you've seen other stuff since?"

"Yes, which is why I knew I *had* seen my grandma's ghost. It's one of the reasons I moved here. To get away from it all. A long time ago, I'd decided to stop telling my parents about the things I saw. Guess it's ironic I ended up in a place that's even more haunted. What about you? When did you know you were…"

"Special? Guess I was a late bloomer compared to you. My first time was in high school right after my best friend Alyssa was killed in a car accident. She appeared to me. After her funeral, I was so angry with her boyfriend. He was the one driving."

"Was he drunk?"

"No, they didn't find any trace of alcohol or drugs in either of them. Anyway, I couldn't forgive him for taking her away. And then, it happened again. One night, as I was coming home from church, I thought I saw Alyssa walking along the road.

"When I passed her, I turned to look at her face, but

her hair was covering it. When I checked the rearview mirror, she was watching me from the backseat. I almost lost it.

"Somehow, I managed to pull over, and I just sat there, gripping the steering wheel and staring straight ahead. When I turned, Alyssa was sitting next to me in the passenger seat."

"Oh, no."

"Yeah. So, I screamed. But when she touched my hand, I felt all my fear melt away. 'I know you're sad for me,' she said. 'But I'm fine. I came here to tell you not to be mad at Zach. It wasn't his fault. There was a dog. Tell him I will always love him.'"

Sarah grabbed the Talisker and filled both their glasses.

"And after that night, I started seeing dead people. Thanks, Alyssa."

"So, you think *she's* responsible for your abilities?"

"Maybe? Oh, and let's not forget that black ninja cloud that seems to want me for something."

"Do you think the two things are related?"

"I have no idea, my dear."

"Is anyone else in your family psychic?" Carter said.

"Not that I know of."

"Whatever happened to Zach?"

"The accident made him a paraplegic. He works at a tech company in Ventura. I haven't seen him in years. You were right when you said I'm sad."

"I didn't mean—"

"It's okay. And now, I'm seeing a ghost in a mirror. And trying to figure out how she died, so."

"Seriously?"

"Yeah. Anyway, I'm stuck. I can't tell you how much I want to help her."

"I know. It's like an itch."

"Sounds like you've done a little sleuthing of your own."

"When I was little. One time, I found my friend's missing cat. Unfortunately, it was already dead. When my parents found out, they made me stop."

Sarah told Carter the whole story, starting with Alyssa's warning and ending with the police chief exhuming Peter Moody's body. When she was finished, the girl shook her head.

"And no one can talk to the relatives because the cops can't afford a plane ticket?" the girl said.

"Pretty much. I could, though. But I'm not a cop."

"You should go, though."

"What?" Sarah laughed nervously.

"I'm serious. I feel like you could learn something from the dotty aunt."

"But Lou isn't going to let me interview her."

"Who says you have to tell him? Look. You saw her info in the case file, right? How hard would it be to find out where she lives? Just go. So what if it isn't 'official.'"

"This is nuts."

"Haven't you ever done anything a little crazy?"

"All the time, but—"

"So, do it. You know you want to."

Sarah looked at Carter sideways. She was arching her eyebrows suggestively, making Sarah smile.

"What are you, my evil shoulder angel?"

"At your service."

"Fine. But there's only one way I'm doing this. And that's if you come with me."

"*What?* But I'm not—"

"That's my offer. Take it or leave it."

"Shit. Sorry. Can I sleep on it?"

"Of course. You have twenty-four hours, starting…*now*."

Carter got off her stool and nearly fell over. Sarah grabbed the girl's arm and helped steady her.

"Whoa. Guess I shouldn't've had that last glass of scotch."

"Okay, that's it. You're staying here tonight, young lady."

"I don't wanna be a bother."

"You're not, *partner*."

"But I haven't said yes yet."

"We'll see."

Sarah got out the pillows and extra blankets and made a bed for Carter on the sofa. When the girl lay down and rested her head, she was nearly out. Sarah looked down at her and brushed the hair from her eyes. Though they had only recently met, Sarah felt she knew her—a kindred spirit. Turning, she noticed Gary on the floor about to hop up on Carter's stomach.

"Nice try, but no."

The cat maowed once and trotted off.

"So, did you ever tell him?" Carter said, her eyes closed.

"Tell who what?"

"Zach. Did you ever tell him what Alyssa said?"

"No, I never did."

"Unfinished business…"

In another moment, the girl was snoring softly, and Sarah went to bed. As she lay there, staring at the ceiling, she thought about what Carter had said. She should've told Zach. There was good chance he was still carrying around the guilt from the accident. Why hadn't she told him?

"Because I never forgave him," she said to Gary, who

lay curled in a ball next to her. "*Now* who's the bass player?"

Sarah awoke early with a headache from the wine and the scotch. She checked her phone and saw that it was a little after seven. She dressed and went to check on Carter.

She found the girl sprawled out on the sofa, Gary curled up on her stomach, looking up at Sarah with squishy eyes.

"Traitor," she said, and went into the kitchen to make coffee.

She'd had the good sense to pick up scones, butter, and jam from the gourmet kitchen shop downtown—just in case—and set them out on the counter as the coffee brewed. Her phone went off and, seeing it was Joe, she picked it up on the first ring.

"Morning," he said.

"Good morning, Joseph."

"You okay?"

"I'm fine, why?"

"I wanted to check in. I'm at Casa Abrigo, waiting for the guys."

"Are *you* okay, is the question?"

Carter walked into the kitchen with Gary trailing close behind.

"I'm doing all right, I guess," he said. "Everything work out with Carter last night?"

Sarah smiled at the girl. "As a matter of fact, she's helping me with my case." Carter shook her head. "It's official. We're a team."

"That was fast," Joe said.

"That's how we roll."

"You're acting weird, you know."

"I'm feeling *empowered*."

"Okay, whatever," Joe said. "So, I'll see you at the office later?"

"Sure."

"Ciao."

"Ciao, baby."

Grinning, Sarah disconnected and turned to get mugs for the coffee.

"How did you know I'd agree?" Carter said.

"Because I am awesome. Oh, and I've decided we're telling Lou. I need him on my side. Come on, we got scones."

Joe was standing in the kitchen at Casa Abrigo staring at his phone when Manny walked in.

"I know that look," the foreman said. "What did she do this time?"

Joe looked up, puzzled. "It isn't enough I have to deal with one woman who sees things that aren't there. Now, she's brought on a partner."

"Hijo."

"Is it too early for a drink?"

"Hey, boss, I meant to tell you. Last night when we were finishing up, I found… Better to show you."

Manny waved a hand, and Joe followed him to the staircase that led to the second floor. He pointed at something.

Joe could see what looked like claw marks that ran across several balusters, as if an angry bear had swiped its paw across them in a single movement.

"Vandalism?"

Manny shook his head. "No way. Nacho just finished sanding and polishing. It happened while we were here."

Joe looked around, as if expecting to encounter an invisible intruder. In all the years he'd been doing this, he had never experienced anything worse than vandalism. Now, strange things—things he couldn't explain—were happening.

"Anything else?" Joe said.

"Memo said he felt someone touch him while he was working in one of the bathrooms upstairs."

"One of your other sons maybe?"

"No. They were out getting us food. And I was in the cellar."

Joe sighed. "Better get this fixed."

He headed for the front door, for the first time in his life experiencing a sense that things around him were closing in. It was almost as if finding that mirror had set something in motion. But what?

"Where you goin'?" Manny said.

"I need to see Sarah."

After Joe left, Manny was standing on the staircase when a shadow fell across the floor. The foreman made the Sign of the Cross and went outside to get his tools.

Nineteen

"Absolutely not," Lou said.

He was standing behind his desk, wagging a threatening finger. Through his dark complexion, Sarah and Carter could see the blood rushing to his face, making his eyes appear huge—manic—under his dense eyebrows.

Sarah smiled patiently. "Look, Lou. You obviously can't pursue this because of your stupid budget. There's no reason why Carter and I can't pop over to Lawrence and, you know, ask a few innocent questions."

"'Innocent'? This is official police business!"

"First of all, please lower your voice."

"Sorry."

"Secondly, it's not like we were going to show up there pretending to be cops. I mean, that would be reckless." Then, to Carter, "Am I right?"

"Totally out of order."

"Great," Lou said. "So, who *were* you going to pretend to be?"

"Reporters."

"Oh, for the love of—"

"Hear me out, Lou. Carter and I have a plan."

"Uh-huh."

He sank miserably into his chair and buried his face in his hands.

"We're a couple of reporters from Dos Santos looking for a story, right? We want to help solve this terrible crime so the family—what's left of them, anyway—can get some closure."

Lou looked up. "'Closure'?"

"Work with me here."

"And what happens when you *do* get the truth and there's no 'big story' for the folks back home to read?"

"So, we talk to some people at the *Dos Santos Weekly* and convince them this story is hot. It's not that complicated, buddy."

The police chief rubbed his temples as if a huge migraine were brewing. He pawed at his desk, hoping one of the empty paper cups still had a few drops of coffee left.

"What about credentials?" he said, jamming his tongue at the bottom of one of the cups. "The family isn't going to let you talk to the aunt without you identifying your- selves first."

"Leave that to me," Carter said. Sarah and Lou turned to her. "What? I'm resourceful."

For several seconds, Lou flipped the police file open and closed. He wanted to solve the case almost as much as Sarah did. While he hesitated, Sarah winked at Carter— she knew she had him. Finally, he pointed his warning finger at the two of them.

"I cannot be involved in any of this. Something happens—they call the cops to have you arrested—you're both on your own. I swear, I'll disavow everything."

"Understood," Sarah said.

"I mean it, Sarah. I'm in enough trouble after that

stunt we pulled out at the cemetery."

"'We'? Oh, I'm sure everyone's forgotten about that. I mean, so what? You dug up a corpse, and it turned out to be exactly who they said it was. No biggie."

Lou lowered his head and talked into his chest. "Lord, give me strength." Then, to Sarah, "Okay. I'll give you the address where the aunt is and the name and phone number of her brother. If they ask how you got the information—"

"We're reporters, remember?" Sarah said.

"Right." He shook his head. "Sarah, don't make me regret this." Then, to Carter, "And you. What're you, twelve? How did you get involved? Did Sarah threaten to steal your bike?"

Carter bristled. "For your information, I'm twenty-four."

Resignedly, he wrote everything on a yellow legal pad, tore off the page, and handed it to Sarah.

She rose. "Thanks, Lou. We'll make you proud. Come on, Carter."

On her way out, Carter gave Lou the stink eye. But he didn't notice—his eyes were closed and he was rubbing his temples again, thinking about the hell he would pay when it came out that a couple of Nancy Drews were doing his job for him.

"Please, God," he said. "If You care about me at all, You won't let Vic find out."

When Sarah and Carter walked into the realty office through the rear entrance, they found Joe and Rachel chatting in the hallway. Both stopped talking and looked at them expectantly.

"Hey, guys," Sarah said. "Carter, you know Joe. And this is my sister, Rachel."

"Your *sister*?" The girl smiled warmly. "I see you in the restaurant like, every day."

"Nice to finally meet you officially, Carter."

Carter turned to Sarah. "I have to change for my shift. See you at six." Then, to Rachel, "Nice meeting you."

"You, too," Rachel said.

They watched as she went out the back to her car, a cute white MINI Cooper.

"Can I talk to you in your office?" Joe said to Sarah.

"Sure." She turned to Rachel and scrunched her nose. "Could I ask a huge favor?"

"Cinnamon mocha espresso cappuccino?"

"Sure *you're* not psychic? Thank you."

As Sarah settled in her chair, Joe took a seat opposite her. He was furiously picking at a hangnail, and she knew immediately he had something serious on his mind.

"This must be bad," she said.

"Some weird shit has been happening out at Casa Abrigo."

"You mean, besides me seeing a ghost in a mirror and a client almost getting killed by a falling lamp?"

"Yeah. Today, Manny showed me the staircase. It looked as if a wild animal had attacked it."

"Oh, no."

"And there are other things—little things that, by themselves don't mean much. Disappearing tools. Stains on freshly painted walls that can't be explained. No wonder the bank wanted to be rid of it."

She dug through her purse, found her tin of Starbucks mints, and popped a couple in her mouth. Then, she offered some to Joe, who declined.

"Why did you have to involve the girl?" he said.

When she met his gaze, she could see that he was angry. "Carter? I don't understand why that bothers you."

Silently, Joe got up, and Sarah thought he was going to leave without answering. Instead, he closed the door and took a seat again.

"I'm worried about you, Sarah," he said. "Something disturbing is happening, and…"

"Oh my gosh," she said, leaning forward. "You're scared."

"Okay, I admit it. In fact, I'm terrified. And then, Carter sees that…whatever it was…and— Now, there's *two* of you to worry about."

Relieved she hadn't mentioned what the evil entity had said about her, she leaned forward and touched his hand.

"Joe, we're grown women. We can take care of ourselves."

"Sure. I'll bet that's what Gail thought, too."

"You think those were *paranormal* birds that killed her? You sound like me."

"All I know is, things are starting to get dangerous. That thing Carter saw? What if it tries to hurt her—or you?"

"I'll throw holy water in its face. We'll be fine."

"Where were you this morning?" he said.

"Visiting Lou."

"Why?"

"Well, you might as well know. Carter and I are flying to Lawrence, Kansas. Tonight."

"What?"

"Well, technically, we're flying into Kansas City and *driving* to Lawrence, but— Look. It's a fact-finding mission. We're going to talk to Peter Moody's aunt and her brother."

"I'm surprised Lou is okay with this."

"Lou's a big pussycat."

"I'll tell him you said that. And Carter is cool with this?"

"Are you kidding? She's excited to be a part of it."

As Joe got to his feet, Sarah stood and scooted around her desk. She took his hands in hers and looked into his eyes.

"Don't be mad at me, okay? I hate it when you're mad."

"I'm not. I'm— I worry."

"I know. And I think it's sweet."

She grabbed his face, pulled him toward her, and kissed him hard on the lips. Embracing her, he laid her head against his chest and stroked her hair.

"Don't forget to stop at Party City on the way and pick up your fake police badges," he said.

"Honestly. We're fake *reporters*."

"Oh, that's better."

She pulled away. "I'd better get going. I have to pack. Carter and I are leaving as soon as she gets off work. Oh, and can you please make sure to feed Gary, give him fresh water, and change his litter box?"

"I don't have time to—"

She kissed him on the nose. "Thanks. You're a sweetheart."

"How long will you two be gone?"

"I'm guessing three or four days."

"Okay." He smiled. "I'll let you know if the ground opens up and swallows Casa Abrigo to the sounds of *Carmina Burana*."

She opened the door and, seeing Rachel walking in with the coffees, followed her sister into her office.

As Joe observed Sarah leaving, his thoughts returned to the morgue. Once again, he was staring at Gail's body, only now it was Sarah who was lying there. Then, Sarah became a little girl who couldn't have been more than ten. Her body was broken and battered, her skin a translucent blue.

He was sixteen and living in New York, he remembered. He'd recently gotten his driver's license. If only he hadn't been in such a hurry that day, the accident would never have happened. And his mother wouldn't have had to... Putting the memory out of his mind, he slipped quietly out the back.

Franklin Chestnut stood staring at a light box filled with a series of radiographs. The coroner had seen the results of wild animal attacks before. Usually, it was the victims' dogs who were responsible. In other cases, it was mountain lions and bears in the forest. But *birds*?

After carefully examining the body and retrieving bits of raven feathers, Franklin concluded that Gail Cohen had been surprised by the ravens when they crashed through the door leading to her balcony. How was it possible those creatures could break glass? He referred to photos taken at the scene and noticed the ghostly images of those first ones that had tried to break through and died. They almost looked as if they'd been painted on the unbroken parts of the glass. The police report indicated that the neighbors who called 911 thought they heard something shatter, followed immediately by the victim's screams and insisted only seconds had passed between the two sounds.

Franklin was tired. He'd meant to call Beverly to let her know he'd be late. She was probably on her way to the restaurant. He shook his head and rubbed his eyes with the heels of his hands. It was their anniversary, and he needed to get going. Something kept nagging at him, though, and he couldn't get a handle on it. It was something about those birds. Sighing in frustration, he put on his jacket.

"Not just any birds," he said to no one. *"Ravens."*

.

———

It was after six and dark outside. Blanca had already left for the evening. Rachel had been so busy organizing her files, she didn't realize what time it was. Shutting down her computer, she decided to lock up for the night. She hoped Eddie hadn't waited for her and had given Katy her dinner.

After the new security alarm equipment was installed, Rachel always followed the same routine. She would lock the front door, then check the computer monitor in the storage room to ensure all the video cameras were working. On her way out the back, she would set the alarm and lock the back door.

As she approached the front of the realty office, the door opened, revealing a man standing in the backlight of a streetlamp shrouded in mist. It was drizzling outside, and the light limned the figure strangely, making it seem other-worldly—possibly threatening.

"Can I help you?" she said, her voice trembling.

"I didn't mean to startle you."

Michael Peterson stepped into the light, letting the door close behind him. It shut a little too loudly, making Rachel wince. As usual, he was dressed impeccably. But there was something off. His hair? No, *his eyes*. They were like dark pools.

"It's okay," she said, glancing around for an escape route. "We're closed."

He acted as if he hadn't heard. "I tried calling Sarah. That's when I decided to come in person. Do you know where I can reach her?"

There was something unsettling about the way he was smiling at her. She couldn't put her finger on it. But she wished he would leave so she could lock up and go home.

Something told her to keep the information vague. "She's out of town, I'm afraid."

"Oh? Business or pleasure?"

"I'm happy to take a message."

"That would be great."

He looked around the office, as if trying to determine whether Rachel was alone. When he looked up, he must have noticed one of the newly installed video cameras, its red light blinking silently as a warning. His expression turned grim.

"Well," he said, his lips transforming into a rictus grin. "Guess I'll wait to hear from her, then. Please let her know I stopped by."

Before Rachel could answer, he headed for the door and grabbed the knob. She followed, intending to lock the door after him. He stopped and turned, and she almost ran into him.

"I only came to find out how Casa Abrigo is coming along. You wouldn't happen to know if it's ready to go on the market, would you?"

Rachel realized she was perspiring. She made a conscious effort to speak evenly so as not to betray fear.

"Well, Joe and Sarah normally handle that side of the business. I just run the office."

"Don't sell yourself short. See you."

He opened the door and slipped out into a cold, hard rain. Exhaling, Rachel scurried to the front door and, her hand shaking badly, locked it after several attempts.

Returning to her office, she grabbed her purse, set the alarm, slipped out the back, and ran to her car as if the devil himself were after her.

As the plane taxied off the runway, Sarah turned her phone on. Carter had just awakened—that girl could sleep through anything—and was yawning and stretching. It had been a long day. They'd flown from Santa Barbara to LAX on United, then hopped on a nonstop Delta Flight to Kansas City International Airport. Sarah groaned when she remembered they still had to pick up the rental car and drive fifty miles to Lawrence. It would be two hours before she could lie down in a hotel bed and close her eyes.

"Sleep well?" Sarah said to her travel companion.

"Great. What about you?"

"I don't sleep on planes."

"Too bad."

Sarah noticed the voicemail waiting for her and was about to listen to it when she saw they had stopped at the terminal and people were getting out of their seats. Putting her phone away, she climbed out and got their carry-ons from the overhead storage. Carter's was Tumi, and again Sarah wondered how the girl could afford such an expensive brand. Maybe her parents had money?

Soon, they were on the rental car shuttle heading for Avis. Sarah had forgotten about the voicemail and was telling Carter about the time she had the best barbecue of her life in Kansas City after her plane was diverted there in bad weather.

As they pulled out of the airport in their Ford Escape, Carter fired up Google Maps on her phone and punched in the TownePlace Suites in Lawrence. She'd chosen the hotel, insisting it was better to be downtown, where they could have quick access to restaurants—and Starbucks. Sarah didn't need convincing, since this was a Marriott property and she would get points anyway.

It took only a few minutes to get to the I-29, and soon they were zipping south doing seventy. Incredibly, they reached the hotel in forty-five minutes. They had reserved two rooms and, after checking in, Sarah realized she was no longer tired and wanted to eat something.

"Meet you in the lobby in thirty minutes?" she said to Carter.

"You read my mind. Gonna grab a quick shower and change clothes.

"Me, too. See you soon."

They were on the same floor, but their rooms weren't close together. As Sarah let herself into her room, she thought about what a nice travel companion Carter was. She wasn't loud, never complained—even when the idiot in front of her tried putting his seat all the way back during the meal service—and she didn't seem to mind being stuck in a middle seat.

Sarah had finished showering and was brushing her hair when she noticed the voicemail again. She picked up her phone and listened to two messages from Joe going on about not being able to find Gary's food and another about how he missed her, one from Katy wishing her a safe trip, and finally, Rachel's message. Her sister's voice sent chills down Sarah's spine. Before calling her back, she listened to the message again, then got dressed.

Sarah and Carter had found a pub within walking distance of the hotel and settled on burgers.

"You seem distracted," Carter said as their food arrived.

Sarah sipped her blueberry cilantro margarita. "I

called my sister. Apparently, she'd had a visit from a client."

"Good news?" Carter took a swig of her Cosmic IPA.

"Well, he seems interested in one of our properties. But he…frightened her."

"How?"

"I'm not sure. Rachel wasn't specific when I spoke to her. She said he seemed *off*. The thing is, he told her he'd called me before going over there. But his number didn't come up on my phone. Anyway, I need to call him." Sarah took a bite of her burger. "So, ready for tomorrow?"

"We're meeting him at what time?"

"Ten. At Starbucks."

Carter toyed with a french fry. "Sarah, do you really think we can pull this off?"

"Remember. If *you* believe you're a reporter, then *he* will."

"I've never been a very good liar."

"Look sincere. Besides, we want to crack this thing, right? Oh, crap. I forgot my digital recorder."

Smiling, Carter reached into her purse, pulled out a small device, and waved it in Sarah's face. "Gotcha covered."

"Carter, my dear, you are nothing short of amazing."

After dinner, they decided to sit at the bar and have a drink. Several men wearing business suits circled them like lions at a luau. Smiling, Sarah whispered something to her friend. She reached over and began stroking Carter's hand. The vultures got the message and wandered away. Sarah and Carter burst out laughing.

Sarah had always had trouble sleeping the first night of a trip and lay in her bed with her eyes wide open. It was late, and she wished she could drift off so she would be refreshed for their meeting. After several minutes, her eyelids became heavy, and she felt herself relaxing. But there was a faraway light shining in her eyes, and she wondered if it might be one of those emergency night-lights plugged into a wall outlet.

Sitting up, she squinted at it. It seemed to be moving toward her. Soon, it was large enough for her to see *inside it.* Sitting in the center of the light on a ratty double bed was a man wearing a T-shirt and boxers, rocking back and forth. He looked familiar.

Soon, the image was large enough that he was almost the same size as Sarah. Frightened, she retracted her feet and pressed up against her headboard. She could hear traffic noises and the sounds of voices. She was in a room in some run-down hotel. Outside, she could see a flickering neon sign from across the street. Though part of it was cut off, she could make out HE TAP HO.

The man continued rocking, and she could hear a soft chanting. He seemed to be doing something with his face —she didn't want to see. As if aware he was being watched, he stopped and slowly turned to face her.

It was Peter Moody. And instead of eyes, he had two dark, bloody holes.

"Eyes on me, Sarah," he said, and laughed like a lunatic.

Screaming, she woke to find she'd been dreaming. She was alone, and the only sound was of a distant siren outside in the night.

She thought about calling Carter, then concluded that at least one of them should be rested for the interview in the morning.

Twenty

Owen Daniels wasn't what Sarah expected. She and Carter had arrived at Starbucks early, wearing tasteful designer jeans, plain shirts, and flats—their idea of how women reporters might dress. Carter wore a black leather jacket and Sarah wore a jean jacket. Carter had sprung for black-frame Italian glasses to help sell their deception. And, in case their interviewee asked, she had made fake IDs that looked remarkably authentic.

As the women sat drinking macchiatos, a silver-haired man who looked like a gentleman cowboy walked in. He wore a modest gray suit with no tie and reminded Sarah of a Rotarian. Seeing the women seated by the window, he strode toward them deliberately.

"Sarah Greene?"

"That would be me," Sarah said.

She rose and extended her hand, but the elderly gentleman was reluctant to take it. She wondered if he might be a germaphobe. After sneaking a glance at his naked wedding ring finger, she concluded he simply might be unused to being around women. After an awkward few seconds, he agreed to shake hands.

"And this is Carter Wittgenstein." He nodded in acknowledgment. "Why don't you have a seat, Mr. Daniels. Can I get you something?"

"Regular coffee's fine."

"Um, sure," she said, frowning at Carter who, to be honest, found the old man to be sweet, as out of place at Starbucks as a nun in a mosh pit.

While Sarah went to purchase a coffee for their guest, Carter took out her digital recorder and a small notepad and pen.

"That a recording device?" Owen said.

"Yes. I hope it's okay. We don't wanna to get anything wrong when we write our story."

"Mm."

Sarah returned with a grande drip coffee and set it down in front of Owen. "I wasn't sure if you wanted cream, or…"

"Nope. Black is fine."

Despite the rough edges, Sarah found that she liked Owen Daniels. She decided he was a no-nonsense man of the old school who didn't slouch or swear. A little awkward around the ladies, but a straight shooter, nonetheless.

Carefully, he removed the lid from his cup with fingers that looked arthritic, blew on the hot coffee, and, squinting, took a tentative sip. He looked at Sarah as Carter hit the RECORD button.

"I have no idea why your paper is interested in digging up all this history," he said. "But I said I'd tell you what I know, and that's exactly what I intend to do."

"And we appreciate it," Carter said.

Sarah opened her notebook. "Before we get started, Mr.—"

"Owen."

"Yes. I wanted to ask how your sister Colleen is doing."

"Well as can be expected, I suppose. She's, um, forgetful. That's why I had to put her in the home. You know, for her own safety. She's well taken care of, though."

"I'm sorry," Sarah said as she wrote in her notepad.

"Of course, she got worse after Morris died."

"Her husband?"

"Yes."

"He was Gerald's younger brother?"

"That's right."

"Can you tell us how he died?"

The old man shook his head and took another swallow of coffee. He looked out the window for several seconds, and it occurred to Sarah that for this man, there was no such thing as an awkward silence.

"Damnedest thing," he said at last. "Had a heart attack driving to the pharmacy to pick up Colleen's prescription. Aricept, I think it was. Ended up drifting into a row of parked cars. He was dead before the paramedics could get to him. Nobody else was hurt, though."

"I see," Sarah said. "And is she…"

"Aware?"

The old man laughed unexpectedly, hard enough to squeeze out a few tears. The women exchanged confused glances. He wiped his eyes with a napkin and took a swallow of coffee.

"She knows, all right. Thing is, she's concocted this wild story about Morris having run off with a waitress. Can you imagine? Thinks the two of 'em are living it up somewhere in Jefferson City."

"That's amazing," Carter said, laughing.

"No, child, that's grief. It's what happens when you can't face the truth and need to find a way to keep going."

Blushing, Carter lowered her head and wrote something in her notebook.

Sarah pressed on. "So, did Colleen and Morris have any children?"

The old man's face turned grim, and Sarah was worried she'd pushed the wrong button. Stiffly, he drained his cup, carefully set it down in front of him, and snapped the lid back on.

"A daughter. Nicole."

"Oh? Does she live around here?"

"She ran away when she was fifteen."

He nearly spit the words out, putting Sarah on the defensive, and it took her a moment to recover her composure. She had no idea Colleen and Morris Moody had had a child. And though the information was not directly related to the Peter Moody case, she couldn't resist going on.

"Can I ask when you last saw Nicole?"

"Summer of 1990. Right before she and her parents left for California."

"What?" Carter said.

"She was always a handful, Nicole was. Kept running away. So, Morris and Colleen thought it might be a good idea if she stayed with Gerald and Vivian out in California for a while. Help straighten her out, you know."

"I'm not sure I understand," Sarah said. "Did she have a good relationship with her aunt and uncle?"

"It was the kids. Those three used to play together all the time when they were little. Peter, Hannah, and Nicole. They were inseparable."

"So, wait," Carter said. "You're saying that after her parents dropped Nicole off in California, she disappeared?"

"Well, no. She spent the summer there. For some

reason, she decided to take off. But she was always like that. Flighty. Despite the best efforts of the Moodys, Nicole ran away. And we never saw her again. Later, the parents were found murdered. It's no wonder my sister is living in a world of her own."

"I didn't mean to get off on a tangent, Owen," Sarah said. "I appreciate the information, though. By the way, can I get you a refill?"

"Doctor allows me one cup a day. Never much cared for doctors."

Winking, he handed Sarah his cup, which she promptly took to the counter.

"You like reporting, Carter?"

"I like people, so."

"Wittgenstein. That's German, isn't it?"

"Yes."

"Used to have a German auto mechanic. He was competent enough but, Lord, did he have a temper."

Sarah returned with fresh coffee and took a seat.

"Okay, getting back to Peter Moody. Can you tell us what happened after his parents' funeral? I understand he returned to Lawrence."

"They both did."

Sarah blanched. *"Both?"*

"Yes. Peter and Hannah. They came back to live with my sister and her husband."

"But I thought Hannah was…"

Carter jumped in. "We weren't able to uncover any information about her."

"Oh. Well, things were okay for a while, I suppose," Owen said. "But then, my sister and her husband noticed that Peter was acting strange. At first, they thought it was because his parents had died so horribly."

"When you say 'strange,'" Sarah said. "What exactly do you mean?"

"I wasn't there, of course. I was living in Kansas City at the time. But I remember the telephone conversations with Colleen. She said Peter had gotten into Satanic rock. Had posters all over his bedroom walls. Refused to keep up his appearance. Things like that.

"She told me that sometimes the boy would be having conversations when no one else was in the room. She'd hear him when she passed his door. Sometimes, he'd be laughing like a crazy person. Then, it'd be like he knew Colleen was there, and he would stop and turn up his music."

"Maybe he was on the phone," Carter said.

"No. There was only one phone in the house, and that was in the kitchen. Things seemed to get worse with Peter. Hardly ate or slept. Did poorly in school. One day, Colleen was cleaning his room. And in the closet, she found…"

"What?" Sarah said.

"A knife with strange carvings on the handle. And a strange metal bowl. Also, there were these little statues that looked like the devil. I never saw these things myself, you understand."

"His aunt and uncle must've been very upset," Carter said.

"My sister and her husband were terrified. They confronted Peter and made him promise to see a therapist. Oh, he did. And after only one session, she recommended that he enter a psychiatric hospital for observation."

"Which one?" Sarah said.

"The Lund Institute. It's not far from Lawrence."

"Isn't that where Vivian Moody was confined for a time?"

Owen smiled. "Well, I believe I am impressed. Yes, she

was. Nervous exhaustion, they said. She always was…sensitive."

Carter cleared her throat. "Owen, do you think your sister and her husband might have been afraid of Peter?"

"Couldn't say. But I know they were afraid *for* him. They were still sad about Nicole—not knowing where she was—and I guess they didn't want to lose Peter, too."

"Understandable."

"What about Hannah?" Sarah said. "What was happening with her while all this was going on?"

Owen smiled. "Hannah was nothing like Peter. She was a model child. Always did well in school, never got into any trouble. Graduated high school with a 4.0 GPA."

"Did she have a good relationship with her brother?"

"She loved Peter. It hurt her when he went away. She used to visit him over at the institute every week."

"Wait," Carter said. "Peter remained in the hospital?"

"Yes. Doctors said he was suffering from psychosis, maybe brought about by his parents' death. They were afraid he might try and hurt himself. He'd already been cutting himself at home."

They had been talking a long time, and Sarah was afraid Owen might be getting tired.

"Did you want to take a break?" she said.

"Like to use the lavatory."

"Sure."

Sarah watched as the old man strode off and turned to her friend in astonishment.

"Hannah is alive?" she said.

"I know. All this time, we've been thinking Peter killed her. But wait, what about the mirror? Maybe the girl *was* Nicole all along."

"Carter, I was convinced it's Hannah. But now, I don't know."

"Well, let's find out what we can about Peter. Clearly, he murdered *somebody* besides his parents. And all signs point to him being a Satan-worshipping nutjob."

Sarah finished her coffee, which had turned cold. "Listen, since we know Hannah is alive—I still can't believe it —we should find out where she's living. She might know everything, including the identity of the girl who died."

"I agree. Hey, do you think we should take a ride out to that hospital?"

"Sounds like something a *real* reporter would do, doesn't it?"

Owen emerged from the restroom and started for their table. He stopped and removed his phone from his pocket. From his expression, Sarah and Carter could see it was not good news. After disconnecting, he continued toward them and picked up his coffee from the table.

"I'm afraid we'll have to continue this another time," he said. "Apparently, Colleen fell." Sarah started to say something, but he raised a hand. "She's okay. Just a bump on the head. I'm going over there now."

"Would you mind if we tagged along?" Sarah said.

"I think it's best if I go alone. You can come by tomorrow morning. She's usually more clear-headed during the day. Say, nine o'clock?"

"Okay, whatever you think is best."

"Thanks for the coffee," Owen Daniels said, and strode purposefully out of the store.

"What do you think?" Sarah said. "Road trip?"

Carter pulled up Google Maps on her phone and did a quick search for the Lund Institute.

It had taken Sarah and Carter only twenty minutes to

reach the stately grounds of the Lund Institute, a psychiatric hospital founded in the early nineteen hundreds by a Dr. Carl Lund, a devout Jungian. The kindly doctor with a penchant for sweater vests and cigars believed in treating patients with compassion, no matter their illness. In his youth, his own mother had been confined in a more traditional facility after an attempted suicide and eventually died there, untreated and friendless. To honor his mother, Lund decided to dedicate his life's work to the less fortunate.

"Glad you made up those IDs," Sarah said.

She and Carter were approaching the stone steps of the massive Romanesque revival building of textured stone and brick. Barred windows embedded in molded semicircular arches looked out over the vast lawn covered in flaming red and gold leaves from the many surrounding trees in front of the building.

Sarah expected the inside to look like a museum. Instead, she found a modern interior. She and Carter crossed the tile floor, their footsteps echoing, and approached a guard station.

"May I help you?" the nondescript man in a dark green uniform said.

"Yes," Sarah said. "We're reporters from the *Dos Santos Weekly*." They removed their IDs and handed them over.

"California, huh?"

"Yes," Carter said, adjusting her glasses. "We're investigating a story and wanted to ask some questions about a patient who was here in 1993."

"Well, all records are confidential."

"We understand," Sarah said. "And we're not interested in those. We were hoping to interview one of the doctors who was here at the time. Maybe ask some general questions?"

The guard handed back the IDs. "Not sure who might have been here then. I suppose I could ask Dr. Martin. She's the chief physician."

"That would be great."

He gestured to an area with several leather couches and chairs. "Feel free to wait over there," he said as he picked up the phone.

The women sat and watched the traffic. Doctors, medical students, and patients' family members came and went. To Sarah, the place seemed more like a university than a hospital.

After a few minutes, a woman wearing a gray knit suit and chocolate brown crocodile pumps hurried through the front door and headed straight for a secure door, security badge in hand. Noticing her, the guard called out.

"Dr. Martin! Dr. Martin!"

The woman stopped mid-stride and made her way to the guard station. Sarah was hopeful the doctor would see them and watched as the guard spoke to her while gesturing at Sarah and Carter.

Sarah could tell the woman, though poised, was overworked and always in a hurry. She wore her brown shoulder-length hair in a side flip, and Sarah knew the woman liked to take pains with appearance. She was pleasantly surprised when Dr. Martin walked toward them wearing a professional smile. Sarah and Carter rose immediately.

"I'm Patricia Martin."

"Sarah Greene. And this is Carter Wittgenstein."

Everyone shook hands. As the doctor took Carter's, she smiled. "I'm sorry, but I have to ask. Are you by chance related to Ludwig—"

Carter smiled. "A distant relative. I'm afraid I didn't inherit any of his abilities, though."

"I see," the doctor said, noticing that both her guests

were staring at her shoes. "I know. A bit much for this place, right? I couldn't resist. I understand you wanted to chat about a former patient?"

"He was admitted in 1990," Sarah said. "We were hoping that someone here would remember him. He's buried with his family in our town, and we're doing an investigative story, trying to solve a decades-old mystery."

"Mm. Well, I started here in 1992, back when all I could afford were chunky loafers. What was the patient's name?"

"Peter Moody."

She hesitated. "Doesn't ring a bell. How'd he die?"

"Suicide."

"Young man?"

"Yes. I believe he was twenty-one at the time."

The doctor looked intrigued. "Look. I was going to lock myself in my office and tackle a pile of overdue paperwork for the rest of the afternoon." She smiled. "I think you two saved me from all that. Why don't you come with me?"

In a few minutes, Sarah and Carter were sitting in Dr. Martin's spacious office, drinking sparking water. The older woman had extraordinary taste, having decorated the room with leather-bound books and tasteful objets d'art from the Middle East and Africa.

"See anything you like?" the doctor said to Sarah.

"Yes, I— Sorry. I was an art major in college. And I guess I love the idea of being a collector." Sarah glanced at Carter. "But on a reporter's salary…"

"I understand."

Dr. Martin got comfortable in her leather chair, slipped on a pair of black reading glasses, and leaned toward her computer monitor.

"Lucky for you all our files are online now. Let me look

up the patient's record. Ah, here we are. Peter Moody." She squinted at the monitor. "My, my."

Silently, Sarah and Carter rose and went behind the desk. They saw a color photograph of a hollow-eyed seventeen-year-old Peter Moody staring blankly into the camera, devoid of personality. He had a number of purplish zits, and his teeth looked as if they hadn't been brushed in years. Without thinking, Sarah extended her hand to touch the screen. A fingered bolt of light threw her back, and it was several seconds before she realized she'd fallen against a bookcase.

"Are you okay?" she could hear Dr. Martin saying, her voice like a buzzing insect.

"Yes, I… I'm sorry."

"No need to apologize."

Dr. Martin and Carter helped Sarah back to her chair on the other side of the desk. Carter handed her friend her water.

"Thanks," Sarah said.

"Feeling better?" the doctor said.

"A bit. Really wish I hadn't done that."

"Uh-huh. Okay. Do you want to tell me the *real* reason you're here?"

"For the story," Carter said, shooting a nervous glance at Sarah.

"My dear Ms. Wittgenstein—if that *is* your real name —give me some credit."

As Carter blushed, Dr. Martin pursed her lips and crossed her arms on her chest, waiting patiently. Carter looked at Sarah desperately.

"Okay, you busted us," Sarah said. "We did give you our real names, but we're not reporters."

"That much I figured out on my own."

"We are, however, very interested in Peter Moody."

"Intriguing," Dr. Martin said, pouring herself a water. "Do go on."

Sarah explained everything, hoping that when she was finished, Dr. Martin wouldn't throw them out of the building.

"That's the whole story," Sarah said. "Are we under arrest?"

Dr. Martin laughed. "Hardly. It sounds to me as if you have a legitimate reason for being here. Don't get me wrong, I'm a woman of science. But there are times when...well, when science can't explain everything. Your reaction, for instance, when you touched the patient's photo. You felt something, didn't you?"

Sarah looked away uncomfortably. She had never told a medical professional about her abilities.

"Yes."

"Well, I would love to delve into *that* some more, but we'll save it for another time. Look, I can't share Peter's actual patient record with you, but I'll tell you what I can. Then, you two can buy me dinner. I've been on a cleanse for the past week, and I am *starving!*"

Twenty-One

"So, how does it work," Dr. Martin said as the three women drank mojitos at a trendy steakhouse in Lawrence. The place was practically standing room only, and Sarah wondered how a "woman of science" could be so refined. The restaurant had been the doctor's choice.

"I haven't had a mojito in ages," Sarah said, savoring the sweetness and avoiding the question.

"You can't imagine what this tastes like to me," Dr. Martin said, "after a week of kale juice." She arched her eyebrows. "Sarah? You haven't answered my question."

"Oh. And here I thought I was doing so well. It just… happens, I guess."

"The flashes, you mean?"

"Yes. I could be in a room minding my own business. I might touch something or come near a person or a thing. Cemeteries are a real problem, let me tell you."

"Mm. Then, I would suggest avoiding the Lawrence Massacre self-guided tour."

Sarah scrunched her nose. "Bad?"

"Not for most people. What else?"

"Or the visions could come to you in a dream," Carter said.

Dr. Martin tsked-tsked. "Carter. Not you too?"

"Afraid so."

"Anyway," Sarah said. "There doesn't seem to be any logic to it."

The doctor raised her index finger. "Actually, there is. I'm not sure about the dreams, but in science, we know that all matter radiates energy. Even rocks. Technically, it's electromagnetic energy. And, I think, you—and Carter—happen to be more sensitive than most. You're like finely tuned radios picking up signals the rest of us mere mortals cannot."

"Including from a computer monitor?"

"Surprising, I admit. But it happened."

"Well, it's annoying," Carter said. "And scary sometimes."

"I'll bet. The danger, of course, is that repeated exposure to these events over time might lead to psychosis."

"Meaning?" Sarah said.

"Meaning you lose touch with reality."

Carter twirled the mint leaf in her drink. "But what if this *is* your reality?"

Before Dr. Martin could answer, a host carrying menus quietly approached the women.

"Ladies, your table is ready. If you'd like to follow me."

Soon, they were sitting in a lovely spot away from the noise of the bar. They'd decided to leave serious business until after the food arrived. Steaks all around with plenty of starchy sides.

"So, what's your story, Patricia?" Sarah said to the doctor. "You seem to enjoy the finer things."

"You mean, I'm not your stereotypical nerd."

"Exactly."

"Well, I went to Smith. My parents have money, you see. I majored in biochemistry and minored in Jewish studies. What can I say? I was trying to get back to my roots."

"But…your name is Martin."

"Courtesy of my ex-husband. It looked better than Finkelstein on my business card. Like you with 'Greene.'"

"Indeed."

"And no one ever misspells Martin. I grew up with nice things, so when I could afford them again, I said, what the hell, and splurged."

"So, your parents are—" Carter said.

"Rich, yes. You see, Carter—and I think you'll appreciate this—I had this crazy idea that I could make it on my own. I only dated doctors and lawyers but ended up marrying a Wall Street investment banker. All while pursuing my career."

"But Kansas?" Sarah said, scrunching her nose.

"It was a good opportunity. Never regretted it. Although I do miss the Bergdorf Goodman sales."

"Any kids in the picture?" Carter said.

"A son. He's a doctor. With a lovely family in New Rochelle. I try to see them as often as I can."

"Wow," Sarah said.

"It's just money, Sarah."

"No, I mean, you seem so…free. I guess you're not what I expected."

"People can surprise you. My patients taught me that. Speaking of which. As I told you earlier, Peter wasn't a patient of mine. I lied when I said I didn't remember him. I do. Absolutely. And even with my lack of experience back then, I always suspected he was faking."

"You mean, mental illness?" Carter said.

"Yes. I reread his file before coming over here. Look, he could have checked himself out when he turned eighteen.

That's the law. Yet, he chose to remain until he was twenty-one. Why? Because he knew he needed help? No." She leaned in conspiratorially and stage-whispered to them. "I think he may have been evil."

"Is that a medical term?" Sarah said.

"I'm a Jew. And, like Catholics, we believe in good and evil. Some people can't help what they are. But Peter. I think he reveled in it."

"The darkness, you mean," Sarah said.

"Yes. I remember he had made friends with another patient. Oh, I wish I could remember his name. A handsome young man. Poor thing suffered from schizophrenia. I was worried that Peter would corrupt him. I remember I approached Peter's doctor about it. I'm not sure if he did anything, though."

"Peter did check himself out, though, right? At twenty-one?"

"Correct. Apparently, we lost track of him after that. Then, as we know, he committed suicide."

Sarah wrote something in her notebook. "Patricia, any chance we could speak with that other doctor?"

"Sadly, he passed away in 2011. Lung cancer."

"I'm sorry. Do you think you could find out who the other young man was? Maybe call us or email the information?"

"I'd be happy to try. Such a tragedy. I remember reading about Peter's death in the paper."

Carter looked at Sarah. "He slit his throat, right?"

"Yes."

The doctor drained the last of her cabernet and looked grimly at Sarah and Carter.

"But only *after* he'd torn out his eyes."

It was late, and Dr. Martin had left to catch an Uber back to her condo, which was located near the hospital. Sarah wasn't tired and wanted to debrief with Carter, so the women returned to the bar and ordered Taliskers.

"That woman can read me like a book," Sarah said, taking a whiff of her drink and throwing it back as if she'd been interrogated by some hard-boiled detective.

"Seriously. Do you think she's psychic?"

"Maybe. Which reminds me. What did Patricia mean when she said *you'd* appreciate that she was trying to make it on her own?"

"I…"

"Carter, you wouldn't be holding out on me?"

"No… Okay, fine. My family is…wealthy. You may have noticed I don't shop at TJ Maxx."

"I was wondering about that."

"It's no big deal. They gave me everything. And, I guess, I was grateful. But…"

"You're special."

"Right. And I didn't wanna stay in Sausalito and put them through the dreams and the visions and everything else that was going on at the time."

"They must worry about you, kid."

"I stay in touch, but I don't provide too many details."

"But why a server in a restaurant? Isn't there something you want to do? Music? Real estate?"

The girl laughed. "I need to work some things out. I haven't exactly been on a traditional path. I have a degree in philosophy from Berkeley and not much else."

"Sounds like me with my stupid art degree. I mean, seriously. How did I think I was going to make a living? So, it sounds like you're following in your great-great-great-whatever's footsteps. I mean, studying philosophy."

"I guess. And Patricia saw right through me as well. I

wanted that feeling of accomplishment when you do something by yourself."

"But, as a fallback, you always have the trust fund," Sarah said, signaling the bartender for another round.

Blushing, Carter lowered her head and tossed back her drink. "That was uncalled for."

"The truth hurts, baby."

"So, what's the plan?" Carter said. "Are we meeting Owen at the retirement home?"

"Although I don't expect to get much from his sister. But we're already here, right?"

"I feel like there's so much we don't know. About Peter, and now Hannah."

"Yeah. We have got to locate her."

Carter laughed. "So, do you think you and I are on our way to becoming psychotic?"

"I hope not. I pray a lot, you know? It helps."

"Our family wasn't religious. I guess I believe in God but…"

Sarah's phone buzzed. She took it out, saw the unfamiliar number, and let it go to voicemail. The new drinks arrived, and the women raised their glasses.

"Here's to pleasant dreams tonight."

"Or no dreams," Sarah said. "Speaking of which, any strange dreams *you* want to talk about?"

"I did dream something last night. I was planning to tell you. There was a man standing far off in a, a mist. I couldn't see who he was, but I knew he wasn't Peter."

"A strange man? Sure this wasn't some sex fantasy?"

"No," Carter said, fake-punching her companion. "Then, another man appeared next to him."

"Okay, this is getting pret-tee gay…"

"Shut up. Besides, they had their clothes on. As I

moved closer, the two bodies—how can I explain?—they melded together into one person."

"Weird. Did this combo-man say anything to you?"

"Not that I remember."

"Definitely beyond my analytical capabilities," Sarah said. "Maybe we should run this by Patricia."

"No way. I'm done talking to shrinks, thank you very much."

"Gotcha. Although, I think she was kind of into you."

"Please stop."

Back in her room, Sarah had undressed and was relaxing in bed, wearing a camisole. She wished Joe were with her and decided to call him when she noticed the voicemail. Hesitating, she dialed her ex-husband instead. He picked up on the first ring.

"Hey," he said.

"Hay is for horses."

"I hope the trip was worth it because I'm really missing you over here."

"Oh, how sweet. Well, I'm afraid I don't have any of those feelings. When we're not working, Carter and I have been entertaining a number of promising young beef salesmen from the greater Kansas City area."

"Very funny."

"If you want to know the truth, I'm horny as hell."

"Said the good Catholic."

"Yeah, well…"

"For the record, so am I."

"Okay, before we lapse into embarrassing phone sex, any more strange happenings at Casa Abrigo?"

"No. But I'm on the lookout. All these random repairs

are burning through the cushion I built into our budget. Maybe we should get a priest in here."

"I could ask Fr. Donnelly. You *were* being serious, right?"

"I wasn't, but maybe it *would* be a good idea. You know, get the house blessed or whatever."

"I think these incidents are tied to whatever is going on with that mirror. Joe, I want to solve this thing and put it behind us, okay? I feel like I won't be able to relax until it's over. Also, it may solve our problem with the house."

"Okay. But what constitutes 'over'?"

"That's a tough one. I guess when the girl's soul is at rest. Who, as we've come to learn, is *not* Hannah. I'll explain later."

"And you think you can make all this happen? Sarah, you're not God. Whatever's going on is—"

"Bigger. I know. But I seem to have this crazy gift, and like Fr. Donnelly said, God gave it to me for a reason. Do you know what I mean?"

"I do. And I love you, weirdness and all."

She laughed. "That's good to hear. Listen, tomorrow, Carter and I have to meet with the aunt. After that, we're coming home. I expect your calendar to be clear tomorrow night."

"I'll see what I can do. Gary can be very demanding."

"Night."

"Goodnight, Sarah."

Sarah lay on the bed, holding her phone and thinking about Joe. Had he meant it when he said he loved her? *Dammit, Sarah. What else do you need?* Hearing his voice, she realized she missed him more than ever and longed to feel his arms around her. She thought about their last intimate encounter, which reminded her she hadn't gone to Confession. She made a mental note to call Fr. Donnelly.

Glancing at her phone, she saw the voicemail again and decided to listen to it. Probably some stupid telemarketer.

"Sarah, it's Donnie Fisk. You know, from *Dubious*? Listen, I'm wondering if you can meet with us at our offices in Burbank. It's about that video we recorded for you at the cemetery. I'd like to show you something. Can you give my assistant a call so we can set something up? Later."

Sarah listened to the message again. She sensed fear in Donnie's voice and wondered what they could have seen that night next to Peter's grave. She laid her phone on the nightstand and reached over to turn out the light when she heard a buzz. Looking down, she saw it was Lou.

"Hello?"

"Why haven't you checked in?" he said, his voice flavored with irritation.

"Who is this?"

"Sarah, come on. I'm being serious."

"Lou, I was going to call you tomorrow on our way to the airport. We still have to meet with the aunt."

"Well, I'll take whatever you got so far."

"Okay…"

Sarah spent the next few minutes catching Lou up on their meeting with Owen Daniels and Dr. Martin.

"Doesn't sound like much," he said when she'd finished.

"Yeah, well. How about this? It turns out Hannah is *alive*. Or at least she was in 1990 when she and her brother returned to Lawrence."

"*What?*"

"There's more. You can add another girl to the mix. Seems there was a cousin, Nicole, who was staying with the Moodys that summer. But she ran away."

"Do you think maybe Nicole is the dead girl?"

"At this point, anything is possible, I guess. But that newspaper photo. I was so sure it was Hannah. Anyway, I'm hoping to get a better picture tomorrow morning when Carter and I interview the aunt."

"Okay, sounds good."

"Oh, I almost forgot," she said. "I got a call from our skeptical friend Donnie Fisk. He wants to meet in their offices in Burbank. I think it has to do with that video they shot."

"Maybe they found something. I think I should be there as well."

"That's what I was thinking. Can you call his office and set up a meeting for Friday? I'll text you the number. I'm flying in late tomorrow and want to take Thursday off."

"Sure thing. Hey, Sarah. Has Joe mentioned Gail Cohen at all?"

"No, why?"

"I was wondering how he's doing. I'll be honest. There's some weird shit going on with that case. Vic Womble sent over a copy of the coroner's report."

"Well, are you going to tell me or…"

"Franklin has this theory that those ravens may have tried attacking her when she was in her car. We found images of birds on the windshield and passenger windows, just like the ones on the glass door in her apartment."

"So, they were already chasing her on the streets?"

"Looks that way. She must've made it into the parking structure and headed up to her apartment. Anyway, her vehicle is in the impound. It's a nice car. Always had a soft spot for black Bimmers."

Sarah's heart skipped a beat, and she pressed the phone closer to her ear.

"Lou, can I ask you something? Is the car by any chance a 328i?"

"Yeah. How'd you know?"

"And did you find red paint on the right front wheel?"

"Are you messing with me?"

"I think I know who broke into our offices that night a few weeks ago. Gail Cohen."

"What?"

"She followed me, Lou. I only lost her because I saw Tim Whatley and stopped. I'm sure it was her. Same car."

"Weird. Well, I can think of better ways to die, other than having your eyes pecked out."

"Her eyes…" Sarah said, her voice distant.

"Yeah. They were gone completely."

"Like Peter."

"What?"

"Nothing. I'll see you Friday, Lou."

"Sure. Night, Sarah. Safe travels."

After she disconnected, Sarah sat on her bed and tried imagining what it must have been like being blinded by a flock of wild birds. She pictured the raven who'd been watching her at Casa Abrigo. Long, spindly fingers of dread enfolded her in a cold embrace as the creature croaked at her, taunting her.

And promising her a slow, agonizing death.

Twenty-Two

By the time Sarah had arrived at the facility, signed in, and gone up to Colleen's room, she wished she could transport herself home where she would find Joe and Gary waiting for her. She would make a show of hurrying toward Joe, then scooping up the cat instead. Joe would be furious. But she was in Lawrence, not Dos Santos. Though she'd spent an awful night without much sleep, she and Carter were on the hook to complete their mission.

Sarah knocked once, and Owen Daniels answered almost immediately. He wore a grim expression that seemed to have aged him another ten years. Sarah felt sorry for him. It seemed all he had was his sister, and she was slipping away from him more and more each day.

"Is this a good time?" she said. "How's Colleen feeling?"

"A little dizzy. But mostly okay."

He stepped back, allowing the women to enter. They found Colleen Moody sitting in a simple wooden chair facing the window. Her head was bandaged, and a purple bruise darkened one side of her swollen face. The curtains were pulled back, and Sarah could see a lovely view of the garden below.

"Colleen dear," Owen said. "You have visitors."

"I don't talk to strangers when Morris isn't at home. You know that, Owen."

"Yes, I know. But they need to speak to you."

She brightened. "Is it about my daughter?"

Owen turned to the women, exasperated. Sarah and Carter exchanged a look, and Carter stepped toward the window. She knelt beside Colleen and took her hand.

"I wish I could have met Nicole," the girl said. "I'll bet she's a lovely girl."

The old woman smiled, her eyes misting. "She is. And I miss her so much. She ran away, you know."

"Yes, I do."

"I don't know what Morris and I were thinking. Taking her all the way out to California."

"To be with her cousins, I thought."

"Those three were like peas in a pod. And the girls. Everyone thought they were sisters. I remember they would have sleepovers. And they always made Peter stay in the living room in a little tent we'd bought him. The girls would sleep in Nicole's bed. Of course, instead of sleeping, they would giggle all night."

"What about Peter? Was he ever lonely?"

"Oh, no. He seemed to enjoy being by himself. Didn't he, Owen?"

"I suppose," he said.

Sarah noticed the old man's expression had darkened.

"There was the one time, though. When he tried sneaking into the girls' room."

Owen stood. "Colleen, don't."

Carter and Sarah stared at the old woman's brother.

"It wasn't Nicole's fault," the old woman said.

Her voice was sharp and defensive. Sarah moved closer, glancing at Owen.

"What wasn't?" Sarah said.

"She never encouraged him. My daughter was sweet and innocent. But that boy—he had the devil in him. He…"

Owen took his sister's hand and gave it a kiss. He turned to the women.

"I think she's had enough for today."

Outside, the air was crisp. Sarah and Carter walked through the garden slowly with Owen.

"I don't understand," Carter said. "What exactly did Peter do?"

The old man became incensed, the blue-green arteries in his aged neck throbbing with anger.

"*Do*? He was *naked*. Naked in front of those poor, innocent girls. And he… my sister claimed he was, you know. *Excited.*"

Sarah stopped and touched his arm. "I'm truly sorry, Owen. It wasn't our intention to bring up all these painful memories. But if that was the case, why did they allow Nicole to stay with the family in California, knowing what they knew about Peter?"

"Vivian insisted he'd changed. He'd been seeing a family therapist, and they took him to church every Sunday. He made his Confirmation.

"I'm sure if Colleen had to do it over again… But you see, Nicole was in trouble. And she missed her cousin Hannah so much."

When he looked at them again, his eyes were glistening. Though Sarah didn't want to put the old man through any more pain, she felt she needed to get what they had come here for.

"Owen, one more question before we leave. The last

time we spoke, you said Hannah returned to Lawrence with her brother. Do you know where we can reach her?"

"No, I'm sorry. When she turned eighteen, she told Colleen she'd decided to get a job. You see, her parents had left Peter and her some money. She bought a car, packed her things, and moved out. She promised to stay in touch, but we never heard from her again."

"Okay, thanks."

Carter gave him a hug. "Thank you for everything, Owen."

He wiped away a tear with a calloused finger. "I hope you learn the truth about Peter's parents."

"So do we," Sarah said. "And we're both very sorry about Nicole."

"It's the not knowing, you see. When she called that one time—"

"Wait," Carter said. "Nicole called? After she ran away?"

"Sorry I didn't mention it before. Mind's not what it used to be. Yes, she called Colleen once. About a week after her disappearance. Said she was fine but wouldn't tell my sister where she was. We never heard from her after that."

"I see," Sarah said. "Thank you again, Owen."

They left him in the garden. As they walked off toward the parking lot, Owen Daniels sat on a lonely park bench, the dead leaves of fall swirling at his feet, and wept the tears of an age.

On the ride back to their hotel, Sarah thought again about everything Owen and his sister had told them. It was clear Peter was disturbed, and it made sense that he would kill himself. But they were no closer to finding Hannah or discovering the true identity of the girl who'd died. Though she'd been sure it was Hannah, she was willing to concede that it might have been Nicole after all. But that wasn't possible either, since the girl had communicated with her mother after her disappearance. Could the dead girl have been a stranger after all? She glanced at Carter, who was reading something on her phone.

"So, any ideas how we track down Hannah?"

"I dunno. Maybe hire a private detective?"

"Not sure Lou would approve. I feel sorry for them, you know? Owen and his sister?"

Carter realized she was still wearing her fake glasses and, taking them off, rubbed the bridge of her nose.

"I know what you mean. That family has gone through so much. I wish we could…"

"What?"

"I was thinking. Where did Peter kill himself? It wasn't at home, right?"

"No. Owen would've said something. Oh, no." Sarah slapped her forehead. "The *dream*."

"What dream?"

"Two nights ago. And it was more of a vision."

Sarah checked her rearview mirror and turned off at the next exit. When it was safe, she pulled over and parked.

"Carter, he did it in a hotel room. Some flophouse, from what I could tell."

"Should we check it out? I know it doesn't get us any closer to finding Hannah, but it might be a start."

"I'm right there with you, sista." Sarah closed her eyes. "I saw a sign outside the window. It was glowing. The words… *The Tap House*. I'm sure of it."

Carter opened Google Maps and did a search. "Oh my God, here it is. It's on Massachusetts Street."

"We need the hotel that's next to it. What time is it?"

"Almost eleven."

"How far?"

"Looks like ten minutes."

"I say we check it out and, if what we find isn't too gross, we get something to eat after."

Carter laughed. "Always thinking ahead. The way you eat, and yet you're so skinny."

Sarah started the engine and got back on the road. "A five-mile run every day and a strict wine and scotch diet. You should try it."

"Maybe I will."

Sarah and Carter stood on the sidewalk, staring up at the gleaming office building. Though part of the street was dotted with run-down storefronts—mostly closed—it looked as if the area was gradually recovering. To their right stood an upscale bar called The Tap House. It looked to Sarah like the type of watering hole businessmen and lawyers frequented.

Carter happened to glance to her right. Slowly, she reached over and tugged on Sarah's sleeve. As Sarah turned, she could see the bloodied bodies of what looked like men and teenage boys in nineteenth century clothes littering the street as cars blindly plowed through them, unaware.

"Lawrence Massacre?" Sarah said.

"I think so."

"Perfect."

They looked away and focused on the building in front of them. Sarah sighed dramatically.

"Well, we're not going to learn anything in there."

When she turned around to face the street, she noticed a tiny, run-down pawn shop that still appeared to be in business. She looked at Carter.

"Worth a shot, I guess."

They went to the corner and crossed the street. When they reached the shop, Sarah opened the glass door and heard the sound of a little tinkling bell. *How quaint.*

Inside, the air was stale, and Sarah could detect a faint odor of old books and man-sweat. Though the floor looked clean, the room was stuffed with cases and cases of old cameras, cassette players, binoculars, and assorted bric-a-brac. There didn't seem to be any organization to the merchandise. It was almost as if everything had remained where it landed.

Behind the counter, a man who looked to be in his mid-twenties, with pale hair and stubble, was examining a vintage comic book in a plastic sleeve. Sarah tilted her head at Carter, signaling her to take this one.

"Excuse me?" Carter said.

At first, the man ignored her. When he looked up and saw the girl, he broke into a huge, toothy grin.

"H-Hey."

"Hi. Um, my friend and I are looking for some information."

The man glanced at Sarah, who was examining an assortment of vintage ladies' watches.

"What kind of information?"

"See that building across the street?" Carter said, pointing. "Didn't there used to be a hotel there?"

"Uh, I guess?"

"Well, we're trying to find out about a man who, um, may have killed himself in one of the rooms. This would've been in 1993."

"Well, I was born in 1990, so."

"Are you the owner?" Sarah said, joining her friend.

"Naw, that's my *papous*. Hey, maybe *he* knows something. He's owned this store for, like, forty years."

"Is he around?"

"Yeah, he's in the back. Want me to get 'im?"

Carter smiled at the clueless clerk. "That would be great."

"Huh-huh. Okay, I'll be right back."

"Looks like you made a new friend," Sarah said.

"*So* not my type."

In a moment, a man of around seventy with male pattern baldness, greasy reading glasses, and a paunch stepped out. Sarah noticed the baggy black suit pants and starched white shirt with the sleeves rolled up, and guessed he might be an immigrant. When he spoke, his heavy Greek accent sealed the deal.

"I am Nikolas. My grandson said you wanted to ask me question?"

Sarah and Carter exchanged a look. They dug out their reporter IDs and showed them to the shop owner. After introducing themselves, Sarah took the lead.

"We're doing a story that involves a man who killed himself in the hotel that used to be across the street."

"Yes, I remember. This was many years ago. Nineteen-ninety…"

"Three."

"Yes. Terrible. That hotel had a bad reputation. But it was good for business. People always pawning things for drug money. They tear it down four years ago. Now, only rich business types over there.

"No one needs a pawn shop. I try to get my grandson interested in taking over so I can retire, but all he can think about is video games and girls."

On cue, the slacker poked his head out from the back and grinned at Carter. She avoided his gaze.

"*Papou*, where do you keep the duct tape?"

"Bottom shelf on the left."

"Thanks."

Rolling his eyes, the old man continued. "My wife don't want me to work anymore. She is not feeling so good these days."

"I'm sorry," Sarah said, getting impatient. "Getting back to the suicide."

"Oh, yes. Very sad. They said that guy took his own eyes out before slitting his throat. Who would do such a thing?"

"Did he ever come in here?"

"Yes, he did. Bought only one item."

"What was that?" Carter said.

Nikolas disappeared behind one of the display cases. When he returned, he was holding something long, black in the middle, and shiny at both ends. Carefully, as if handling explosives, he set it down on the glass counter.

"What is that?"

Sarah paled. "It's a melon baller." She stared at the old man. "Is this the one he used to, to…? You know."

"No. There were two. Other one end up with the police. Evidence, I guess."

Carter had picked up the instrument and was examining its silver bowl, which made Sarah wince.

"It's almost exactly the same size as a human eye."

The old man laughed hoarsely. "This was what the woman said."

Sarah touched his arm. "'The woman'?"

"Yes. That man come in with some woman. Young and pretty. Blonde. Nice legs. I think she was his girlfriend."

"Hannah," Sarah said to Carter. Then, to the shop

owner, "Did they say anything else? Like where they were going or…"

"No, nothing. Pay in cash and leave."

"I see. Well, thank you. This has been very helpful."

"Anytime. You're reporters. Sure you don't need a camera, maybe? Or a tape recorder? Everything is thirty percent off."

"No, we're good," Carter said, and they left the store.

Outside on the street, the girl took a deep breath of Kansas air. "So, The Tap House for lunch?"

"Why not? I wonder if they have fresh melon on the menu."

"Good one."

But Sarah hadn't meant the remark to be funny. In fact, seeing that instrument had filled her with a dread that clung to her bones like kudzu, or the supernatural bird-storm that had been responsible for Gail Cohen's death. And the woman? It *was* Hannah, she was sure of it.

Hours later, she and Carter were on a plane bound for LAX. Sarah hoped flying at thirty-five thousand feet would prevent any visions from piercing the first-class cabin she'd been upgraded to.

Hildy knocked softly and entered to tuck in Colleen for the night. But instead of finding the old woman in the chair she always occupied by the window, the aide found her on the bed face up and still. Terrified, Hildy rushed over.

Colleen was breathing—thank God. Her eyes were open wide in sheer terror. She tried speaking but could only manage to babble incoherently.

"Colleen, what happened? Are you all right?"

"Here."

"What?"

"He was here."

She looked at the aide, petrified by the presence of some unseen intruder. Despite her uneasiness, Hildy checked the closet, bathroom, and draperies, and found nothing out of the ordinary.

"Who? Your brother?"

"No. *Him.*"

Hildy helped the old woman into a sitting position and propped her up against the headboard with two large pillows for support. She went into the bathroom and filled a glass with water. When she offered it, the old woman pushed it away.

"Colleen, did someone…try and hurt you?"

"Yes."

"But who was it? There's no one here."

Colleen took the glass and drank. Swallowing hard, she looked at the aide, her eyes like two cold flames.

"It was my nephew. It was Peter."

———

By the time Sarah got to her house, it was after 1 a.m.—too late to call Joe. So, she settled for having Gary in her bed with her. At first, she couldn't sleep. She kept thinking about the pawn shop and that cursed melon baller. Eventually, the sound of Gary's gentle purring relaxed her, and she drifted off.

When she opened her eyes, she found herself moving down a dark corridor that smelled of mildew. Was she sleepwalking? The dark carpet with the faded floral pattern looked threadbare in places. Faintly, she could hear the sounds of television sets behind closed doors, and she realized she was in that same run-down hotel. She didn't want to be here and tried going back. But as she reversed course, she met with a solid wall.

Continuing on, she reached a door with worn brass numbers that spelled 1408. She could hear whispering inside. Shaking, she forced herself to grab the doorknob. When she turned it, the door opened easily. Inside, she found Peter Moody sitting on the bed, naked. He was saying something she couldn't understand. On the nightstand there was an offering bowl and a dagger with a black handle.

Hannah walked in from the bathroom, wearing a sheer white nightgown. She looked so grown up now. The light from the grimy window illuminated her breasts under the fabric. She was holding something, but Sarah couldn't see what it was. Unable to look away, she watched as Hannah approached her brother and mounted him, her eyes looking at the ceiling as she undulated her hips rhythmically.

Peter continued chanting, and soon, he grimaced in a prolonged shudder of sexual release. Hannah raised her left hand. The melon baller she was holding gleamed in the weak light. Instinctively, Sarah reached her hand out, trying to stop what was about to happen. But it was no use. Hannah kissed Peter full on the lips and, saying something unintelligible, plucked out his right eye in one swift motion. She did the same to the left. Though Peter didn't scream, Sarah could tell he was crying as his sister pressed his bloody face against her breasts and stroked his hair.

Now, Hannah reached over and picked up the offering bowl. She placed the severed eyes inside and grabbed the knife. Sarah tried screaming, but nothing came out. Peter took up his chanting again, and Hannah joined him. She lifted his head and, placing the bowl under his chin, watched calmly as he took the knife and slit his throat. The dark blood flowed into the bowl, droplets splashing on Hannah's nightgown. When the bowl was full, she stood and, leaving her brother to bleed out on the bed, stared at the yellow moonlight pouring through the hotel window.

The scene in front of Sarah seemed to be getting smaller, and soon, the hotel room was a pinpoint of light. As she opened her eyes again, she found herself safe in her bed. She felt exhausted and couldn't bring herself to cry.

Twenty-Three

LOU FIORE FINISHED his coffee and set the cup on the floor. He was feeling sleep-deprived and wished he could lick the rest of the dark brown sediment off the bottom of the paper cup, but he was worried Vic Womble might say something. Sighing, he leaned back in his chair as Franklin Chestnut used a pointer to refer to the radiographs on the light box.

Lou wondered whether Sarah was awake yet. He was aware she'd gotten in late, and was anxious to talk to her about what else she and Carter had learned in Lawrence. Instead, he had to endure a morning with Vic, although admittedly, it was generous of the homicide detective to have invited him to the briefing.

"And you're certain no human could've done this," Womble said. He was chewing on his pen again, something Lou knew he'd picked up after quitting smoking.

Franklin shook his head. "Not a hundred percent. I suppose someone could've fashioned a pair of gloves with sharp instruments…"

"Like Freddy Krueger?" Lou said, grinning.

He nudged Vic, but the dour cop wasn't having it.

"My point being," Vic said, "we can rule out homicide as the manner of death."

Franklin nodded. "Unless somehow you can prove that these were trained birds."

"Still," Lou said. "I've never known a flock of ravens to attack anyone like that."

"It is unusual, I'll admit." Franklin smiled. "But not unprecedented."

Vic was squinting at one of the X-rays and scratching the corner of his moustache. He glanced at Lou and turned to the coroner.

"Frank, are you saying this has happened before?"

Franklin grinned. "As a matter of fact."

"What?" Lou said.

"Something about the raven attack kept nagging at me. I had my assistant do a search in our database, and we got a hit."

He crossed to the last X-ray and pointed. Both cops squinted at the spot.

"This isn't Gail Cohen. It's a man who was found murdered in *your* neck of the woods, Lou."

"When was this?"

"1970."

"Have you got the autopsy report?" Vic said.

"Right here. Made you each a copy."

Lou pored over the photos. A man estimated to be in his mid-fifties had been found nude in the forest, partially eaten by wild animals. His face and neck showed signed of a vicious bird attack. And like Gail Cohen, his eyes had been pecked out. According to the report, he'd been dead for days. No one knew who he was, and no one had filed a missing person report. An unlucky local family had discovered the body while on a nature hike with their dog.

"Whaddya think, Lou?" Vic said.

"Looks like another cold case. I'd ask Sarah to look into it, but I don't need her distracted right now." Then, to Franklin, "Who else have you shared this information with?"

"Well, it's in the official report, so everyone."

"Okay. Vic, I'll see what I can find out, but it looks like you've got a helluva mystery on your hands."

"Sarah Greene may come in handy after all," the coroner said to Vic.

"Whaddya mean, Doc?"

"Old Testament. Jeremiah 7:33. 'And the carcasses of this people shall be food for the fowls of the heaven, and for the beasts of the earth; and none shall frighten them away.'"

Lou looked at Franklin Chestnut with a serious expression. "I know that verse. It's about dealing with the wicked in Gehenna."

"I'm impressed."

"Eight years of Catholic school. Frank, are you saying the attack on Gail Cohen might have been *punishment*?"

"I'm saying, as a pathologist, I don't have a good explanation."

Womble rubbed the back of his neck. "I'm not making this into something. I guess we leave it as undetermined." Then, to Franklin, "You'll support me on this?"

Franklin sighed. He'd been excited to make the connection and wanted to pursue an investigation. On the other hand, he was well aware there would be no way of ever proving that something supernatural was responsible.

"I won't change my report. Undetermined it is."

"Thanks, Frank."

Lou was disappointed. He knew in his gut other forces were at work. And he also knew Vic felt it, too. Vic was a good cop—very thorough. Maybe he was tired and wanted nothing more than to put a bow on this one and move on to the next thing.

"Thanks for everything, Frank," Lou said.

Vic shook the coroner's hand. "Yeah, thanks."

Outside next to Lou's vehicle, Vic spoke to Lou in low tones. Lou knew the man well enough to read the signs. He was unsure.

"Things like this just don't happen," Womble said. "People die. But it's usually by accident or foul play."

"That's been my experience. I have to say, though, Vic. After working with Sarah, I'm starting to see things differently. We can't explain everything using science. And I think we're going to have to leave ourselves open to…other possibilities. But hey, this is your case. You do what you feel is best."

The men shook hands and said goodbye. On the way back to his office, Lou decided he wasn't going to let this lie. Something was going on—something unexplained. He decided he would call Kyle Jeffers to see if he might remember anything about that dead man in the woods. But first, he needed coffee. Bad.

———

It was almost nine when Sarah opened her eyes. She was beyond exhausted. She thought again about calling Joe, knowing he'd be there in a heartbeat. But she felt conflicted, wanting to be with him yet not wanting to watch as her best friend made his way through a new series of romantic entanglements. They'd done that already, but back then, they were just good friends. And now?

She couldn't bear the thought of seeing him with other women. But what had she thought? That they would keep going the way they were forever? Till death do us part? As her sister had rightly pointed out, might as well be married.

Thankfully, there hadn't been any more nightmares—only dreamless sleep. She could hear Gary padding into the room. A moment later, a thump as the cat landed on the bed and began purring loudly.

"You know where your food is."

He rubbed his head on her hand, encouraging her to get out of bed.

She closed her eyes. "I'm sleeping."

He began maowing urgently and kneading his paws on her stomach.

"Fine. Come here, you."

She picked him up and scratched behind his ear. Yawning, she set him gently on the floor and got out of bed. When she checked her phone, she was surprised at how late it was. She needed coffee and remembered Carter was working today. She would head over to The Cracked Pot, then to the office to speak to Rachel about her bizarre encounter with Michael Peterson. Later, she would try seeing Joe, maybe for lunch.

Her phone went off, startling her as it vibrated in her hand. Lou. Shit, she'd forgotten all about him.

"Hi, Lou." She faked a yawn. "Yeah, pretty late. I know. Give me an hour and we can meet at The Cracked Pot, okay?"

Still dragging, she took out underwear from a dresser drawer and picked out a "day off" outfit from her closet, which involved jeans, boots, and her beloved leather jacket. She contemplated a biscuit-colored, long-sleeved silk shirt that looked great on her. But then, she remembered how it could've used another button at the top. That together with Lou's occasional wandering eye made her rethink the outfit. She went for a high-neck wool sweater that screamed church lady.

"So much for my life being my own," she said to the cat, and went to take a shower.

Joe peered at the spreadsheet on his laptop. Day by day, their profit margin on the property was shrinking, mostly due to the mishaps and destructive occurrences that had plagued the project since they began. He adjusted himself in his chair and scooted closer to the small wood table he'd brought into the kitchen at Casa Abrigo that served as his remote office.

Over the years, Joe had heard his share of strange stories. Mostly from other realtors. Dos Santos had a history—a bad one. And there were bound to be bodies in the closet, although thankfully, *he* had never discovered one in any house he'd purchased at auction. Well, until now.

He recalled when he first moved here and began researching the town's history in the local library. The town's founder, John Dos Santos, had been a war hero. Yet, inexplicably, he and the men he served with were buried not at the Santa Barbara mission with the other important families but at what was at that time a paupers' grave without dignity or fanfare.

Old newspaper articles had hinted at "shady doings" by Dos Santos. Questionable real estate deals and dark scandals involving young, unmarried women and, in several cases, teenage boys. And there were rumors of Satanism. Add to that everything that was happening at Casa Abrigo. Was the town, in fact, cursed? Joe didn't believe in curses. He was having a string of bad luck, he told himself.

Manny came up the stairs from the cellar and got himself a cold Jarritos from the ice chest.

"Any luck getting that stain out?" Joe said.

"Not much. Come have a look."

Joe followed him down. The cellar looked immaculate. The boys had finished staining all the wine racks. The room had been freshly painted, and the windows sparkled. Manny waved and led Joe into the small storage room. They had replaced the bare bulb with a beautiful mahogany bronze four-light pendant. His heart sinking, Joe stared at the smoky black stain on the floor. It was in the shape of a narrow rectangle and located at the very spot where the mirror had stood. The stone was still wet and Manny's cleaning implements lay nearby.

"It's in the stone, boss."

"What do you mean, *in* the stone?"

"I mean, I've been scrubbing that *mancha* for, like, an hour, and *nada*. I think maybe we need to replace it."

"Did you try the acid?"

"Yes. It lightened it a little. There, you can see where I put it."

Joe got down on one knee to get a better look. He momentarily lost his balance and pressed a hand to the floor to steady himself. What he felt surprised him. He looked up at Manny.

"It's warm."

"Madre de Dios," Manny said, and made the Sign of the Cross.

———

As Carter refilled Sarah's cup, Lou drained the last of his double espresso and pushed the demitasse and saucer aside.

"Want another one?" Carter said.

"No. Maybe some water."

"Sure thing."

Sarah squeezed Carter's hand before she went off. They hadn't caught up since arriving back in Santa Barbara. She felt it should have been the *three* of them meeting to talk about their trip. But her friend was working today, and it wouldn't look good her taking a seat to join them. She hoped Carter wouldn't be too butt-hurt about it.

She stared at the double order of crispy bacon sitting untouched on her plate. She hadn't had her run yet today and had decided to stick to protein and caffeine. She grabbed a slice, broke it in two, and chomped on it. When she looked up, Lou was smiling at her.

"What? Do you want some?"

"No. I guess I'm amazed that with all this going on, you can still eat."

"What can I say? I'm a nervous eater." Thank God she'd decided to wear the sweater. So far, the police chief was playing it cool.

Lou had been discreet about bringing autopsy photos into the restaurant and had only brought along two. One was a close-up of Gail Cohen's face, and the other was a similar shot of the unidentified man in the forest. Sarah compared them.

"The marks do look similar," she said.

"I spoke to Kyle Jeffers, and he told me that in the case of the John Doe he personally never ruled out homicide. But they were never able to collect enough evidence. And back then, there were no DNA tests, so they couldn't identify him."

"So, they file it under animal attack and call it a day?"

"Pretty much."

She smiled. "Well, you could try sweet-talking your

buddy the judge over in Santa Barbara and get another exhumation order."

"Forget it. Besides, this man's body was cremated." He handed her a slip of paper.

"What's this?"

"It's from the Old Testament. Frank seems to think there may be a supernatural element to these killings."

"I thought it was birds."

"That's how the final report will read. Vic doesn't want to prolong the investigation."

She smiled. "But you think otherwise?"

He looked away, a little embarrassed. "Maybe you're rubbing off on me."

No longer hungry, Sarah pushed aside her bacon, picked up the coffee cup, and held it in both hands.

"Hey, Lou. I'm sorry we couldn't get more information for you. But at least we know Hannah was probably with her brother before he killed himself."

"Which means it's likely she's alive. May I?" He reached over and helped himself to Sarah's plate.

"Be my guest."

He crammed the rest of the thick-cut bacon into his mouth. Sarah noticed Lou's lips shiny with grease. It occurred to her that men eating was not attractive. In fact, eating in general wasn't, and she wondered how distasteful *she* looked when putting food in her gob. No wonder some women ate very little on dates. Why was she thinking about dates? *Sarah...*

"Lou, I've been thinking. If Hannah *is* alive, then who's the ghost that's been plaguing me?"

"I dunno. What about the cousin?"

"Nicole? Unfortunately, no. She made a call to her mother a week after disappearing."

"Maybe Peter Moody picked someone up. You know, a

runaway. It would've been easy for him to lure someone to the house with the promise of food and a place to stay. Maybe even drugs."

"But why does the ghost look so much like Hannah?"

"Okay, how about this? We know he was having sex with his sister. Maybe he was looking to change it up a little."

"Not sure what you mean."

"I'm talking about a twin fantasy. He could've found a runaway that looked like Hannah."

"What is it with men and twins?"

Lou coughed uncomfortably. "I'm sure I don't know."

"And anyway, why would he kill her?"

"She didn't want to play along?"

"Maybe."

"What about that other lead?" he said, wiping his mouth with a napkin. Didn't you say Peter Moody made a friend in that mental hospital?"

"Yes, supposedly. Dr. Martin is checking on it. But I don't expect anything to come of it."

"Oh, almost forgot," he said. "We have an appointment tomorrow morning in Burbank with your friends from *Dubious*. To be honest, I'm a little surprised. I mean, aren't they—?"

"Arrogant asshats? Yeah, I was pretty surprised, too. Maybe I should hide a little hex bag in their offices and see what happens."

"Don't even joke about a thing like that."

"Not to worry, Lou. I'm Catholic, remember? Too much guilt to pull a stunt like that."

When they were finished, Sarah waited for Lou to leave and went to find Carter. She walked back toward the restrooms and, as expected, found the girl having a smoke outside.

"Sorry about not including you," Sarah said.

"It's okay."

"You're not mad?"

"No, why should I be? What did Lou think of our little expedition?"

"Too many unanswered questions. Oh, and now he's developed this theory that Peter Moody was living out a twin fantasy by bringing home a stray."

"Ew."

"Take a look at this." Sarah handed her the autopsy photos.

"God, their eyes."

"The other victim was a man who died years before. Ever seen anything like it?"

Carter dropped her cigarette butt and crushed it. She took a closer look. Sarah noticed the delicate line of Carter's jaw and the high cheekbones. With better hair, she'd be a knockout. Why would a girl hide her beauty? She handed Carter the slip of paper.

"Jeremiah," Sarah said. "Guess in those days they were big into death by bird."

"I think I remember this verse. I took a world religion class at Berkeley, and we studied the Old Testament. Well, parts of it. And you think the—"

"Ravens."

"These ravens are acting as punishment? What in the world was Gail Cohen into to deserve that kind of death?"

"No idea," Sarah said. "But I do know someone who might be able to shed some light on it."

"Who?"

"Fr. Brian Donnelly." Then, to herself, "Guess I'm seeing my old pal sooner than I thought."

"A priest? Good idea."

"Want to come?"

"You bet. I get off at three."

"I'll pick you up."

Sarah's phone vibrated. Though she didn't recognize the number, the area code looked familiar, and she decided to answer.

"Hello? Sarah Greene."

There was a pause. Then, a voice she immediately recognized as Owen Daniels's came on.

"Sarah?"

"Yes, Owen. How are you? Is everything okay with—?"

"Colleen passed away last night."

"*What?* Hang on, I'm putting you on speaker. Carter's here with me."

She pressed a button and held the phone horizontally in front of her, as if offering it to some invisible guest.

"Go ahead, Owen."

"It was her heart. I think… She, she seems to have had a bad fright."

"Did she say what…"

"Said it was her nephew. They insisted it must've been a dream. But she was adamant."

The old man described how the aide had found her alive and notified the on-staff doctor. They had given Colleen a sedative. When someone came to check on her in the morning, they found she was not breathing. She had been dead for hours. The women could hear the old man choking back a sob.

"She was so scared. I'm making funeral arrangements and wanted to let you know."

"I'm glad you did."

"I found an old photo album in Colleen's room. I'm sending it to you. Thought it might help you with your research."

"Thank you."

"Owen, we're so sorry," Carter said, and looked at Sarah. "We're sending flowers, okay? Can you give us the address of the mortuary?"

"I'll text it to you later. Thank you, ladies."

The man was so formal, it broke Sarah's heart. Before she could say goodbye, he disconnected. As she stood staring at the phone, she thought over what Colleen had said about seeing Peter. Then, she recalled what the girl in the mirror had told her.

Not dead.

Twenty-Four

"I was so scared, Sarah."

Rachel was sitting at her desk, an untouched chai latte sitting in front of her. Sarah sat across from her sister, watching her intently. She remembered when they were teenagers. She was fifteen; Rachel was thirteen. It was right after Alyssa's funeral. Something had changed after the girl's death. Sarah no longer saw Rachel as the annoying little sister, and from then on, she became Rachel's protector. She'd already lost her mother and her best friend. Could it be she was afraid of losing her sister, too?

Soon, Rachel was going everywhere with Sarah. Dances, football games, the mall. Just as Alyssa had done, Rachel spent hours in Sarah's room, and eventually, Sarah found she had a best friend again. Somewhere along the line, boys started noticing Rachel, and her big sister was there to keep them in line. By the time Sarah went off to UCSB, Rachel knew how to look after herself. At Santa Barbara City College, she met her future husband, Paul, who, after a successful dinner at the family home, received Sarah's stamp of approval—and Eddie's blessing.

Sarah reached out her hand and took her sister's. "Your tea is getting cold."

"Oh." Rachel took a sip. "It's good."

"Did Michael threaten you?"

"That's just it. It wasn't anything he said or did. Maybe I was imagining the whole thing. It was dark, and I was alone in the office."

"But you sensed something was wrong."

"Yes."

"You should never ignore that feeling."

Sarah thought back to how oddly Michael had behaved at the singles' dance when Fr. Donnelly arrived. And then, his interest in buying Casa Abrigo. Coincidence? That house was too big for one person. What was he *really* up to?

"Sarah?"

"Sorry, what?"

"I said, what do you think we should do? I mean, nothing happened."

"I'll talk to Joe. One thing's for sure, I don't want you or Blanca staying late anymore."

"Well, I'm sure Katy will love seeing me on time for dinner."

Sarah stood and opened the door. "I need to run some errands."

"Have you seen Joe yet today?"

"No. He's on my to-do list." Sarah turned to go.

"Hey, sis?"

"Yeah?"

"Thanks. I mean it."

"No problemo," Sarah said.

Talking to her sister had upset her in ways that surprised her. Why would Michael Peterson want to harm Rachel? She left before her sister could see the threatening tears.

———

Sarah jogged her way up San Marcos Pass Road at a steady clip toward Casa Abrigo. She'd decided she needed to clear her head, and the best way to do that was to go for a run. She could feel the rising road in her calves and picked up her pace, all the while keeping an eye out for loose gravel. Once, she'd stepped on a rock and was laid up for a month with a torn tendon.

The trees looked darker up here against the graying sky. Or was that her imagination? It was definitely colder than at her house. In a clearing, something glowed faintly. Probably a patch of sunlight that had made its way through the thick cloak of clouds that promised rain.

She could see the house at the top of the rise. Stark, threatening. Joe's truck was parked outside with the others, and the sight filled her with happiness. She'd missed him so much and completely forgot her feelings of caution toward him. Heading toward the house, she decided to continue on instead. She hadn't run in several days, and she wanted to get back into shape. Another five miles wouldn't kill her.

As she made her way through the forest, she could hear the wind rushing through the trees and the distant croaking of a raven. She followed a well-worn trail leading to Devil's Bluff, where she would enjoy the view for a few minutes, then return to Casa Abrigo. She was sure she could con Joe into driving her home.

Other than the wind, the forest was strangely quiet. Pacing herself, she continued on toward the Santa Ynez River. Three more miles. She could hear the faint sound of rushing water. Now she thought she heard wings beating.

The last time she'd heard that sound, it was at the public storage facility when she and Joe went to visit the mirror.

The trees opened up into a clearing, and she could see Devil's Bluff. It felt warmer, and she removed her hoodie, revealing the T-shirt she'd received at last year's Pier to Peak Half-Marathon. Breathing hard, she approached the precipice and stood looking out at the beauty surrounding her. She checked her pulse. A flock of ravens streaked across the sky, croaking angrily, sending a jolt of fear through her. A noise startled her. It sounded like a rush of wind.

Before she could turn around, she felt something driving her forward. She was already dangerously close to the edge and cried out. Thinking fast, she darted sideways, turned, and began running away from the cliff. Something invisible was pursuing her—she could sense it—and it terrified her. As she approached a fallen tree, another strong push drove her down. She didn't have time to scream and fell forward onto the tree. Excruciating pain tore through her side, and for a moment, she couldn't catch her breath. Silently, she prayed to St. Michael.

When she recovered her senses, Sarah found she was lying next to the gigantic log in a chaparral bed of scrub oak and wild lilac. She could feel something wet on her face, and when she went to touch it, she found blood. She sat up and checked her arms and legs. Nothing broken, thank God. *My ribs.* She was in agony. Her heart was beating rapidly and, rather than risk hurting herself further, she decided to call Joe. It took him only a few minutes to maneuver his truck to where she was sitting.

"Sarah? What happened?"

"I'm not sure. Help me up."

He extended his hand. When she'd gotten to her feet, she let out a loud moan.

"Where does it hurt?" he said.

"My side."

"I'm taking you to emergency."

"No, I'm okay. The pain has lessened."

"Take a deep breath." She did as he asked. "I'm going to have a look."

"Playing doctor, are we?"

"Be quiet."

Gently, he pulled up her T-shirt, exposing her bare midriff. The area on one side looked badly bruised. Gingerly, he probed it.

"One a scale of one to ten?"

"Maybe a six."

"Okay. *Carefully* twist your body from side to side."

He watched as she followed his instruction.

"Well, I don't think you broke any ribs. Come on, let's get you up to the house."

"This is why most people hate exercise, you know," Sarah said, leaning on Joe's shoulder as she adjusted her shoe. When she looked up at him again, she noticed he was staring at something.

"What is it?"

He pointed to a branch that had broken off, leaving a sharp point sticking straight up out of the log.

"You could've lost an eye," he said.

"That's a comforting thought. Oh, my hoodie."

She pointed off somewhere, and he went to retrieve it. Then, he helped her into the truck.

"What happened anyway?" he said, turning the vehicle around and heading back.

"Do you want the truth? Or should I cop to being a klutz?"

"The truth."

"Something pushed me."

"What? You mean, like an animal, or…"

"No. Something *invisible*. Joe, please don't give me that look. It sounded like wind. First, it tried shoving me over the cliff. I ran, but it knocked me down."

At the house, they made their way toward the front door. Sarah found she was limping and realized she must've injured her knee, too. Nothing a nice hot shower wouldn't fix, though.

As they reached the open front door, Joe stopped her and laid his hands on her shoulders. He was about to say something when he smiled sadly and pressed her close to him. Surprised and happy, she held him. Looking up, she kissed him, leaving a blood smear on his face. Laughing, she wiped it off with the sleeve of her hoodie.

"Maybe now is not the time to bring up the budget," he said.

"Bad?"

"The good news is, we're way ahead on the other properties."

"And the bad?"

"We're taking it in the shorts here. Feel up to seeing the cellar?"

"I guess."

Overcoming her fear, Sarah walked into the storage room in the cellar and knelt on her good knee to examine the stain. It looked like someone had created it using charcoal, and she could see it was deeply embedded in the stone.

"This is where we found the mirror."

"Yeah. Sarah, I don't know what's going on. I mean, do we bring an exorcist in here, or what?"

"I'll speak to Fr. Brian about it. I'm seeing him later today." She reached her hand out behind her. "Give an old lady a hand, will ya?"

In the kitchen, Sarah grabbed a water from the cooler. As Joe applied a bandage to the cut on her face, she told him about the bible verse. Manny and the boys were at lunch, and it was just the two of them. The house was beautiful, and Sarah wished it was another *normal* property. But something dark had the place in its grasp—she could feel it. Maybe a blessing would help.

"I don't understand," Joe said. "A biblical punishment?"

"It's only a theory. I'm hoping Fr. Brian can help."

He sidled up to her and brought her in close. She loved his strength and readily succumbed.

"What are you doing, mister?"

"As long as you're seeing him, do you think you could get a preemptive Confession to cover tonight?"

She laughed. "A *preemptive* Confession?"

"Yeah. Because I want to come over tonight and, you know, take care of you."

"I see. So, you think I can store up Confessions like a bank and spend them as needed? Maybe I can ask Fr. Brian for a line of absolving credit. Get it?"

"Okay, never mind." He kissed her forehead and took a step back. "Can't blame a guy for trying. Come on, I'll drive you home. Sure you don't want to at least go to urgent care?"

"I'm fine, Joe."

"What about your knee?"

"I've had worse. Besides, I need to shower and change. I'm picking Carter up at three."

"I thought we could have lunch."

She hesitated. "You know, lunch would be great."

"Okay, I'll drive you home and meet you at—"

"The Japanese place. Rache and I went there the other day, and it's good."

"Whatever you say."

Sarah could hear the sound of vehicles outside, followed by laughing voices chattering in Spanish.

"Hey," she said. "I'd rather the guys didn't know about what happened. Let's leave it at I bumped my head, okay?"

"Sure."

Sarah and Joe left as Manny and his sons were walking in.

"Hey, guys," she said, hoping no one had noticed the bandage.

Sarah peeled off the bandage and examined the cut on her face. It had already closed, and she guessed she could cover it with makeup. She stepped into the steaming shower and let the soothing water pulse against her back. Since coming home, her whole body was feeling stiff. She would swallow a couple of ibuprofen tablets later, after she got some food in her. Taking her time, she washed using a new eucalyptus and tangerine body gel that was supposed to relieve stress. Maybe if they had seen fit to mix in some scotch, it would've worked. She was starting to feel better, though.

Stepping out, she used a soft bath towel to dry herself, then walked into her bedroom and put on her underwear and bra. Standing in front of her dresser mirror, she examined her injured side. Turning sideways, she froze. On her shoulder blade was a large, dark bruise that resembled— no, it couldn't be.

A *hand*.

Sarah pulled in front of The Cracked Pot and parked to

wait for Carter. It was after three. The girl was probably changing. While Sarah waited, she thought about Joe. Seeing him again at lunch had been a comfort. She had decided not to say anything about the bruising on her back. Instead, they discussed what to do about the incident with Michael Peterson. Since nothing had happened, they decided not to say anything to Lou. Joe advised Sarah not to contact Michael and to wait and see if he made an appearance again.

Carter walked out, wearing jeans and a Free People top and carrying a cute Lululemon black duffel. Grinning, she tossed her bag into the backseat and climbed in on the passenger side.

"I can't get over this car," Carter said. "Makes me wish I knew how to drive a stick."

"I could teach you."

"Maybe someday. So, is the priest expecting us?"

"Yeah, although I didn't go into any details on the phone."

Traffic was light, and it only took a few minutes to get into Santa Barbara. Sarah parked on the street near the church, and they walked in. School had already let out, and the campus was deserted. As they made their way toward the office, Carter happened to glance across the street at the field. Looking away, she followed Sarah into the building.

Inside, the assistant, Mrs. Ivy, was nowhere in sight.

"Fr. Brian?" Sarah said.

The priest's door was partially open, and she could hear two voices. Then, "Come on in, Sarah."

Sarah walked in first and was disconcerted to find Harlan Covington sitting in front of the desk. When he saw the women, he rose and smiled, sending a chill down Sarah's spine.

"Ms. Greene," he said, extending his hand. "Nice to see you again."

Reluctantly, Sarah took it, noticing again the onyx ring.

"Mr. Covington. This is my friend, Carter Wittgenstein."

When the introductions were finished, Sarah said to Fr. Donnelly, "I wasn't aware you two knew each other."

Fr. Donnelly forced a chuckle. "Harlan and I go way back. He is a very generous donor. I've been trying to convince him to replace that dodgy furnace of ours."

"I'll see to it right away, Brian," the old man said. "Now, I must run. Ladies?"

Sarah watched as he walked out, his back straight and his step sure. Although he'd never done anything to her, there was something about him. What was the word? Arrogant? No. Something else. When the three of them were alone, Sarah closed the door, and the women took seats across from the priest.

"You've got a problem with Harlan, Sarah?"

"Me? No. No problem. Well, okay. It's just that… Don't you think he's a tad…"

"Imperious?" Carter said, trying to suppress a grin.

"Oh my gosh, that's it exactly." Then, to Fr. Donnelly, "What she said."

"Well, he is a bit stodgy, I'll admit. From the old school. But so am I. And he's been a great friend to the Church."

"How long have you known him?" Sarah said, genuinely curious.

"Ooh, let me see. Well, as long as I've been at the parish. More than twenty-five years, I suppose."

"How did you meet?"

He smiled. "Another time." Then, to Carter. "Are you Jewish, Carter?"

"Me? No. I'm, um. Well, originally, my family was. But

with the anti-Semitism and such, they converted to Catholicism. I'm not really anything, though. Guess I never bought into the whole God thing. No offense."

Fr. Donnelly laughed. "'The whole God thing.'" Never heard it put quite like that. Well, prayer is a powerful arrow in your quiver, young lady. You might consider it one day."

Sarah had been observing Carter and noticed she wasn't in the least offended by the priest. In fact, she seemed fascinated. Leave it to an Irishman to charm the socks off a girl.

"So, Sarah, why have you two come?"

"Ah, business." She grabbed the manila envelope that was sitting next to her purse on the floor, removed the photos and bible verse, and slid them across the desk.

"Those photos are of two different victims who died almost fifty years apart. Both were attacked by birds. Ravens, to be precise."

"And what does Jeremiah have to do with it?"

Sarah glanced at Carter. "We're thinking maybe the deaths were…"

"Punishment?"

"Exactly."

The priest sat back. "Well, of course, the Old Testament God was a little less forgiving than Our Lord and Savior. Back when that verse was written, his chosen people—some of them—were arrogant. Many historians believe the kings of Judah sacrificed children to false gods at Gehenna and were therefore to be punished."

"By birds," Carter said.

"Yes. And the beasts of the earth. Just a minute. I think I have…"

He rose and went to a bookcase. Scanning the spines, he found what he wanted and returned to his desk.

"This is the old testament in Hebrew. I used to be quite fluent. Let's see."

Sarah and Carter waited patiently as Fr. Brian paged through the book.

"Ahh, here it is. *Vehayetah nivlat ha'am hazzeh, lema'achal, le'of hashamayim, ulevehemat ha'aretz; ve'ein, macharid.*"

Carter was looking intently at the photos. "So, if God doesn't do that sort of thing anymore, what about some evil entity carrying out a death sentence?"

"That's very astute," the priest said. "The devil can also visit punishment on those who offend him. You said one of the victims was recent?"

"She was found dead the other night in her apartment."

"Oh, yes. I remember reading about Gail Cohen."

"How did you— I mean, the police haven't released the name."

Fr. Donnelly stood. "Oh, I'm sure I saw her name somewhere. Well, if there's nothing else, I'm late for a school board meeting."

"Okay," Sarah said. She and Carter rose. "Well, thanks for seeing us, Fr. Brian."

"My pleasure. And nice meeting you, too, Carter. I hope we'll see more of you around here."

"Careful, Carter," Sarah said, laughing. "Before you know it, he'll have you volunteering to be a greeter at Sunday Mass."

Carter extended her hand. "Thanks, Father. It was great meeting you, too."

"Hey, Carter, can you wait outside for a sec? I need to speak to Fr. Donnelly privately."

"Sure."

Sarah smiled at the priest as the girl left the office and closed the door.

"I, um…" she said.

He glanced at his watch. "Oh, for heaven's sake." Making the Sign of the Cross, he absolved her.

As Sarah and Carter exited the building, the girl looked again across the street and noticed the lone woman standing in the grayness wearing half a face. She sighed heavily.

"No rest for the wicked."

"What?" Sarah said.

"Nothing."

It was late—after ten. Patricia Martin sat at the laptop in her office, a browser window open showing a freeze-frame of a patient. A time code displayed in the upper left-hand corner. Outside her office, the hallway was silent. The only sound came through the closed windows, a strong wind bringing rain and sleet.

The patient in the video looked distraught. She clicked the PLAY button again and sat back to re-watch the clip. Off-screen, a doctor was speaking.

"And the dreams?" the doctor's voice said.

"Same. I-I know they're not real, but that's what *they* want me to think. So they can operate on me again and take my soul." He laughed. "But they won't find it. No, I-I've hidden it somewhere… Who are you?"

"Dr. Brody. You remember me. We spoke yesterday."

"I'm not telling you anything. *They'll* hear."

"Who will?"

"*Them.* They're everywhere." He gestured wildly at the air with both hands. "Floating around here—can't you see them? I can. All the time."

"I'm afraid I can't. Maybe they've gone."

"What?"

The patient looked around. Grinning, he stared into the camera.

"Good job, Doctor. You've scared them away."

Dr. Martin paused the video again and looked down at her chart. She would have to let Sarah and Carter know— she promised. Stretching, she closed her laptop and stood. Grabbing her purse, she left her office and locked the door after her.

Outside, the wind was getting stronger. As if something were trying to discourage her from what she knew she had to do.

Twenty-Five

HARLAN COVINGTON HAD HAD a horrible night. He'd kept turning over in his mind Fr. Donnelly's warning. *Protect Sarah.* Impossible. There was too much at stake, and the priest knew it. But he'd been insistent—asking the attorney to promise in the name of the Holy Trinity. The sentimental old fool. It wasn't fair.

And how was Harlan expected to keep some meddling psychic safe while cleansing the town of this latest scourge? As it was, he didn't have much time. Though the proton beam therapy had seemed to arrest the cancer in his prostate, he knew the cursed disease would be back. Like the creeping evil that was consuming Dos Santos. It was ironic. For almost half a century, he'd practiced celibacy. Now, this.

When Harlan first met Sarah, he'd seen her as an amateur. Someone who'd stumbled into something she didn't understand and was woefully ill-equipped to overcome. Sure, she might have gifts. In fact, he sensed in her an extraordinary power. But she was unaware of what she possessed and would most likely end up blundering blindly to her death through no fault of his. He felt certain The Darkness was after her. And so, apparently, did Brian Donnelly. Which was why the priest was unwavering. Sarah was to be protected at all costs. Reluctantly, Harlan had promised.

"And what about her friend Carter?" he said to himself. "Am I supposed to protect this child, too?"

Morning light leaked in through the shuttered windows. Harlan's bedroom felt cold, as if something ominous and unseen had settled there. Groaning, he rose and did a few stretches. He followed this with his customary workout: one hundred each of push-ups and sit-ups, then thirty minutes on the treadmill. Other than the cancer, he was in excellent shape, he felt. Strong enough to fight.

As he wiped the sweat from his brow, Mary Mallery, his longtime housekeeper, entered with a tray. On it was a berry smoothie—his favorite. All of the ingredients were organic. And, he knew, she'd boosted the concoction with antioxidants and a little whey powder for protein. He watched as she set the tray down on one of the nightstands.

"Will there be anything else?" she said.

"No, Mary, thanks."

He stepped off the treadmill and crossed the room to enjoy his smoothie. As he drank, he could feel the cooling froth trickling down his throat. When he was younger, he did all the things young men did—dined frequently on red meat, drank whiskey, and smoked cigars. And the women. What was it St. Augustine had prayed? *O Lord, help me to be pure, but not yet.*

These days, he was virtuous and watched his diet carefully, his only luxury strong, black coffee. Combatting the dark forces required not only strength but discipline.

Thank God, his mind was sharp. Still so much to do. And only the Almighty knew how much longer he had.

After finishing his drink, he burped. Smiling, he recalled when he was a child and had belched magnificently at the dinner table. His mother had ceremoniously wiped her mouth with her napkin and said, "Go to your room." There was no other punishment, but Harlan felt so deeply ashamed, he never did it again. Now, in his seventies, he no longer cared.

"Go to *your* room, Mother."

The finger wearing the ring throbbed, reminding him of what remained to be done. So much killing. He recalled when he first visited Dos Santos after training in Rome. That was fifty years ago. He'd immediately sensed the evil in the town and wasted no time getting to work. The result? A man engaged in human trafficking and who had been responsible for abducting countless runaways, left for dead in the forest with his eyes pecked out.

Harlan wished he could receive absolution, but for him there was none. He would have to face God with blood on his hands and hope for forgiveness. He looked down at the ring.

"Soon," he said. "Soon, this will all be over."

Sarah was surprised at how small and unremarkable the offices of Bad Blond Productions were. The unattractive building, located near NBC Studios, was the home of *Dubious*. Originally, she and Chief Fiore were supposed to attend the meeting, but Sarah insisted on bringing Carter.

It was after ten. As the three of them walked in from the parking lot, they were greeted by a pleasant-looking woman who looked to be in her fifties.

"You must be our guests," she said, extending her hand. "I'm Lillian."

Before they could introduce themselves, she led them through a narrow hallway lined with huge framed posters, each of which showed Donnie and Debbie Fisk in some dramatic pose, the word Dubious emblazoned across the top. Eventually, they arrived at a conference room. A large TV was mounted on the wall, and the table was surrounded by comfortable-looking leather chairs.

"Can I get anyone coffee?" the assistant said.

Lou smiled. "That would be great."

"Anyone bring their autograph pens?" Sarah said.

Donnie and Debbie walked in. Everyone exchanged greetings.

"I appreciate you guys coming down," Donnie said.

He removed his thick glasses and cleaned the lenses using a shirttail. Lillian returned with a tray of coffee mugs, enough for everyone.

"Thanks, Lillian."

She distributed the drinks and exited, closing the door after her. Debbie smiled through collagen-swollen lips, like an oily press secretary. Sarah and Carter exchanged a look.

"Sarah, you all are about to see something that's, well, a little odd." She looked at her brother and tittered.

"*More* than a little odd," he said.

"And after you've had a chance to look at it, my brother and I have a question for you. So. Is everyone ready?"

Sarah felt like she was back in kindergarten. She wondered if they'd be asked to take a nap on the floor after. She looked at her friends, and the three of them took their seats.

"Good," Debbie said. "Donnie?"

Donnie turned out the lights and switched on the TV.

The video they were about to watch was already cued up. He hit the PLAY button, and Sarah saw herself approaching Peter Moody's grave. When the scene had finished, Donnie stopped the video.

"Did anyone want to see that again?" he said. No one said anything. "Okay. I'm going to show you something else. It was taken accidentally after Sarah's investigation. Apparently, the kid moving the equipment switched on the camera by accident. Just watch."

He hit PLAY again. There was a lot of bustle. People moving in and out of frame—no sound. The camera moved and, as the lens pointed away toward one of the walls of the cemetery, a figure in white could be seen standing there, the eyes glowing. On the video, a hand waved in front of the lens, and the video stopped abruptly.

"Can we see that again?" Carter said to Donnie.

"Yes. And there's another one after this."

Sarah strained to see the figure, her heart thudding. It looked as if it was not fully formed. Debbie's voice startled her.

"Everyone ready?"

Donnie played the last video. "We digitally zoomed in to get a better look."

For effect, he freeze-framed the final image. Sarah, Carter, and Lou leaned in. The room was dead silent. There was no mistaking it—no trick of the light, no shadow, no cheesy visual effects.

It was the girl in the mirror.

The lights came on, and Sarah found Donnie and Debbie staring at her intently, like joke cops waiting for the perp to confess. Their faux-friendly demeanor had been replaced by one of mild hostility. Sarah looked at Carter, who also seemed confused by the sudden change in attitude.

"We want to know how you did it," Donnie said, his voice even.

"Did what?"

Debbie sighed and took a seat across from Sarah. She shook her head and glanced at her brother.

"We're not amateurs, you know."

Donnie joined his sister. "Our goal is to make it to a hundred shows—enough for syndication. We've been all over the country, documenting so-called paranormal events. And this season, we're planning a trip to Australia. *And* we have a script in development over at Universal."

"People are always trying to pull shit on us," Debbie said, her voice rising. "Pardon my French. They rig up projectors and sound systems playing creepy noises. But it never works. Want to know why? Because we're *professionals*."

"Okay," Sarah said. She pointed at the frozen image of the girl visible on the TV screen. "Are you suggesting that I *created* that? How would I—?"

"It wouldn't be the first time."

Sarah had had her fill of these two. "Let me explain something to you, *Debbie*. Ghosts are real. And that up there? Also real. I think we're done here."

Choking back anger, she got to her feet. Carter and Lou did the same. Lou approached Donnie, standing within inches of him. Donnie tensed.

"We have an active investigation going on," the police chief said, "and I'm going to need a copy of everything you showed us. Plus, if there's any more…"

"I don't believe I need to give you anything."

Lou smiled to himself. "Okay, hardball it is, then. I'll get a subpoena. And while I'm at it, I'm going to need both of you to come up to Dos Santos for further questioning."

"*What?*" the brother and sister said, their voices higher than normal.

"That's right. And I'm also going to get a warrant to search the premises for any other evidence you might be 'withholding.' I'll call you if I think of anything else."

"But we didn't do anything!" Debbie sounded like a petulant teenager.

Lou smiled graciously and leaned toward her. "Where I come from, *that's* how you play hardball, sister."

Sarah and the others walked out and were about to get into Lou's car when the receptionist came scurrying out, waving something.

"Wait!" Lou walked over to meet her halfway. "Donnie told me to tell you this disc contains everything you asked for. Oh, and he's sorry for any misunderstanding."

Lou accepted the offering. "Tell him thanks for me. See you later."

As Lou started the engine, the three of them watched the assistant trudge back into the building.

"Remind me never to get on your bad side," Sarah said.

Carter joined in. "I'm guessing this is not a good time to ask you to fix my parking tickets?"

"That's it, guys," he said. "Keep pushing my buttons and see what happens."

Whistling tunelessly, he pulled out and got back on the road, glad to be leaving beautiful Burbank.

It was almost noon by the time they reached Santa Barbara. Lou had offered to buy Sarah and Carter lunch, but Sarah wanted to check something first. At the police station, she took her car and drove Carter to Casa Abrigo. She was sure Joe wouldn't mind.

"It's lovely," Carter said as they made their way to the front door.

The property had been newly landscaped, and the house looked like something out of a magazine. The front door, which had been freshly stained, stood partially open. Carefully, Sarah pressed on the door handle, and they entered.

"Oh my God," Carter said. "How much did you say you're selling it for?"

"Why? Interested?"

"You never know."

The interior was immaculate, and Sarah had to catch her breath when she saw the open kitchen leading to the dining room, where new high-end lighting had been installed. She tried imagining it filled with expensive furniture.

"Joe?" she said.

"In the cellar."

She smiled at Carter. "Come on."

They crossed to the kitchen and descended the stairs. The wine racks had been put back in place, and Joe and Manny were rolling up the drop cloths. The smell of sealer was strong and made Sarah a little lightheaded.

"Don't mind us," she said to the men. "By the way, Joe, Fr. Brian is a go for the house blessing."

"Fantastic."

"This way," Sarah said to Carter.

She led the girl to the storage room. The door was closed. Carter looked at her apprehensively.

"You first."

Sarah smiled. "No, I need to know your impression."

Smiling nervously, Carter grasped the knob and turned

it. Slowly, she swung the door open. As she did, she felt as if a cold wind had pushed her back, and she gasped.

"You okay?" Sarah said, touching her shoulder.

"There's a lot of energy in that room."

"Right?"

"Don't make me go in, though, okay?"

"No, I think I got what I needed."

Water bottles, plates and napkins, and pizzas from Papa Pepito's took up one end of the conference room table at Greene Realty. Sarah and Carter had turned the space into a war room. Bulleted facts about the case were listed on the whiteboard. Lou stood there, staring at what they had so far, chomping on a slice of salami and mushroom.

"Don't forget that biblical verse," he said, pointing a greasy finger. "It might be important."

Sarah arched her eyebrows. "Right."

In a separate corner, she scribbled the name Harlan Covington, followed by a question mark.

"You think he's involved?"

"I think he knows more about Peter Moody than he's letting on."

Carter took a red marker and made a circle. Under it, she wrote *Cellar!* "Whatever's going on in that house is concentrated in that room."

"So, basically," Sarah said, "what we have is a lot of useless facts."

Lou wiped his mouth with a napkin, grabbed a water bottle, and stepped up to the board. "You have to find the thread." He took a swig and read across. "It's here. We just can't see it yet."

"The dead girl *is* the thread," Sarah said.

Carter turned to her. "When's the last time you saw her?"

"Let's see... It was in a dream. I was back in that storage room in the cellar."

"What about the mirror?"

"After we moved it to public storage, I went there with Joe. Nothing."

"Maybe you should go back."

"That's a good idea. You seem to have a feel for this, Carter. Maybe *you* can get her to come out and play."

"I don't like the sound of that," Lou said.

Sarah returned to the board and underscored the name Michael Peterson twice. Rachel poked her head in.

"Anyone want coffee? I'm making a run."

Lou's hand shot up. "Double espresso, please. No, make that—"

"A triple, I know," Rachel said.

Lou stared at her, surprised. "But how did you—?"

"Can I have a chai latte with an extra pump?" Carter said. "It feels weird giving my order to someone else."

"Nothing for me," Sarah said.

"Got it." Rachel paused and stared at the board as Sarah drew a line connecting Michael Peterson and Gail Cohen. "Are you saying those two are connected? That's a stretch."

"Rache, don't you think it's odd that they both came into our lives at almost exactly the same time?"

"A coincidence," Lou said.

Sarah shook her head. "My little woman says otherwise. And while we're on the subject, why was Gail Cohen murdered?"

"Who says she was?"

"Come on, Lou. Birds from hell?"

"Okay, I'll admit that *is* weird. But it doesn't prove—"

"Fine." She erased the line.

"Well, I haven't got any better ideas," Rachel said, and left.

Sarah fake-pounded her temples and groaned loudly. "I feel like the answer is right here. But I can't seem to…"

Her phone, which was lying on the conference table, went off. She ignored it. Carter happened to be closer and glanced at the number.

"Hey, Sarah, you might wanna get that. Looks like a Kansas area code."

"Holy crap!"

She dropped her marker and practically leapt for her phone. "Hello? Sarah Greene. Dr. Martin? Hang on, I'm putting you on speaker."

She set the phone down and cranked up the volume as everyone crowded around.

"Dr. Martin, can you hear me?"

"Perfectly."

"Carter is with me. And we've also got Chief Lou Fiore of the Dos Santos Police."

"Hey, Doc," he said.

"Hello, everyone. Okay, as I explained, when Peter Moody was here, he made friends with another patient—a young man. It wasn't easy, but I managed to get a name. But I'm not going to give it to you without authorization. I can, however, provide some details about him."

Sarah's stomach twisted into a knot. "Okay, go ahead."

"The patient in question was being treated for schizoaffective disorder. Symptoms included hallucinations, depression, manic behavior, and suicidal ideation. There were also indications of self-harm. According to his chart, he'd been taking various antipsychotic medications. From what I can tell, they were marginally effective."

"Dr. Martin?" Carter said. "Can you tell us what

happened to him? I mean, was he still there after Peter Moody checked himself out?"

"That's the strange part. The hospital's recommendation was that he stay until treatment was complete. But under state law, adult patients can discharge themselves, unless a court determines otherwise. He left around the same time Peter Moody did."

Lou leaned toward the phone. "Dr. Martin, Lou here. We're going to need a name and address. If I need to, I'll get an administrative subpoena for the patient records."

"Well, according to HIPAA regulations, I'm supposed to ask if this is relevant to an active investigation."

"It is."

She sighed. "You won't need the subpoena, Chief. I'll fax you the file now."

"I appreciate it," Lou said. "Thanks."

Sarah gave out the fax number, and they said their goodbyes. Moments later, Sarah could hear the sound of an incoming call on the fax machine in Rachel's office. Excited, she headed across the hall and, rather than waiting for the entire file to be printed, grabbed the cover sheet and first page. When she read the name on the file, she gasped. Carter had come in, followed by Lou. The girl looked over Sarah's shoulder, her face losing its color.

"So, who's the patient?" Lou said.

Sarah handed him the pages and sank unsteadily into Rachel's chair.

"Michael Peterson?" he said. "Looks like you were right."

Sarah rested her head on the desk. "I think I'm going to be sick."

Twenty-Six

"SOMEONE HAS TO PROTECT HER," Rachel said, on the verge of tears.

Everyone had gathered in the conference room again. As the others got their drinks, Lou ignored his and spoke softly to Rachel.

"I'm not letting anything happen to your sister. I'll assign an officer to keep an eye on Sarah's house."

Rachel wiped away a tear. "And what if that man shows up *here* again?"

He put his hand on her shoulder. "I *will* protect her, Rachel."

"What about private security?" Carter said.

Rachel scoffed. "What, like a bodyguard?"

"Well, I don't know."

As the others argued, Sarah sat slumped in one of the chairs, her head on her chin, stunned over what she had learned. The whole situation was unreal. Michael Peterson? He'd been so charming. And that schizo-whatever diagnosis? He'd exhibited none of the symptoms Dr. Martin mentioned. But there *was* something. His intense reaction to seeing a priest, for example. And to think Sarah had daydreamed about a romantic relationship with him. Rachel stopped talking and, noticing her sister, she sat next to her and massaged her shoulders. Sarah turned to Rachel, her eyes glistening.

"I need Joe."

"I called him. He's on his way."

Soon, Sarah's ex-husband stormed into the room. Ignoring everyone else, he went to Sarah. When she saw him, she stood and pressed herself against his shoulder as the room went silent. Joe turned to Lou, his expression grim.

"I'm putting you on notice. If I so much as *see* that guy come near Sarah, I'll break his legs."

Sarah sat on her sofa, Gary on her lap purring, and her legs tucked under her. Joe walked into the room, carrying a FedEx package.

"This was left at your front door," he said. "Looks like it's from Kansas."

"Colleen's photo album." She waved toward the coffee table. "Leave it. I'll look at it later."

He laid the box down and sat next to her. Then, he began gently stroking her hair with the backs of his fingers. That simple gesture always soothed her; it reminded her so much of her late mother. She hadn't thought about her mother for a long time. But now, she was foremost in her mind. She'd died from pancreatic cancer, as Alyssa had warned Sarah six months earlier. Sarah had just turned seventeen. She recalled the endless parade of doctors in the hospital room toward the end. The whispered conversations between the nurses. Her father alone in a corner, pretending not to cry.

Her mother had lost so much weight during those last days and hardly resembled the beautiful, smiling woman Sarah remembered from a family photo. In that picture, her mother was laughing; her long, flowing hair like Sarah's billowing. It was that image of her mother Sarah treasured.

Then, one day, she was gone.

Sarah's mind traveled back to Hannah. She *had* been with her brother that day at the pawn shop, Sarah was sure of it. And that meant she was out there somewhere. They needed to find her. She was the key to unlocking the mystery of Michael Peterson and his connection to Peter Moody. Her thoughts were interrupted when Joe got up, sending the cat to the floor.

"What are you doing?" she said. "This is your job now. Looking after me. It's why I refused a police detail."

"I have to pee. There, I said it. Also, I'm starving. I was going to cook us up something."

"But you don't cook."

"I'm making us omelets. I'm guessing there's wine and bread, so I think we're in good shape."

"Do you want me to help?"

"Sarah, I'm perfectly capable of making an omelet. And if you're nice, I'll draw a smiley face on the plate in Sriracha sauce."

"Wow, who could resist an offer like that?"

He kissed her forehead and headed for the bathroom. "Why don't you watch television to take your mind off things? I'll be back with some wine in a sec."

Yep, he still adores me. She glanced at the FedEx package sitting on the coffee table. Coaxing Gary onto her lap, she switched on the TV instead.

All of the local news programs had ended. Unenthusiastic, Sarah cycled through the channels looking for something that would take her mind off the current situation. She stopped when she reached The Discovery Channel. A rerun of *Dubious* was playing. Despite the enmity she felt for Ken and Barbie, she decided to watch.

This time, Donnie and Debbie were in Atlanta, Georgia, visiting a famous plantation home that was supposedly haunted by the ghost of a young girl from Boston who had been staying there with relatives. Apparently, she'd gone for a walk and never returned.

As usual, Donnie and Debbie interviewed the locals, one of whom was an elderly African-American woman who lived in the area. Her grandmother had worked for the family at the time of the disappearance and had kept a journal. The old woman read from it.

> Everyone says Delilah run away. They thought she was a harlot. Her parents sent her down to get her straight. But I spoke to the girl and knew she t'weren't no harlot. It was that man, the mass'r. He's the one tried to make her bad.

Joe returned, carrying two glasses of red wine. He handed one to Sarah and gawped at the TV.

"Am I in the wrong house?"

"Shh."

Silently, he slid in next to her. Donnie and Debbie were exploring a cellar.

"They say this is where she appears," Debbie said, her voice low and husky for effect.

Sarah watched as the two personalities explored the cellar, making snarky asides along the way. A ghostly mist began to materialize, which they dismissed as steam from the furnace. By the end of the episode, the two "proved" once and for all that there was no ghost. Finishing her wine, Sarah switched off the TV.

A sudden flash of light behind her eyes startled her. She could hear Colleen's voice in her head. *Those three were like peas in a pod. And the girls. Everyone thought they were sisters.* She stared blankly at Joe.

"Obviously, you think there *is* a ghost," Joe said, referring to the TV show.

She got up, grabbed the box, and practically ran into the kitchen. Concerned, Joe followed her and watched as she found a pair of scissors and cut through the packing tape. She ripped the top of the box off and removed the photo album. Joe stood next to her as she flipped through the pages and pages of family photos.

"What are we looking for?" he said.

"I am such a *yutz*. Did I use that right?"

"Yeah, but what—"

"Hang on…"

She continued until she reached a color snapshot of three children—a boy of eleven and two little blonde six-year-old girls. Peter, Hannah, and Nicole. It looked as if it had been taken in the backyard. They were wearing swimsuits, and their bodies were glistening with water droplets. Behind them, a colorful toy sprinkler was giving off a huge spray of water.

Sarah continued staring at the photo, her mouth falling open. The boy was standing off by himself, and though he was smiling, his eyes were hooded and distant. But the girls. It was remarkable—they looked like *twins*. She noticed they were smiling at each other, as if sharing a secret.

"Which is which?" she heard herself say. She turned to Joe. "I was so wrong."

"What do you mean?"

"All this time, I thought Peter had murdered his sister, right? But she turns up alive and living in Lawrence with her brother."

"Then, you thought it was the cousin."

"Right. But that couldn't be because, one, the ghost I saw was a dead ringer for Hannah. And, two, Nicole called her mother a week after her disappearance."

"Didn't Lou say he thought the girl could've been a runaway?"

"Yes, who *looked* like Hannah. Although, I always thought that was a stretch."

"So, who have you been chasing all this time?"

"Joe, Nicole never called her mother. *Hannah* did, pretending to be her cousin."

Her hand trembling, Sarah looked at the photo again, concentrating on the girls.

"The girl in the mirror *is* Nicole."

"I still think she ran away," Joe said as he and Sarah dug into their omelets.

"That's what everyone else thought. Joe, this is good, by the way. What did you put in it?"

"It's a secret."

"Fine. Jewish cooking. Who knew? Look, Peter had been obsessed with both those girls since they were little."

"How do you know?"

"Nicole's mother, Colleen. I think when her daughter came to stay with the family, Peter must've seen his chance to finally seduce her. But unlike Hannah, she wasn't having any of it. So, he killed her."

Joe was about to take another swallow of wine when Sarah took it away from him.

"What are you doing?"

"I need you sharp. Look, I think Nicole's body is buried in the forest somewhere. And *I* know how to find out where."

"I'm afraid to ask."

"You're taking me to the storage facility."

"*Now?* Great, and you *had* to turn down Lou's offer of a bodyguard."

"That's where you come in. And thanks to me, you've only had one glass of wine."

"What about Carter? I thought you wanted her to see the mirror."

"I'll update her later. Apparently, she and the band have made up, and they're rehearsing tonight."

Joe got up and cleared away the dishes as Sarah went to get a jacket. By the time she returned, he'd put everything in the dishwasher.

"Time to charm a ghost," she said.

With practiced silence, Mary closed the library door after her and returned to her room upstairs. She would come for the coffee things later, after the guest had departed. When the man arrived, he was well dressed and polite, but there was a look in his eyes—an unspoken anger mixed with desperation, and it unsettled the housekeeper. She'd seen that look before. It was when that woman—Gail Cohen— had come to see Mary's employer. She, too, had looked desperate.

Once inside the safety of her bedroom, Mary crossed to the small writing desk by the window and sat. She found her rosary lying by itself, the once-black beads worn from use. She'd received it when she entered the convent as a novitiate.

She had gone there to spend the rest of her life in prayer. Prayer for the sick, the lost, the fallen. Back in the secular world, working for a strange man with access to dark powers not officially sanctioned by the Church, she never stopped praying and would continue until she breathed her last.

In the library, Harlan Covington poured out two cups of strong black coffee and brought them to his guest. He set one down on a side table and kept the other for himself. Taking a seat, he faced a grim Michael Peterson.

"Thank you for coming," the old man said. "Try the coffee. It's Ethiopian."

Though Michael seemed uninterested in refreshments, he picked up his cup and took a sip.

"It's pretty good."

"This particular blend is very hard to come by. I get it from a supplier in San Francisco."

Michael's hands began shaking and he set the cup back on the table, spilling the hot liquid onto the saucer. When he looked at Harlan again, his eyes were fierce, as if he'd transformed. As he spoke, he stammered.

"Wh-where… where is th-the mirror?"

"I've had my people following Joe and Sarah, but no luck, I'm afraid."

Michael stood. "I'm running out of time."

"I am aware. Please sit down."

"No!"

Sighing, Harlan set his cup down carefully and wiped his mouth with a white linen napkin.

"We both want the same thing: the mirror. I *will* find it, but you must give me more time."

"I told you, I don't—"

"Have more time. So you said. Give me until the end of the week. In the meantime, I suggest you lay low."

"You mean, l-like Gail?"

The old man looked away. "Her death was unfortunate. A tragedy."

"Sh-she was *murdered*. Why c-can't you…find—?"

Harlan stared coldly at Michael, his eyes dark and intense. Whatever it was he was conveying without words, it disconcerted the other man.

"You would do well to remember who you're speaking to."

Covering his mouth to suppress a sob, Michael turned toward the door. Harlan stood stiffly and walked him out. As they approached the foyer, Harlan could feel the phone in his pocket vibrating. At the front door, he shook hands with his chastened guest and, after he had departed, closed the door.

When he brought out his phone, the attorney saw one missed call. He returned to the library, unlocked the phone, and dialed.

"What have you found out?" Harlan said.

"It looks like they're moving the mirror."

"Are you sure?"

"Yes. I overheard Sarah talking about Casa Abrigo. I think they might be bringing it back to the cellar."

"That's good news. Will it be the two of them?"

"No. The chief will be there."

"I see." Harlan looked up for a moment. "Looks like we'll need a distraction. Stay close to them, but don't let them see you."

"Right. Speak soon."

The old man disconnected and absently rubbed the finger wearing the ring. He thought of Sarah and the promise he'd made to keep her safe. That might no longer be possible. Sighing, he dialed his phone.

"Michael? Sarah is on her way to Casa Abrigo. And she has the mirror. You should go there now."

Harlan disconnected and left his office to make the final preparations.

Tim Whatley returned the phone to his pocket and, using binoculars, continued observing Joe and Sarah as they loaded the mirror onto the bed of Joe's pickup. Except for these two, the storage facility was deserted. A lightning flash lit up the sky, followed by thunder.

He felt a chill that reminded him of the darkness descending on them all. As he had so many times before, he wondered whether Harlan Covington was a part of that darkness or its sworn enemy. He prayed that it was the latter. If Harlan's plan failed, Sarah Greene could very well wind up dead.

He heard a noise somewhere nearby, which spooked him. Seeing nothing, he returned to his unmarked vehicle and waited for Joe and Sarah to leave.

Twenty-Seven

As JOE MADE his way in the darkness up San Marcos Pass Road, Sarah gazed out her window at the still blackness. The rain was coming down hard, and Joe had to keep his speed down so he wouldn't damage the mirror.

"One more time for the record," he said. "Are you sure this is a good idea?"

Smiling, she touched his hand. "We need to end it. And I feel like this is the only way. Besides, Lou and his gun will be there."

There was something up ahead. Why wasn't Joe slowing down? The headlight beams fell on a naked figure standing in the middle of the road in the rain. Her hair was matted, her skin almost translucent. Her eyes were missing.

"Joe, watch out!"

He slammed on the brakes, causing the truck to shimmy, then glide to a stop. Breathing hard, he turned to Sarah.

"Okay, do you want to tell me what——?"

"There was a woman."

He reached over to the glove compartment and retrieved his flashlight. Then, he climbed out and pointed a beam into the darkness. The only sounds were the rain and his engine idling. He went around to the truck bed and checked the mirror. Secured tightly by ropes, it appeared to have survived the jolt without any damage. Eventually, he returned to the truck.

"There's no one out there, Sarah." He put away the flashlight. "Let's try to get to the house in one piece, okay?"

As Joe fastened his seatbelt, Sarah could sense something close. When she turned toward her window, she saw a woman with blonde hair and no eyes standing next to the truck. Her face was contorted in pain. She opened her mouth in a silent scream and, impossibly, hundreds of ravens flew out into the night.

"Joe!" Sarah said.

"Now what?"

When Sarah looked again, there was nothing but the rain.

"Just drive, okay?" she said.

A few minutes later, they reached Casa Abrigo. The outside lights were on a timer, and they should've been on. But the house was drenched in darkness.

"So, where's Lou?" Joe said as they got out.

"He'll be here. Let's get the mirror inside."

He dropped the tailgate, grabbed a carpeted dolly, and set it on the driveway. Carefully, he and Sarah lifted the mirror and set it down. They rolled it toward the house. At the front door, they stopped, and Joe got out his key. He tried putting it into the lock, but his hand was shaking. Gently, Sarah put her hand on his and helped guide the key in.

"Thanks," he said. "I need to turn off the alarm."

As she swung the door open, she could hear a soft,

electronic beeping. Joe flipped on the lights and strode across to a far wall. He opened the alarm panel and disabled the security. Then, he helped Sarah roll the mirror in. Without speaking, they continued into the kitchen and toward the cellar door.

"Here comes the hard part," Joe said. "Lou should've been here by now. Why don't you call him?"

"Good idea."

She retrieved her phone from her pocket and dialed the police chief. The call went to voicemail immediately.

"He's not picking up," she said. "I think we should get started."

Sighing, Joe opened the cellar door and switched on more lights. Carefully, they removed the mirror from the dolly. He entered first and waited for Sarah to grab the other end of the mirror. It was not only heavy but large and awkward. Sarah almost missed a step, causing the mirror to shoot forward. Fortunately, Joe recovered and steadied it.

They were halfway down. Outside, Sarah could hear the rain pelting the ground. She thought she heard the wind and wondered if they'd forgotten to close the front door. She would have to send Joe upstairs to check once they got settled.

Finally, they were on the ground. Rather than use the dolly, they carried the mirror into the storage room. Manny had replaced the blackened stone, and Sarah couldn't distinguish between the new and the original.

"Did Manny redo the whole floor?"

"No, just the stained part. Where do you want it?"

"We'll have to estimate."

They positioned the mirror. When Sarah was satisfied it was standing more or less in its original spot, she removed the heavy moving blanket. Standing in front of the mirror, she saw nothing but her reflection.

"Joe, I think we left the front door open. Can you run upstairs and close it?"

"Are you sure you want to be down here by yourself?"

"I'm fine."

"Okay. Call me if you need me."

He leaned in and, laying a hand on her shoulder, kissed her. She squeezed his hand and smiled apprehensively as he left her alone in the storage room. She could hear his faint footsteps as he ascended the stairs. Then, silence.

No sooner had Joe left her than the temperature in the room dropped. *Showtime.* Sarah concentrated on the mirror and waited. Ice crystals appeared on the glass accompanied by faint crackling noises. Though Sarah was frightened, she was certain Nicole wouldn't harm her. For no reason at all, she thought of Donnie and Debbie Fisk. They would've dismissed this as some sort of parlor trick. Something far away began taking shape in the mirror. It was an amorphous, billowing entity that wafted toward her. Soon, Sarah was able to make out the face of the girl. *She's so young.*

Without warning, a blue-white hand tore through the glass and took hold of Sarah's wrist, hurting her. Before she could scream, it yanked her into the mirror. Sarah felt her breath leave her as she was dragged forward through a long, dark corridor. She had a sense of lightness and couldn't feel her feet on the ground.

"This way," the girl said, her voice frightened.

"Nicole, wait. I'm not supposed to be here."

Their voices sounded distorted. Ignoring Sarah, the girl kept pulling her toward a small door made of aged, splintered wood standing at the end of the corridor. As they approached, the door creaked open. Effortlessly, they passed through, and soon Sarah found herself in the middle of a dark cave.

"What is this place?"

"This is where I died," the girl said without emotion.

Ignoring his buzzing phone, Lou drove through the pounding rain, looking for the right house. He didn't like Carpinteria. It was too far from his home turf. He'd been down here once years ago when Vic Womble organized a poker game shortly after his divorce. Vic had purchased the home at a bank auction and, from the looks of it, it was probably all he could afford. None of the other guys in Homicide felt close to Vic, but they'd all agreed to be supportive, including Lou. Divorce was way too common in the cop world. Lou had seen good cops go to shit because they didn't have any emotional support. Most felt Vic had a broom handle up his ass, but he was still a good cop.

There was a house on the corner, Lou recalled, whose lawn was filled with gnomes. *There.* Checking his rearview mirror, he swung right and pulled up to the correct house. The lights weren't on. Weird. He checked his watch and saw that it was after eight. He should've been at Casa Abrigo with Sarah and Joe. But the message from Vic had sounded urgent.

He got out and crossed the red brick walkway to the front door. When he pressed the doorbell, a soft chime went off inside. Seconds passed. This wasn't like Vic. Finally, lights came on inside. The front door opened. Vic was dressed in jeans and a T-shirt. Barefoot. From his expression, he clearly wasn't expecting visitors.

"Lou, what's going on?"

"Whaddya you mean? You left a message with my dispatcher telling me to get over here."

"Huh?"

"Something about the Gail Cohen investigation?"

Vic scratched at his beard stubble and swung the door open wider. "Come on in."

Lou took a seat on a bar stool in the kitchen as Vic opened a couple of beers for them. He handed one to Lou and took a seat next to him.

Lou took a deep swallow. "Okay, this is weird. I get a message—supposedly from you—saying to meet you here right away and that it's urgent."

"Did the message provide any details?"

"No, but it mentioned Gail Cohen. I thought maybe you'd changed your mind about the manner of death."

"Lou, honestly? I didn't leave any message. And besides, why wouldn't I call your cell?"

"Good point."

"And no, I haven't changed my mind."

Lou sighed and took another swallow. "Are you sure? I keep thinking about that other John Doe from 1970."

"Okay, I'll admit they're similar. But with Gail Cohen, we still have no motive."

"Sounds like you're ready to close the books on this one."

Lou finished his beer and stood. He glanced over at the sink and noticed the dirty dishes and the dishwasher door lying open.

"Looks like I interrupted."

"I was going to do some reading. Fiction for a change."

"Anything good?"

"Dean Koontz. Maybe *he* knows what those birds were up to."

"Thanks for the beer." Lou left the bottle on the countertop and went to the front door with Vic following.

"We should have another poker night," Vic said.

"Yeah, sure. Why don't you reach out to the guys and let me know."

"Will do."

"Night, Vic."

"Sorry you had to come all this way. I'll ask around tomorrow to see who might've left that message."

"Something tells me it wasn't anyone at the station. See you."

The rain had become a steady drizzle. On the way back, Lou thought about the message. Who was on dispatch? Laurie. She was new and wouldn't have known whether the person on the phone identifying themselves as Vic Womble was an impersonator. Innocent mistake. But why would— Shit, *Sarah*.

Whoever it was wanted him far away from Casa Abrigo. He tried calling her. No answer. Checking his mirrors, he stomped on the pedal. It was early. He could still make it to Dos Santos in time.

Sarah could see shafts of moonlight outside the cave. And she heard the sound of rushing water. When she turned, she saw Nicole standing over something. Afraid, Sarah slowly made her way across the cave floor and looked down.

It was a girl's body dressed in blue jeans, a yellow crop top, and dirty white sneakers. Wisps of blonde hair clung to the skull around a jagged hole in the temple where the bone had been crushed. The bones of the arms and hands were intact and, except for the fact that this was a skeleton,

Sarah could imagine the teenager getting up as if from a long, lonely sleep.

Tears filled Sarah's eyes as the reality of what had happened hit her. She turned to Nicole, who was holding herself, rocking softly and muttering.

"Tell me what happened."

Their voices sounded natural now and echoed softly off the moist cave walls.

"It was Peter. He wanted to… He wanted me to do things. Like he did with Hannah."

"And you refused?"

"At first, he laughed it off. Said he was only joking. But after a while, he became more insistent. I threatened to tell his parents. He said if I didn't say anything, he would leave me alone."

"And did he?"

"Yes. I spent the rest of the summer with Hannah. One day, she invited me down to the river to swim. I was worried Peter would be there, but she promised it would just be the two of us. We hiked for a long time, talking like we used to when we were little. When we got to the river, we laid our towels on the rocks and went in. I remember the water was so cold.

"Hannah said there was a cave we could explore. It sounded like fun. We got out and dried ourselves off. Hannah showed me this secret entrance through the boulders. It could be our special place, she said. We went inside. It was dark. I was scared and wanted to leave. She took my hand."

As the ghost spoke, Sarah could picture the girls who looked so much alike making their way through the darkness of the cave, hand in hand. Like Alyssa and her on one of their preteen ghost adventures. Sarah felt a deep connection to Nicole and wanted so much to comfort her. But all she could do was listen. The girl pointed.

"We stood over there. It was cold, and I had goosebumps. Hannah smiled at me in this strange way. Then, she put her hands on my face and...kissed me on the lips. I didn't know... I mean, I felt like it was okay. We'd known each other all our lives. And Hannah was... I loved her, I guess."

Sarah reached out her hand and took the girl's. It felt smooth and cold and didn't weigh anything.

"It's okay, Nicole."

The ghost stared at her, her expression turning violent. As she jerked away, her hand felt sharp and rough like rusted metal, cutting Sarah's palm. Then, Nicole fell to her knees, her image stuttering in the darkness.

"And then, *he* was there."

"Peter?"

"It was like when we were little. Me and Hannah wanting to be by ourselves. And him always *ruining* it." She began sobbing. "They held me down. Peter, he..."

"He raped you?"

"After, I didn't want to go home. I was so ashamed. I remember him telling me that if I said anything, he would find a way to hurt me. I got dressed and went outside. Peter and Hannah were already walking back. I was so angry. I screamed at them. Told them both to go to hell. I said I would tell his parents.

"Peter got really mad and came back. I tried running, but I kept slipping on the wet rocks. He caught me and dragged me back into the cave. I screamed for Hannah, but she never came. Then, Peter said, 'Eyes on me, Nicole,' and hit me in the head with a rock. It was the last thing I remember."

The ghost let out a shrieking sob that echoed and

collapsed next to her bones. She'd finally been able to tell her story, and Sarah prayed the girl's soul could move on.

Sarah knelt next to the girl. "Nicole, do you know if Hannah is alive?"

"Dead. Killed by the ravens."

"No, that was Gail Cohen."

The girl looked up at her as if Sarah were stupid. Her eyes were on fire, her teeth sharp and fierce.

"There is no Gail Cohen."

"What?" Sarah felt faint and wavered. "Oh my God, it was Hannah all along."

"But *Peter* is alive."

The ghost said this like a little girl reciting a nursery rhyme, her voice sing-songy.

"Peter is uh-LIE-uv, Peter is uh-LIE-uv."

She was giggling in a way that unnerved Sarah. She tried desperately to understand.

"But I saw him buried in the ground."

Nicole became quiet and looked at Sarah with dead, intense eyes. Sarah wanted to run but didn't know where to go.

"All those years," the ghost said. "I watched and waited, unable tell anyone. Until *you* found me."

"Nicole, I'm sure Peter is dead."

"No! He *lives.*"

Sarah sank to her knees, swooning from an intense heat. When she opened her eyes, she was back in the storage room. The temperature was normal. The mirror was dark. She heard a scraping noise behind her.

"Joe?" A dark figure approached her. "Thank God. Help me up, would you?"

She reached out her hand and waited for Joe to take it. She wanted him—*needed* him—to stay with her, she was so frightened. The figure stepped into the light. But it wasn't Joe.

It was Michael Peterson, grinning like a demon.

"No, get away. Please, Michael… Leave me alone."

As he moved closer, she wondered where Joe was. Why had he left her alone with a madman? She noticed Michael was gripping a crowbar she recognized. It was Joe's. She wanted to scream, but couldn't.

"You don't have to do this."

Grabbing her by the hair, he moved in close and made her look at him. As she fought him, he forced a wet cloth over her mouth and nose, and held it there until she breathed in the pungent fumes and began to lose consciousness. Then, in a deathly whisper like burning paper…

"Eyes on me, Sarah."

Twenty-Eight

By the time Lou reached Casa Abrigo, the sky had cleared and the moon shone brightly. Up ahead, he could see a nondescript vehicle parked on the street. Inside the house, the lights were on, and he guessed everything was all right.

He parked behind the car and jogged up to the front door, which was closed but unlocked. Tentatively, he pushed the door open. The house looked empty as he stepped inside.

"Hello?"

No answer. They were probably in the cellar.

"Sarah? Joe?"

A lonely silence filled the interior. Lou's cop instincts took over and, unholstering his weapon, he went immediately to the kitchen, where he found Joe sprawled on the floor, unconscious. He checked for a pulse and, finding one, turned Joe onto his back. Gently slapped his cheeks to see if he could get a response. He found a half-empty water bottle on the counter and dumped its contents on Joe's face. In a few seconds, Joe's eyes fluttered, and he tried grabbing Lou by the throat. Lou scooted back and waved his hands in front of him.

"It's okay, Joe. It's me."

"Lou?"

"Yeah. Come on, let's get you up."

He helped his friend into a sitting position. Grimacing, Joe felt the back of his head. No blood.

"Do you think you can stand?"

"Yeah."

It took two attempts, but eventually Joe was able to get to his feet. He stood with his arms propped against the kitchen counter for balance. Lou got him a fresh water and handed it to him.

"Thanks."

"You want to tell me what happened?"

"Whoever it was clocked me from behind."

"Did you happen to get a look?"

Joe took a huge gulp and set the bottle down. "No. Shit, my head." He looked around. "Where's Sarah?"

"Sorry, I just got here. You rest a minute. I'm going to check the cellar." He crossed to the door. "Sarah? You down there?"

When there was no answer, he made his way down the stairs, still holding his weapon. All the lights were on. He saw that the door to the storage room was open. He crossed over to it and went in. Shattered glass lay all around the mirror. Leaving the room, he checked the rest of the cellar and trotted back up the stairs, where he found Joe sitting at his makeshift desk.

"She's not there?" Joe said.

"No."

"Lou, what the hell happened? You were supposed to meet us here."

"I'm sorry, Joe. But someone led me on a wild goose

chase. They wanted me far away from here. Any idea who could've done this?"

"Had to be Peterson. Who else?"

"You're prob'ly right. Come on, we need to find Sarah. You up for this?"

"Yeah. Let's go."

The men made a complete search of the house without any luck. They decided to walk the perimeter, in case Sarah had fallen outside.

"The pool," Joe said.

They went through the French doors leading to the backyard where they found the rectangular swimming pool with a stone deck. Joe ran to the edge and peered down. Nothing but shallow, brackish water.

"Let's check the front of the house," Lou said.

As they made their way around, Joe immediately noticed the empty driveway and stopped. He looked toward the street and saw the unfamiliar car parked there. He bolted down the driveway and, standing in the middle of the road, glanced in both directions.

"Sarah!"

Lou joined him and saw the look of sheer desperation in his friend's eyes.

"He's got my truck," Joe said. "And he's taken Sarah."

Sarah was floating in murky darkness, the rumbling of a vehicle in her ears. Fighting for consciousness, she managed to open her eyes. When she did, she found herself in the front seat of Joe's truck, moving down a familiar trail through the forest. But how? She reached for the door handle, and that's when she realized her hands were bound with thin nylon rope.

She lifted her head and looked to her left. Michael Peterson, his face grim, was driving. She could see the determined look in his eyes. He drove with purpose through the damp forest toward—*Devil's Bluff?*

"Why are you doing this?" she said.

"I have to. He-he's making me."

"Who is? Peter?"

"Shut up. It'll all be over soon."

"Michael, you can stop this. I know about you. You were never meant for this."

"He-he helped me. Made me...*normal.*"

"How?"

"I couldn't be...a normal person. Peter made a deal. He would live in me and I would be healthy. No more nightmares. No more thoughts of..."

Sarah finally understood. Somehow, Peter had arranged things so that when he died, his soul would possess Michael Peterson. It was as if he were a demon, controlling this poor, sick man. And, in exchange, giving him the semblance of a normal life.

"Michael, he's made you a slave. And Hannah? She stayed with you, didn't she? Pretending to be Gail Cohen. But it was the two of you again. Then, she died."

Michael seemed to be driving dangerously fast, frightening Sarah even more.

"Someone took her from us. But I'll find them and make them suffer in ways they could never imagine. You have no idea the power I possess." *He said "I."*

"Peter?"

His voice was different. Menacing. All of the fear and the stammering were gone, leaving a coldness that chilled Sarah. It was as if she were speaking to the devil himself.

"Why did you kill Nicole?" she said.

"She threatened to expose everything."

"And your parents?"

"Turns out they already knew about Hannah and me. Too bad, really. Mom made the best grilled cheeses." He let out a high-pitched laugh.

"Peter, how did Nicole get into the mirror?"

"My, so many questions."

"I need to know."

He became angry and hit the steering wheel with his fist.

"I don't *know*. She must've found her way to it somehow. I'd performed a speculum ritual on the mirror and was using it to commune with forces you could never understand. And they were in *my* power. *He* gave me that."

"Who?"

"I'm not one to name-drop, Sarah. Unfortunately, my body was weak. It couldn't withstand the awesome power I had been given. It was my heart, you see. I was dying."

"So, you gave your eyes as a sacrifice?"

"Yes."

"And then, you killed yourself."

"Only to be reborn. Just as he had promised me."

He peered through the windshield and, leaving the trail, drove purposefully through the trees.

"There's one more sacrifice I need to offer to ensure my survival." He smiled at her wickedly. "Almost there now."

Lou had worked fast to bring together a volunteer group to search the woods. Soon, cops with dogs and a few townsfolk were combing the dark woods looking for Sarah, their flashlight beams piercing the thick blackness. Joe had called Carter, and now the two of them made their way through the darkness together. Everyone, it seemed, was calling Sarah's name. But their voices were met by stillness, broken only by the hooting of an owl and the mournful cries of coyotes.

"Where do you think he's taking her?" Joe said to Lou.

"Hard to say. Devil's Bluff is that way. Maybe he's intending to—"

"Don't say it."

"We'll find her, Joe."

"I wish I'd been with you guys tonight," Carter said.

She was crying. Joe took her hand.

"This is not your fault, Carter. I was with her and she was still taken."

Voices continued calling out into the night. Only one word.

"Sarah!"

As Sarah stood next to the truck, Michael untied her hands. Immediately, she reached for her medal, but it was gone. As she tried digging in her heels, he dragged her toward the cliffs. She thought she could hear her name on the wind. Her heart fluttered at the thought that Joe, Lou, and possibly others might be close on her trail. Michael glanced back.

"They can't help you."

"Let me go, Michael. You can still get away."

"Why are you talking to him, Sarah? *I'm* in control."

"Hannah is *dead*. You've lost, Peter."

He stopped and, grabbing her wrists, forced her to her knees. The look in his eyes was terrifying, and she began to cry.

"I'm nothing if not loyal. You may have certain gifts,

Sarah Greene, but you don't see the big picture. Your dying is all part of the plan. Not *my* plan, of course. You know, in a way, it was lucky you found the mirror. Because that's how he was able to find *you*. Now, get up."

Michael dragged her to the precipice. Looking down into the darkness, she could make out the boulders shining white next to the river. If she fell, she would be crushed. Something occurred to her. Peter was twenty-one when he died. He was a kid in a man's body.

"You're angry," she said. "I get it. You wanted one life. And they kept forcing you toward another."

"A little amateur psychology to lighten the mood?"

"You're a child. Acting out because you didn't get what you want."

"Shut up."

"No, I won't. Poor Peter. All he wanted was to screw his sister in peace, and also his pretty cousin. But the big, bad parents said no. And he got mad."

"You better stop, bitch."

"Or what? Apparently, you've already made up your mind to kill me. Let me ask you something. Weren't you also promised Hannah? Why is she dead?"

"Someone is working against me."

"Oh, I see," Sarah said. "You mean, someone *smarter*."

Michael took hold of his temples and let out a mournful cry that echoed off the cliffs. Sarah saw her opportunity and ran. But it was dark, and she didn't notice the jagged rocks jutting up from the ground. She tripped and fell, breaking her fall with her right hand. As she scrambled to her feet, an intense pain shot through her wrist.

As Michael came for her, she stepped back and slipped over the edge. Before she fell, she managed to grab an exposed tree root with her good hand. Desperately, she tried getting a foothold. She could see Michael coming toward her, his eyes filled with rage.

"Looks like you saved me the trouble," he said.

She felt her hand slipping. "Please help me!"

"I think it's best we end this."

"No, please."

Through her tears, Sarah could see something huge blotting out the moon as it raced toward them. Then, she heard the beating of wings. When the dark mass was close, Sarah knew what it was.

Ravens.

There were hundreds of them. And they were coming for Michael. When he saw them, he cried out and tried running. But it was too late. As the birds surrounded him, croaking with fury—the sound of their beating wings deafening—they pecked out his eyes. Covering his head, Michael stumbled back toward the cliff as the birds relentlessly attacked his head and hands. He tumbled backward off the cliff and, shrieking like hell itself, he fell to his death as the birds vanished into the nighttime sky.

Too frightened to scream for help, Sarah clung to the tree root and prayed. Somewhere far off, she could hear someone shouting.

"Sarah!"

"Here," she said, struggling to pull herself up.

She glanced down. There in the moonlight, she could see Michael Peterson's body sprawled on the rocks like a bloody mannequin. The voices were close now. Two hands reached out toward her, and she recognized Joe and Lou as they grabbed her free arm and pulled her up, the pain causing her to scream.

Joe examined her wrist and shook his head. "I think it might be broken."

"No, it's a sprain. Joe, are you okay? I didn't know what happened to you—I was so worried."

"Well, I'm wearing a bruise in the shape of a crowbar, but I'll live."

She kissed him deeply as a bright beam shone on them. A Santa Barbara PD helicopter was hovering above. Sarah's heart was pounding as she realized how close she'd come to dying. As she sat on the ground, Carter dropped to her knees and hugged her friend.

"Thank God you're okay."

"Ow! Watch the wrist."

"Sorry."

Lou glanced around them and looked at Sarah. "Where's Peterson?"

She barely heard him. "Down there."

The men peered over the cliff as others in the search and rescue arrived, the intense beams from their flashlights illuminating the area.

"What happened?" Lou said.

"He was trying to kill me. I guess he lost his footing and went over."

The cop took a closer look at the cliff. "And I'm guessing he tried taking you with him. What, did he grab your leg?"

Sarah hesitated. She didn't want to talk about what had happened. Not yet.

"That's right. But I managed to kick him in the face."

"Makes sense. Glad we got here in time."

Carter noticed something on the ground and crouched to pick it up. It was a black feather. Pocketing it, she approached Sarah.

"How do you feel?" Carter said.

"Tired."

"Come on, let's get you up."

As Carter helped her friend to her feet, Sarah whispered something in her ear.

"Peter is dead. But this is far from over."

Joe and Carter led Sarah to Joe's truck. As she made her way toward the vehicle, she had the feeling she was in a dream. Her wrist throbbed as the image of the ravens coming for Michael played in her head on a loop. She didn't realize Joe had helped her into the passenger side of the cab. When she looked down, she saw something familiar and reached for it with her good hand. It was her St. Michael medal. She held it close to her heart.

Wiping away her tears, Carter hugged her friend again. "Let's go home, Sarah."

"I can't. I have one more thing I need to do."

Lou entered the cave first, his flashlight playing against the shiny walls. Sarah followed, then Joe and Carter. Carrying her arm in a makeshift sling, Sarah moved ahead and stood at the exact spot she'd seen in her vision. Looking down, she could see the bones, partially dressed in jeans and a yellow crop top.

"It's Nicole," she said. "This is where Peter murdered her."

Lou knelt and poked the remains with his flashlight. "With Hannah's help, right?"

"Yes. Nicole needed to tell her story to someone. That someone was me. I hope she's at peace."

"And Hannah?" Carter said.

Sarah lowered her voice—she didn't want Joe to hear. "Gail Cohen *was* Hannah all along."

"My God."

"I think in many ways, she was as much a victim as Nicole. Maybe there's forgiveness for her, too."

Two other cops carefully placed the girl's remains in a body bag. As they carried her out, a corner of the cave was glowing, and Sarah had to shield her eyes. When her vision adjusted, she could see Nicole standing there, smiling. She was wearing a pretty white dress Sarah remembered from the photo album. Sarah wondered if anyone else had seen the girl. Then, the glow faded, and Nicole was gone.

"You saw her, right?" Sarah said to Carter.

"She was so beautiful."

Lou stuck his face in between them. "See who?"

The women exchanged a look. "Nothing," Sarah said. "Caves give me the creeps. Let's get out of here."

Twenty-Nine

SARAH, Joe, and Carter sat in the front pew with Owen Daniels and several family friends. The celebrant looked to be around thirty with warm brown eyes and a youthful tousle of wavy brown hair. The altar was beautiful, enclosed in a series of nested arches leading the eye to the spare wooden crucifix hanging in the center. A blue sky painted above gave the impression they were already in paradise. On the left in a little raised alcove stood Mary, hands beckoning, wearing the traditional blue and white. And on the right, Joseph, holding the child Jesus. In the center on the floor stood Nicole's closed casket.

The Mass went quickly. A cantor led the congregation in song at the appropriate moments. Sarah didn't sing. The priest's homily was short. He didn't know the deceased and relied on generalities that included various bible verses, including Isaiah, Lamentations, and this from Corinthians:

> We shall not all fall asleep, but we will all be changed, in an instant, in the blink of an eye, at the last trumpet.

Hearing this, Sarah was reminded that it would be a long time before she was okay again. She'd almost died out there at the hands of a madman, saved by something unbelievable. In fact, whenever she closed her eyes, she could still picture Michael's horrified face without eyes as he fell to his death.

When the Mass ended, pallbearers that included Owen and Joe carried the coffin to the hearse waiting outside. A procession of cars would make their way to Mount Calvary Catholic Cemetery, where Nicole would be laid to rest next to her parents.

Joe drove Sarah and Carter to a cousin's house in Lawrence. In the front passenger seat, Sarah looked out the window at the passing scenery. Kansas looked so flat. Visually, there didn't seem to be any relief. She turned around and smiled sadly at Carter, who was drawing something in her journal. She recognized Nicole's coffin.

"I thought the service was nice," the girl said.

Joe reached over and touched Sarah's hand. "So, do you think that's the end of it?"

"You mean, is it safe for us to list Casa Abrigo?"

"Well, that's not what I—"

"I'm kidding. Sheesh. Yes, I think it's over. This part, anyway. Nicole has been laid to rest and Peter has, um…"

"Gone straight to hell?" Carter said.

Sarah forced a laugh. "Something like that."

"What about the mirror?"

"We'll burn what's left of it."

When they arrived, the house was filled with friends and relatives. Everyone wore black, which seemed wrong to Sarah. They should be celebrating. After all, Nicole had been *freed*. She remembered that none of these people knew what had happened to her. For them, this was the story of a family member who had gone missing decades ago and was recently returned to them in a box full of bones.

When Owen saw the three of them, he walked over and shook hands but lingered when he reached Sarah.

"Thank you," he said. "I meant to ask how you broke your arm."

"It was my wrist. A stupid accident. I'm sorry it turned out this way, Owen."

The old man tried to smile. Without warning, the tears came. He squeezed her hand and did something unexpected. He kissed her cheek. That simple gesture had done it. Sarah cried openly and pressed herself against Owen's newly cleaned suit jacket.

"I am so sorry," she said.

As she straightened up and wiped her eyes, he smiled at Sarah and Carter, who was also crying.

"You two managed to save Nicole. You brought her home. And I'll always be grateful. God bless you both."

He excused himself and left to speak to some other guests who wanted to offer their condolences.

"I never thought we saved anyone," Sarah said, dabbing her eyes with a tissue.

She peered around the room hoping to spot an open bar where she could grab a stiff drink. There must be something. Who ever heard of a dry wake? But there was nothing. People held cups of coffee and soda. More than ever, she wished this were Boston and the family Irish.

Patricia Martin walked in, carrying a gift bag. She was wearing a beautifully tailored St. John Collection black suit with modest heels. No purse. When she saw Sarah, she smiled and strode over.

"Dr. Martin. So glad you could make it."

The doctor handed the gift bag to Sarah, who peeked inside and found a bottle of Talisker. Sarah's mouth fell open as she grabbed the neck.

"Thought you could use this."

"You have no idea."

Conspiratorially, Sarah led the good doctor toward the kitchen, with Joe and Carter in tow. They found seats at the country kitchen table while Sarah rummaged through the cupboards looking for glasses. Exasperated, she settled for Dora the Explorer juice glasses. She picked Swiper for herself. Before anyone could speak, she had poured drinks for everyone and taken a seat. Closing her eyes, she savored the smoky, peppery goodness and sighed.

"Thank you," she said to Dr. Martin, feeling herself relax.

"No problem. Thanks for inviting me. Sorry about your wrist."

"I'll live. Surgery is scheduled for next week."

"Great to see you, Carter," Dr. Martin said. Then, to Joe, "Ex-husband, right?"

"Yep."

"Sarah neglected to mention you were hot."

Joe reddened, and the other women almost did spit-takes.

"Sorry, I tend to say what I think. The real reason I decided to come was to ask about Michael Peterson."

"He's dead," Joe said.

"Oh, I'm sorry. What happened?"

It took two slugs of single malt, but Sarah finally broke down and told everyone the *real* story of what had happened at Devil's Bluff.

"It's hard to believe," the doctor said. "I mean, there *are* documented cases of someone exerting a strong influence on a person. You've heard of a Svengali, I'm sure. These are individuals who can hold a person as an emotional hostage. But what *you* seem to be talking about is—"

"Possession," Carter said, reaching for the bottle.

"Dr. Martin," Sarah said, "the Michael Peterson I met—who Joe and I met—was smooth. In fact, he was a real charmer. Nothing like what was described in his file."

"I thought the guy had it together," Joe said. "You know, a smart businessman with money looking to buy his next house."

The doctor knitted her brow. "That doesn't jibe with the videos of him I watched." Then, to Sarah, "And he tried to *kill* you?"

Sarah refilled her glass. "Yeah."

"Well, I've always said, science is good, but it can't explain everything. Are you sure you didn't imagine those ravens, though? I mean, it would be understandable considering your stress level."

Sarah smiled. "There you go talking science again, Doctor."

Dr. Martin reddened. "Right. 'There are more things in heaven and earth.'"

"And in Dos Santos, apparently," Carter said, smiling at Sarah.

They spent the rest of the afternoon chatting about nothing important. Joe had switched to ginger ale early on but decided to let Sarah cut loose. The afternoon wore on, with new people arriving every half hour. Dr. Martin headed out early. Then, other guests started leaving. Soon, it was time for Sarah and her entourage to go. The bottle of Talisker stood on the table, less than half full. Sarah made a frowny face.

"I suppose a doggie bag is out of the question?"

Owen walked in as they were about to leave.

"We have to have catch a plane," Joe said as Sarah tried drawing a smiley face on the bottle with her finger.

"Sure." He pointed at the bottle. "That yours?"

"Yeah. Should we dump it, or…"

"Not much of a drinker myself. But today I'm making an exception."

Owen poured himself a drink and raised his glass. "To Nicole."

Scrambling, the others found their glasses and raised them. The three Californians made their goodbyes and headed out. Sarah was more than a little tipsy, and Joe and Carter had to guide her to the car.

"Love you guys so much," she said as she wiggled into the passenger seat, her cast in tow.

"We had no idea," Carter said, grinning at Joe.

It took three tries, but Sarah was finally able to fasten her seatbelt for the trip home.

———

"I ask for your blessing and your mercy."

Harlan Covington ignored the pain in his knees as he knelt facing the confessional's screen. The last time he was here, Gail Cohen had been killed. The old man had come seeking absolution and was denied. Now, he was back. And this time, it was Michael Peterson who had been destroyed and Peter Moody along with him.

As always, the ritual to summon the ravens had been grueling but necessary. The town of Dos Santos was corrupt—like Sodom—and since accepting the power of the ring, Harlan had vowed to fight the terrible evil until his dying breath.

"You know I cannot forgive your sins," Fr. Donnelly said.

"You are Christ's representative on earth—a direct descendant of the Apostles. You have the power to grant absolution."

"I do. But in this case, my hands are tied, as you well know."

The old man wept. "Please. I don't want to go to hell."

They'd had this conversation many times before, and it always ended at the same place. The priest thought a moment. How many deaths had his friend of twenty-five years been responsible for? It was no matter that those he had dispatched were evildoers and that he was following instructions. It was not up to men to take a life for a life. That was God's domain. And yet.

Harlan Covington had willingly taken on this mission —a secret mission not sanctioned by the Vatican—to fight evil in the world. And sometimes, that necessitated killing those who committed the evil. What mattered is whether the penitent was truly sorry. But was he? There was no way the priest could know. Only God could see into a man's soul.

"I meant to thank you for saving Sarah," Fr. Donnelly said.

"I'm not certain I can promise to *keep* her safe. Now that *he* knows, he won't stop until she's dead."

"You must do your best. Ultimately, it's in God's hands." The priest sighed. "Alright. Tell me your sins."

"I killed a man."

"Are you sorry for what you have done?"

Harlan thought a moment. Though he *was* sorry he had to carry this terrible burden, he was not sorry for causing someone's death. This was a holy war. And in war, soldiers were required to kill their enemy to protect the innocent. Would God punish His soldiers when they were only doing their duty?

"No," he said. "I am not sorry."

"Then, you must pray for God's mercy."

Thirty

THE REHEARSAL SPACE was packed with millennials, and Sarah had to put up with pushing and shoving as she, Joe, Rachel, and Katy teetered at the edges of the makeshift stage. Thank goodness there wasn't a mosh pit.

Though this wasn't her kind of music, she'd promised Carter she would attend the impromptu concert. She owed so much to the girl, who had kept her grounded during those horrifying last hours of the case.

In the beginning, they had planned to pass along the gory details to the *Dos Santos Weekly*, hoping they would run the story so they wouldn't end up as liars. Carter volunteered to write an online article—something Sarah hadn't expected. And what she turned in was immediately accepted by the paper. Sarah had sent the link to Owen and Dr. Martin.

The band took the stage, and the room erupted. It had been a long time since Sarah had attended a live concert, and she was a little in awe of her friend.

First, the other band members appeared—the drummer, lead guitarist—and then the bass player who, it turned out, was an attractive young woman with tattoos all up and down her arms and straight, platinum blonde hair. As they tuned their instruments, Carter ascended, wearing black skinny jeans and a black tank top with the words *Never Surrender!* imprinted on the front in silver lettering. Everyone in the audience went wild. Apparently, Carter had a lot of fans.

The band performed a set of what Sarah considered typical alternative rock. As the lead singer, Carter sounded wonderful. Her voice was strong and confident. The rapport Carter had with the bass player was evident, and it didn't take long for her to understand why those two were an item.

The music was very loud, and Sarah found she was getting a headache, which added to the throbbing in her wrist. After forty minutes, Carter turned to the band and said something Sarah couldn't hear. When she turned back around to face the audience, the band broke into a ballad, surprising Sarah.

Carter sang "Ill Wind" by Harold Arlen and Ted Koehler. She'd remembered listening to a record in her father's collection that Sarah Vaughan had made in, what was it, 1961? Norah Jones had also covered it in the early 2000s.

Carter's voice sounded bluesy and sad, capturing the pain and weariness evident in the lyrics. Sarah was in awe. Most of the audience didn't know what to make of that song but listened politely. When it was over, they clapped, unsure about what they'd heard.

"I loved that last song," Katy said to Sarah as she and the others made their way to the car.

"Me, too." Then, to Rachel, "Wish Eddie could've heard it."

"See you tomorrow in the office?" Rachel said.

"Yep." She held up her cast. "'It's just a flesh wound.'"

Sarah's sister hugged her, careful to navigate the cast. "I'm so glad you're okay. I—"

Sarah tried a laugh. "Hey, you're not getting rid of me that easy."

Sarah kissed Rachel and Katy and watched as they got in their car and drove off. Tomorrow, she intended to have coffee at The Cracked Pot and tell Carter how wonderfully she sang. Joe was somewhere getting the truck, and Sarah took the opportunity to think.

She could see a glimmer in the distance. In another moment, Sarah recognized Alyssa, floating in the middle of the dark, empty road. And she knew things weren't going to be peaceful for long. More trouble was coming, and Sarah would be forced to confront it, even though she was sure she could never face a ghost again.

A hand touched her shoulder. She turned and found Joe smiling at her.

"Hey, let's get out of here. You okay?"

Sarah looked back. Alyssa was gone. But she knew her friend would return with some new dire warning. Tomorrow. She would deal with it tomorrow. For now, she would be with her friend, her lover. Her protector.

"Yeah," she said. "Let's go home."

Afterword

Thank you for reading *The Girl in the Mirror*. I sincerely hope you enjoyed it. Will you take a few minutes to post a review and tell your friends? Word of mouth is an author's best friend and is very much appreciated. Peace and love.

Steven Ramirez

Ready for the next Sarah Greene Supernatural Mystery? *House of the Shrieking Woman* is on sale now. And to stay informed, sign up for the newsletter at stevenramirez.com/newsletter and choose "Supernatural Suspense."

House of the Shrieking Woman—At a women's shelter, Sarah Greene investigates a series of disturbing incidents that began with the arrival of a troubled young woman from Guatemala. Soon, Sarah discovers a possible link to the evil infesting Dos Santos—an insidious presence known as The Darkness.

CPSIA information can be obtained
at www.ICGtesting.com
Printed in the USA
LVHW041216170420
653844LV00001B/123